The
Unburied
Dead

First published by Blasted Heath, 2012
copyright © 2012 Douglas Lindsay
This edition by Long Midnight Publishing 2017

www.douglaslindsay.com

ISBN: 978-1-54956-363-8

THE UNBURIED DEAD

DOUGLAS LINDSAY

PROLOGUE

Wildflowers? It smells like wildflowers, but then, how can something actually smell of wildflowers? There are hundreds of wildflowers. They must all smell different. All the wildflowers together?

His mind churns.

Wildflowers. *I don't know any stinking wildflowers.* Wildflowers. The word tumbles through his brain. His head twitches, a sudden snap, eyes closed for a second, and it's gone. Now the smell of the underground tunnels: rotten cabbage. Rotten cabbage, sewage, decay. They should bottle those.

He glances over his shoulder at the woman three seats behind. Dark brown hair. Almost black. Shoulder length. She's not looking at him. It must be her, the wildflowers. There's no one else in the carriage that would wear that kind of scent.

The train rumbles to a halt, emerging from the tunnels into the drizzle and cold dark night of Dalmarnock station.

He doesn't turn all the way round, but looks at the woman's reflection, catching her eye in the window. A fleeting glimpse then she looks away. He smiles at her too late, but can feel her shudder.

He looks along the length of the carriage. Two old women, grumbling, voices too loud; a man asleep, face pressed against the glass; four teenagers, talking about the weekend and passing around a bottle of cheap wine.

He sucks his teeth, runs his hand across the stubble on his chin and looks at his reflection in the window. Five days growth. Needs to shave. Not good for business, but he likes it. It's more him than the man he has to present to the world every day. His mind rambles on, a trail of confusion, his eyes attracted over his shoulder every few

—

1

seconds to the woman behind.

Wildflowers. If a wildflower grows in a garden, does that make it a garden flower? Maybe there's another name for it. Maybe it smells different. Would it smell different?

The doors fizz slowly shut. He looks up at the route map. Seven stops to go, and she'll have to get off at one of them. He wouldn't do anything on the train. Too much chance of an interruption.

A quiet back street, with gentle drizzle, broken streetlights and a dog barking half a mile away. That was the place for your first murder.

Is that what he's already thinking? Murder? Does he want to murder Jo? Of course not, but it's almost happened before. Must be realistic. He wants her. Wants to feel her and hold her. Smell that floral scent close up, breathe it in, taste it as he licks her neck. Feel her gasp as he thrusts his hand between her legs.

Maybe she'll want it too, or maybe she'll fight. If she fights.... Then you can never know what's going to happen.

He imagines the newspapers. He thinks about the newspapers all the time. Sometimes his name is in the papers, but not often. Never for something like this.

If she wants him, if she comes willingly, will the newspapers care, will anyone care? And if he rapes her, will anyone care? But if he leaves her body on the ground, raped and dead, maybe then they'll notice. Maybe then they'll start talking about him.

He looks out of the window, at the lights and wet streets of Rutherglen, as the train crawls towards the next stop. Shouldn't think like that. It's wrong. It's stupid. It's not very helpful. It doesn't help. *Are you listening, Dad?* It doesn't...fucking...help.

His eyes slither round again and he looks straight at her. She avoids his gaze. He loves her hair. The same hair that Jo had, just touching her neck. The hair that fell over his stomach when she was fellating him. Twitches at the thought of her, tries to push it from his mind. Bloody Jo.

—

2

But the thought is there now. Her tongue all over him, and not because he was forcing her. She'd wanted it. All the time. Always wanted him; him deep inside her, her hands all over him, his tongue all over her. All the time.

Then she'd started to sleep with other men. And then she'd left.

The woman bites her nails, looking round at the first damp run of the platform as the train shudders slowly into Rutherglen station. Pretty face, slightly overweight, small nose, red lips, getting very frightened by the strange guy two seats away who is staring at her.

The train comes to a halt beneath the M74. Again he glances over his shoulder at the woman as the doors open. Why should he hide it now? She knows what's coming to her.

There's giggling from up the carriage as the four teenagers drunkenly make their way off the train, pushing, laughing, arguing, shouting *fuck* into the night as loudly as possible.

He looks back to the woman. She's staring at him now, and this time looks away more slowly. He swallows. Maybe she does want him. Maybe she likes the attention.

He turns away and looks up the carriage. He smiles. He lowers his head. He can smell her, her scent filling the air. The two old women are looking at him, as if they can read the intent on his face.

'What?' he says, a bit disconcerted. 'What?' he repeats, and their eyes avert.

The sleeping man's head bobs up from a silent slumber, then flops back onto his chest. The doors start their slow fizz. There's a stamping on the floor behind. He is still perturbed by the attention of the old women, the women who can somehow look into him and can read every thought running through his brain, every bloody nightmare splitting his head apart.

He is slow to turn, and then suddenly realises what he's missing. Turns quickly now, but she's already out the door, the doors already closed. He runs to them, stands at the

—

glass. She waits on the platform, crying out for the train to move off; breathless. He starts pulling at the rubber between the doors. Makes some headway. An inch. She doesn't wait. Two inches. She sees the teenagers disappear through the door into the waiting room, one other passenger making the slow walk along the platform, and runs after them. The train starts to move off. He's tugging desperately at the door but he's not getting any further. He's still there pulling at the rubber as the train pulls past the woman hurrying to the exit, and their eyes meet one last time. He drinks in the hair, hoping he will remember her, but all these women look the same. She shudders, then feels like crying with relief as he steps back from the doors and is gone as the train accelerates away into the rain, the still of the night.

He returns to his seat. Looks at the old women, who stare back this time, and he feels intimidated. His eyes drop.

'Bloody Jo,' he mutters.

The woman climbs the stairs to the bridge over the railway tracks. A lucky escape. She feels the relief, and already she is beginning to put it out of her mind. Men. They're all the same; and she starts again to construct her defences for when she has to explain to her husband where she's been all evening.

1

Why does anyone join the police? I mean, seriously? What a colossally shit job. Toss in overworked, underpaid, and the fact that nearly everyone hates you, and you have to question the motives of anyone who wants to do it. A variation on that Groucho Marx line about not wanting to be in a club that would have him as a member. Presuming Groucho actually said that. The world's full of misattributed quotes, though it's usually John Lennon or Maya Angelou.

So, who knows what my fellow officers are thinking? A calling? A need for power? The need to do good? Or the desire to be above the law, so you can manipulate it, or break it. On and on, a thousand reasons for a thousand officers.

I joined in '96. I'd been back from Bosnia for over a year. Still drifting, still suffering. I didn't turn to drugs, I didn't turn to drink. I mean, I drank a shitload, but not so's I thought I was using it as a crutch. Mostly, I turned to women, as many as I could find. They seemed quite happy about it, until I left, or they found out what number they'd been that month.

Yep, I was an asshole. All that fucked up, PTSD bullshit coursing through my veins, all those images of bodies dumped in the stinking heat of a Balkan summer, all those sounds of screaming women in my head, were nobody's excuse. I should've spoken to someone. I didn't. Tried to work through it, but just never seemed to grasp that sex wasn't helping.

Then finally, I got someone pregnant or, at least, someone told me I'd got her pregnant. This coincided with the arrival in the public consciousness of Detective Sergeant Jonah Bloonsbury.

Jean Fryar left school at the first opportunity. No 'O'

levels, no future. Started working in a newsagent's up the old Edinburgh Road. I used to go in there sometimes on a Saturday for my twenty Marlboro. I had a detached look that the women liked. I never looked interested. Never looked like I wanted them.

Worked every time, although probably only because I wasn't trying to get it to work.

Don't even remember whether the first time was at her place or mine. There was something about her, although it was probably just that when I lay back and she sat on top of me, it was so damned good I almost managed to get the images out of my head.

One night or other the condom got left in my pocket, along with my brain. I'd been doing a reasonable job up until then.

Unsurprisingly, I'd moved on by the time she called me up saying she was pregnant. She seemed to believe I might be interested, and because I wasn't doing anything else at the time, I said I'd marry her.

I know. I didn't deserve her, not with that attitude. Didn't deserve anything, other than what I got.

It didn't take long for her to start badgering me about getting a job. I think what she actually wanted was for me to go abroad again. She envisaged me sending my pay cheque home from a distant, war-torn land. She was keen on Chechnya. If things had worked out well for her, I would've been killed, and she'd have received compensation from someone.

However, a story started appearing in the newspapers. A young sergeant in Glasgow called Jonah Bloonsbury cracked a murder inquiry which had defeated the most senior detectives in the city. The guy was nine years older than me and he had his fifteen minutes. Front page news, detective of the month. He'd acted alone on a hunch all the others had ignored and had nabbed his man after a long chase on foot over open moorland up beyond East Kilbride. Reading between the lines, it was apparent that in the end he had taken the guy down and kicked the shit out of him before the bloke had been taken into custody.

I could do that, I thought. I could kick the shit out of people. And the police would give me shift work, and I wouldn't have to spend too much time at home.

We got married on a staggeringly warm summer's day in 1996, then three weeks later Jean had a miscarriage. So, the child was gone and, messed up and insensitive beyond reason, I immediately contemplated losing my wife as well. I didn't do it straight away, but that was the beginning of the end.

The police no longer seemed necessary, but I was there, and right enough, it kept me out of the house for long periods. I didn't have to put up with her drinking, and she just didn't have to put up with me.

By the time I'd finished my first year, I had met Peggy and was seeing her behind Jean's back, and by the time I finally met Jonah Bloonsbury, Peggy and I had been married for eight years and the marriage had long since drifted into disinterest. By then Bloonsbury was a drunken detective chief inspector, living on past glories and suffering the same sort of marriage as the rest of us.

That first murder case wasn't his only big success. There were several others, though none so high profile. But somewhere along the way the pressure became too much for him, and he drowned in alcohol. I don't know when he hit the downward spiral, but by the time Bloonsbury reached fifty he was wasted, viewing everyone with suspicion through the dregs of a bottle of cheap blended malt.

There was one last crowning glory over a year ago, plucked from nowhere, to temporarily save his wretched career and wasted reputation, but since then his life has been nothing but a fast drop in the elevator to Hell. And now he's just a guy, drifting through his fifties; overweight, ruddy-faced, bleary-eyed. A waste of a good man, but there are many more where he came from.

So, it could be said I joined up for two illusions – a child that never came, and the total lie that is the career of

—

7

Jonah Bloonsbury – but in reality, I joined because I felt like my brain had been taken out and refitted the wrong way round.

I bumped into Jean Fryar again a few months ago. She slapped me across the face, we went for a drink, compared divorces and children – three and two for me, two and four for her – and nearly ended up in bed. I like to think we both thought better of it in the end, but really the decision was all hers. And that's all there is to say about Jean Fryar.

The story of Jonah Bloonsbury limps on however, while the rest of us watch it pass by – mourners at a wake – as he reaches for one last success; or perhaps merely hangs on, hoping to receive a full pension, with as much dignity as a man with a bottle of whisky attached to his face can do.

Meanwhile my brain turns slowly, occasionally almost clicking back into position, but never quite making it.

And still an asshole.

Monday morning, three days before Christmas. Sitting at the desk with a colossal hangover, the memory of the weekend still burning. The football didn't go well – Partick Thistle lost three-nil at Ross County – and I ended up in bed with a horror out of the *No Oil Painting* catalogue. Clearly, we were made for each other. Don't remember a thing about the night either, so have no idea if it was worth the self-loathing. At least I wasn't called in, and any weekend without that is something of a success.

Taylor isn't in yet, not that he'll care if he's judged. It's just me and Herrod and a collection of marginally post-pubescent constables. The Superintendent's in of course, letting all us men know who's boss, crushing us all beneath her size six stilettos.

Passed Alison on the way in this morning. I was married to her for twenty-nine days a year or two ago – something which I did in a fit of idiocy after my divorce from Peggy came through. She was working downstairs somewhere, walking by with a criminal on her arm. He looked good on her. We smiled. Very cosy. We get on a lot better since the divorce, although we avoided each other for nearly a year afterwards. She's marrying Sergeant McGovern in June, which is unfortunate.

Herrod lifts his head from some paperwork, tossing the file into the out-tray as he does so.

'It's bollocks, Hutton,' he says.

Can't argue with that.

'That you found the meaning of life again?'

He sticks his feet on the desk and lights a cigarette. Of course, there's a no-smoking policy in the building, but there's no one here to police it. The man smokes B&H same as everyone else. That's one of the reasons why he never gets any women, although, to be honest, there are a lot of reasons why he never gets any women.

I'm still smoking Marlboro, but generally don't at work. Trying to be a good little soldier, obeying all the directives from the top.

'Got this guy, right? The bampot says he was at his sister's all night. The fuck spends the night with their sister? I haven't seen my sister since she was twelve. I'd vomit on my sister.'

I'm fully prepared to believe that Herrod has in the past, at some time, vomited on his sister.

'But not this guy. This guy spends the night with her. Very cosy. The sister backs him up, of course. And all the while, as they're tucked up under the sheets, or whatever they're doing, his warehouse is going noisily up in smoke. Full insurance, nothing to do with me, mate, I was in bed with my sister.'

'Aye?'

'It's bollocks.'

'You said. We know. We're not here because it's anything else.'

'It used to be different, didn't it? You came in here on a Monday morning, you did your job, you took from it what you could, and every now and again you arrested some eejit and kicked the shit out him. Tell me that didn't make sense.'

'You sound like an advert for the force in the Sunday Times.'

He shrugs, spits out a sigh, shakes his head.

'I don't know. I've just had enough, you know. All this crap, all these eejits. Every last fucking one of them.'

He finishes his lament, stubs the cigarette out in an overflowing ashtray. My heart bleeds for him. I almost want to give him a hug.

'Shut up and stop feeling sorry for yourself.'

He grunts at me and moves another report from In to Out without looking at it.

The door opens. One of those dashing young constables walks in looking like the before half of a Clearasil advert, followed by DCI Bloonsbury – a man who hasn't slept for a month – reeking of alcohol. The model detective. We nod at him; he ignores us, walks into his office and slams the door shut. A couple of shots of J&B, two cups of coffee, half pack of Bensons and he'll be ready for us.

The man's downhill slide has picked up some momentum in recent months. Word is the Super's on the point of kicking him into touch but, for all the hard act, you can tell she's soft on stuff like that. Likes to take care of her men.

Bloonsbury's door reopens almost immediately, half an hour before schedule. Got a face on him like a flat tyre and a piece of paper in his hand, which he waves in the air, like a drunk Neville Chamberlain.

'Herrod?'

'What?'

Bloonsbury looks at the piece of paper and gives it another shake.

'Rape case? Stonelaw Road?'

Herrod nods. Looks a little sheepish, if so grotesque a man can even remotely resemble a sheep.

'Well, what the fuck are you doing sitting about? Get your arse over there.'

The door slams. Herrod stares at the floor, then looks up as he fumbles for another smoke.

'See what I mean?' he says.

I ignore him and feel sorry for the victim. As if the horror of the night before wasn't enough.

*

Quarter to three. Dispatched to the far end of Rutherglen Main Street, Detective Constable Morrow, PCs Kelly and Bathurst in tow. Spent most of the day working on a big theft – two hundred TVs in a lorry up at Bothwell services – then I got called away to come and stand with Morrow while he does his best to ask the right questions. And it's a no-hoper right from the off.

Fight broke out between three Begbies not far from the town hall. Two against one, rather than all three for themselves. The one comes off worst, ends up on the ground getting his head beaten to a pulp. He'd already been whipped off to the Victoria by the time we got here, but there've been enough people to tell us what he looked like after the attack. Massively swollen head, face bloodied and purple, no teeth left to talk of. Shit. Presumably he survived because they didn't hit him anywhere near his brain. I've seen enough of these stupid bastards who've had too much to drink, think they're Clark Kent and end up with heads the size of basketballs. Seen enough of that, seen far too much of a lot worse.

So, at two fifteen in the afternoon, three days before Christmas, when Rutherglen Main Street is as mobbed as it ever gets these days, no one sees a thing. Plenty of folk saw the guy lying on the pavement looking like dog food, but no one saw the incident take place or the assailants in question.

There are two things to do at a time like this. Forget it and go back to the station; or hang around for five hours questioning everyone over the age of three, all the while getting nowhere. If the bloke dies, of course, then the papers get hold of it and all of a sudden you've got to look as if you're doing something. But if he walks, then damn it, what's the point?

Now I would have had Morrow down as a sad young thing, keen to make his mark. Thank God that doesn't pan out. Morrow turns out to be human. Seems as disinterested as I am. Asking the right questions; looking concerned, being seen to do his bit, but fully aware it's pointless; just dying to get back to the station for a cup of tea. I admire that in a young detective. Look good in front of the public, then forget about it half a minute later. The way forward.

Constables Kelly and Bathurst do their bit. Kelly looks moderately perturbed at the obvious lack of interest from CID, but he ought to know better. Hard to tell about Bathurst. A closed book. She has a very impressive cover mind, although she's probably too young for me.

Probably is, as they say, doing a lot of heavy lifting there.

DC Morrow appears from a shop, looking like a man who wants to be elsewhere. I detach myself from an old lady who claims to have seen everything, but is likely basing most of her testimony on a fight scene from the start of last week's episode of *Casualty*.

'What's the story, Rob?'

Consults his notebook. Very efficient.

'Got a bit of a description from the shop assistant. Not great, but enough to stick into the computer, see what we can get. Apart from that, not much.'

I nod, turn away, look up and down the street. Cold, grey afternoon, the Christmas lights on, bringing a fitting air of melancholy.

Still haven't bought anything for Rebecca. I have no idea what you buy twelve-year-old girls these days. Don't want to look like a fool. Buy her some toy they advertise on the TV, when for all I know she's already busy doing drugs and boys. Can't go for the latest piece of tech, because I've no idea what her mother will have bought her recently. Tough decision. I'll do my usual and ask one of the women at the station.

Already got the boy his Rangers change strip. Nearly choked in the shop when I had to buy it.

I shrug. 'Cup of tea?'

Morrow nods. 'Sounds brilliant.'

A last look around the scene of the crime. Kelly and Bathurst appear to be running out of people to interview. Nothing much else to do. You might never know an incident had taken place.

'Right then, constable,' I say, and off we fuck.

*

Taylor's there when I get back. My immediate boss, sitting in his office behind the fog of depression.

The first time I ever talked to him was at a Dylan concert. We kind of bumped into each other, realised that we were from the same station. It was a bit awkward. Then we found that we were both Dylan freaks, and that was even more awkward. It was like, *I want to be the Dylan weirdo around here!*

We ended up having this grudging kind of Dylan bitchslap comparison thing. He'd seen him seventeen times in concert, to my twelve; I had two iPods full of Dylan – about twelve hundred tracks – he's a traditionalist, doesn't like unofficial bootlegs or concert material, so just had all his studio albums. About four hundred tracks worth or so.

There are two kinds of people reading this. There are those who are thinking, *goddamned Dylan losers, get some proper music on your iPod, for fuck's sake.* And then there are the genuine Dylan freaks out there who are thinking, *seventeen concerts... twelve hundred tracks? That's not a Dylan freak, that's a passing interest. That's barely knowing he exists!*

When I was told I was working for Taylor I wasn't too impressed, but then of course we sat in his car to go somewhere on the first day and *Knocked Out Loaded* was on the CD player, and who else was likely to be listening to that around here? It's been fine ever since.

I stick my head around the door.

'How are we doing?'

He looks away from his computer. Tired. Not thinking about work.

'Quiet,' he says. 'You can take off early, if you like. Go home and make yourself beautiful for tonight.'

'Seriously?' A beat. 'Wait, you're kidding.'

'Check the big brain on Brad,' he says. 'You're not in the Brownies anymore, son. Get us a cup of tea, eh?'

I nod ruefully.

'It's Brett,' I mutter, as I head out the door, and he laughs.

3

He is at the cinema. Enjoying the dark. His common retreat, a small, art house cinema, a twenty-minute bus journey away. Can't stand multiplexes. Comfortable bucket chairs, drinks and food at extortionate prices, virtually every film aimed at glutinous, popcorn-devouring children, and those damned adults with the viewing habits and mental capacity of the under-14s.

He comes here a few times a week, doesn't mind what he's watching. Tonight, a small and beautiful Korean film. *3 Iron*. He finds himself in love with the girl, even though she looks nothing like Jo. Elegy and melancholy, love and sadness. He is entranced, drawn in by the romance. The silence. With beautiful perfection, the lovers never speak.

There are fewer than ten people in the audience, as is often the case, but tonight there is someone special. At first he'd thought it was Jo herself, here in the flesh. She had come here often enough with him in the past, why wouldn't she be here now?

The more he looks, however, the more he sees the differences. It's not Jo, just someone who dares to look like her. Yet he also convinces himself of the similarities. She sits alone, and he wonders what kind of woman goes to the cinema unaccompanied, particularly to such a romantic film? What message is she sending out?

It will be dark when they get out; the streets will be quiet. He could talk to her. He could take it a bit further. He imagines leaning in towards her, her hair in his face, breathing her in. Hesitation before he kisses her or touches her. That lovely moment of anticipation. A finger drawn softly across her neck, his lips touching the bottom of her ear.

As the film progresses, he becomes agitated. He is distracted, until eventually the film has lost him. Not a

15

long film, but by the end he cannot wait for it to be over. There's someone in the cinema with whom he has business, and that business knocks everything else from his mind.

And as the credits finally roll, and the woman who might well be Jo rises from her seat, he bides his time, listening to the thumping of his heart. It had been like this the first time with Jo too. And the last.

The cinema is quiet, the few people in attendance with nothing to say, as if influenced by the silence of the principal characters.

The woman who is not Jo is also distracted, also did not allow herself to be completely immersed in the film. As she leaves the cinema, she wonders whether to call her boyfriend – getting as far as taking her mobile from her bag – but at the same time knowing that she will leave it until she gets home.

There is a stupid argument to be continued, and it would have to be continued that evening, but she's prepared to leave it for as long as possible.

However, on this particular evening, she will never reach her front door.

4

Monday night, Christmas bash. Private room at the Holiday Inn in the centre of town, well out of our patch. DJ playing all sorts of dance chart trash. Can't really expect him to play Dylan all night, can we? We've still got the horrors of the karaoke to come. We're all expecting to hear Bloonsbury's drunken rendition of *Can't Help Falling in Love* for the three hundredth time, and a lot worse besides.

There was a lot of ethnic cleansing in the twentieth century, but how come no one ethnically cleansed the bastard who brought karaoke to the western world?

Probably shouldn't say that out loud.

It's just after midnight and already the party's beginning to break up. You get the sensible crowd who disappear home early, then you can guarantee the remaining hard core will be here until it's time to go to work tomorrow morning. There's always a lottery to get the day off, which I never win, but since Peggy kicked me out, I spend half the year going into work straight from a long night before anyway. One more day just before Christmas doesn't make any difference.

The Super is long gone. The chocolates were hardly off the table and she was out the door. Her old man gets in from D.C. tonight, so she's off back to the castle in Helensburgh to warm up the bed, though from what they say she'll probably be asleep by the time he shows up.

Herrod looks miserable. I expect Bernadette's got a chastity belt on him and has melted down the key. She's got her two kids and now there's no need for any further sex. Every time I meet her, I wonder what on earth he was thinking. On the other hand, one also has to wonder what she was thinking. Maybe, in the blessed name of this year's Richard Curtis romcom, they were just perfect for

---

each other.

'Same again, Sergeant?' Dragged from people-watching by the familiar chant. Raucous, bloody noise, *Born This Way* and a few poor saps making an idiot of themselves on the dance floor. Including, I can't help but notice, PC Bathurst, absolutely stunning in a skin-tight white number. She's got a few of her type running after her but I think I might make a go of it myself, over twice her age though I am. Not quite drunk enough yet.

'Aye, please,' I say to the boss. He asks the same of Herrod then plods morosely off to the bar.

Taylor has been on edge all evening. Seems to think that if he lets his concentration slip, he might end up in bed with DS Murphy from Westburn, as he did last year. Don't think he's told Debbie about it, but it's plagued him ever since. I've said to him, if you're going to screw around behind your wife's back then it's the same as anything else. You've got to give it a hundred percent, balls out, or it won't work out.

He never listens. One drunken night, then he fended Murphy off for a couple of months until she lost interest. He's spent the last year feeling like a bastard, hoping Debbie never finds out. I suspect, however, that she might not even care.

Time passes in a carnival of noise and alcohol. Herrod drains a Bacardi and Coke. I mean, a forty-six-year-old man drinking Bacardi and Coke, it's almost deviant, right?

'Jonah's been saying all month he's not singing this year. It's offensive to the King, he says.'

I laugh, but have to admit to it being a snort by now. That's vodka for you.

'So, what's he been doing for the last ten years?'

'Blaspheming. Says he's repented. Never again. '

We both look over at Bloonsbury, the great Elvis apologist; three tables away, spectacularly fucked out of his face on cheap whisky and in the process of making a monumental idiot of himself over some young thing from out of our patch.

'Who's that he's drooling over?'

Herrod shrugs. 'Some scrubber from Shettleston.'

'He's got a chance though.'

Herrod grunts, shakes his head and turns away. Jealous. 'Bastard.'

Taylor, the white knight, returns with the alcohol. Notice, with dismay, that he's moved onto orange juice. He parks himself, distributes the booze, looks morosely around the dance floor. In the midst of the tumult the DJ has for some reason stuck on that tragic ode to psycho-women everywhere, *Someone Like You*, sending most sane men running to the hills, and everyone else onto the floor in rapturous convulsions, slabbering all over each other and practically having sex where they stand.

'What's the matter with you?' I say to Taylor.

He doesn't notice. I repeat it. He looks round, shrugs.

'Debbie,' he says, reluctantly.

Have a horrible feeling that if I pursue my line of enquiry, he's about to get maudlin. None of us want that.

'Herrod says Jonah isn't going to do Elvis this year. Blasphemy, apparently.'

Taylor grunts. 'Fucking Elvis,' he mutters, disdainfully.

We look at Bloonsbury, his face now surgically attached to that of his salvation from Shettleston. If she sucks all the alcohol out of him, he might wake up to what he's letting himself in for. I have no idea what she's thinking, though.

'If we're lucky, he'll be too carried away with Kitten Heels there,' says Herrod, 'and the singing'll pass him by. What d'you think?'

Kitten Heels? Jesus…

We descend into morose silence and watch the doings on the dance floor. I could be wrong, but it seems that Constables Forsyth and Bennett are having sex. Hard to tell and I strain to see properly, finally laughing as I get the visual confirmation. Holy shit, what a couple. Those two are players on the dance floor.

The music comes to a halt, couples detach, apart from

---

the players who waddle over to a dark corner, then the DJ starts exhorting passengers on the ship of fools to step up and sing. Everyone looks at Bloonsbury and the man does not disappoint. Accepting the rapturous and ironic applause, he removes himself from his Juliet and makes his way towards the microphone. Mumbles something to the DJ and turns to his audience. Winks and points at the girl. Herrod and I laugh harshly.

And then, as if Elvis is watching and can't stand to be blasphemed, we are treated to some divine intervention. A sober officer with a moustache walks through the room. Everyone looks at him. He stands out a mile. Makes his way towards our table. Me and Taylor look at each other and mouth 'crap', just as Bloonsbury fluffs the first line of his song, smiling at Juliet as he does so.

The moustache arrives. We are unimpressed. Bang goes my tryst with Bathurst that I've started to imagine is some sort of shoo-in. He stands at the table, looks down at us. The lot of the police officer: to get your life constantly interrupted by work, even when you're not having a good time.

He bends forwards, starts shouting into Herrod's ear. Herrod's face drops onto the table and he looks morosely over at Bloonsbury. 'Shall I stay?' he's warbling, and no you bloody well shan't, is the reply. You're obviously out of here, mate, with crime to investigate. Taylor and I nearly reach over and kiss each other. No pleasure greater than thinking you're about to be dragged off then finding it's some other poor clown who's in the soup.

Herrod gets up, head shaking and looking like a freezing wet day in Largs. Taylor and I clink glasses and watch him mince over to Elvis and mutter something at him. Then with a 'Fuck's sake' shouted into the microphone, Bloonsbury removes himself from the stage and starts the long trudge back to work. Grabs his coat, gives the girl a grimace, then he and Herrod troop out to the ribald cheering of the rest of us.

It's times like this that make it all worthwhile.

I survey the scene with renewed good humour. Constable Edwards gets up and starts a passable Robbie impersonation, taking his top off as he goes – really, these young plods should learn to keep everything undercover until they've got some chest hair – and I, flushed with unexpected romantic bravado, decide it's time to make my move on Bathurst.

I down the rest of the glass and excuse myself from Taylor. He nods, doesn't mind – he's smiling at last – and I worm my way over. She's standing with her back to the wall under a picture of John Lennon in a policeman's helmet – someone's idea of a joke – and looking gorgeous with a glass of clear liquor in her hands. She smiles at me and she's alone. Good start. Like scoring a goal in the first minute. I manage to stop myself doing that drunk thing where you lean on the wall next to the girl and drool on her. Keep a respectful distance.

'How you doing, Evelyn?'

A reasonable opening. Nothing fancy, nothing smart. Nice and easy does it.

She smiles and nods, not intimidated by having a drunk, forty-four-year-old detective sergeant hitting on her.

'I'm fine,' she says. 'You? That's a nice jacket you're wearing.'

Two-nil.

I smile – there's a lot of smiling going on. I hope nobody's watching, or they might vomit. It's got to be done, though.

'You're not looking too bad yourself.'

'You like this dress?' she says. No, not says, gushes. Her lips are moist, her nipples are hard and straining against the material, her eyes are showing glorious signs of intoxication.

'It's stunning, Hen.' Hesitate, think about it; might as well jump in headfirst. 'You're stunning.' Classic.

She laughs. Three-nil. Think she's going to say something, but doesn't. Her eyes say it all though. She's

21

probably heard about me from at least fifteen other women at the station. I'm drunk, horny, and I feel about eighteen-years-old. There's no stopping me now. Caution to the wind. Give it half an hour and she and I'll be back at my place, drunk, naked, and wild.

'I was thinking of leaving here,' I say. 'All this karaoke crap. Fancy coming back to mine?'

She laughs again. I could drink that laugh.

'I don't think so.'

Uh-oh? Three-one.

Time. Slows. Down.

'Why not?' Stay calm.

'Well, it wouldn't be right.'

Three-two.

'You think?' Maintain control.

'Well… it'd be like shagging my dad.'

Fuck me.

An equaliser, a winner and at least fifteen more goals just to rub it in.

She has the decency to look a bit embarrassed but once the ball's in the net, it's in the net. Contemplate a rearguard action, possibly a scorched earth policy, decide the better of it. Everyone's interests will be best served by a quick and quiet withdrawal.

I shrug. 'Right enough, then,' I say.

She laughs, looks embarrassed again, doesn't say anything. The final whistle blows, I turn my back and walk off. Imagine that every other guy in the place is laughing at me. Find Taylor sitting alone at the table, sullenness having returned.

'Missed the target, then?' he says.

I nod, shrug, start to make my way to the bar. There's a bubbling annoyance in my head, but that's just the embarrassment. 'Want something stiffer this time?'

Taylor thinks about it, then says, 'Johnnie Walker.'

Right. Off I go, feeling utterly emasculated and determined to get even more tanked out of my face than usual. Look to the middle of the floor to watch Edwards nearing the end of his Robbie Williams. Not surprisingly, he's completely naked and making a total dick of himself. He may have no chest hair, but at least his knob is in fine form.

5

Tuesday morning, the top end of Cambuslang, nearly to Halfway. A cordoned-off road, with the usual ghouls a few hundred yards away.

The body's long gone, and will currently be under the knives of Baird and Balingol, this year's pathologists. Butchery with a sharp knife and a smile. I didn't see it, of course. Only got here this morning. Herrod said it was horrific. A bloody mess. Shredded. Glad I missed it. Dead bodies give me too many flashbacks, and I have a hard enough time keeping all those buried memories in their place as it is.

Crawled in, massively hung over, just after eight this morning, to find the station had gone berserk. A major murder three days before Christmas. All hands on deck, with Bloonsbury in charge of the sinking ship. Very brave. He's back there now, coordinating. Taylor's been roped in as well, not too happy about having to answer to the call of drunken Jonah, but that's the way it has to be. Seniority.

They didn't do much last night, but the shit's flying this morning. House to house all the way up this street, and back out along the main road. They'll branch out soon, see what they can get from the surrounding area.

At the moment they're estimating the time of death between ten and eleven-thirty. Most of these people were in their beds by then, or watching TV. The drudgery of normal life. The body was found by some bloke about to take the dog for a walk. Didn't recognise her, such was the disfigurement of her face, but we've since learned that he knows her. We'll ask the right questions. You never know what people will do, but instinct says it wasn't him. The guy's in shock. He'll probably need therapy – it's the modern way. If he can find someone to sue, he'll do that as well. These days you can't solve anything in life without employing a psychotherapist, a solicitor and a life coach. The supermarkets'll be offering those services soon, wait and see.

Herrod's up the other end of the street, house to house. In a better frame of mind this morning. He enjoys murder. Thinks it justifies his existence. Sometimes you'd think he'd commit murder, just to give us all something to investigate.

Bathurst is out there somewhere too. Saw her briefly this morning and she was decent enough not to give me a 'made a tube of yourself last night, didn't you?' smile. Very professional, although she just looked miserable. Regrets turning me down, I expect.

PC Edwards approaches, closed notebook in hand, looking like a man who stripped naked in front of his peers last night, and is regretting every minute. He was another one to make a move on Bathurst, I believe, and was no more successful than I.

'Didn't get much sleep, eh, Constable?'

He shakes his head. Daft bastard.

'Nice y-fronts, by the way. Think you'll ever get them back?'

He shifts uncomfortably. Itching to tell me where to go, I suspect. Can't, of course, so he goes for the quick change of subject.

'There's a woman over here you might like to speak to, sir. Knew the deceased.'

Fair enough. Can't spend too much time laughing at young constables when there's been a murder. I nod and follow him to a terraced house, not far from the close where the body was discovered. Perhaps the street won't be such a barren desert of non-information after all.

Don't feel up to interrogation, and hope the woman wasn't a close friend of the victim who'll spend the interview blubbing. That's how it is nowadays. Everybody cries. We have the blessed Diana to thank for making it respectable. Or, at least, those who murdered her.

Walk into the front room. Ground floor house, where

---

the sun never shines. Maybe in late afternoon. A drab little room, a few desultory Christmas decorations, and a drab young woman sitting in the middle of it, looking as if she's upset because she's run out of Frosties. A cup of tea held between the hands, TV on, sound off.

I sit down opposite, and she notices me for the first time. Constable Edwards stands by the door. Hope I don't look as bad as he does.

'Detective Sergeant Hutton,' I say.

She nods, drinks a noisy sip from her tea, looks at the silent television.

'Mrs. Eileen Sprott,' volunteers Edwards from the door.

Hold my hand up to him. See him nod and retreat further behind that rough exterior. Other things to think about, such as how to explain to his fiancée all those photographs of him naked which have probably already start turning up on the Internet. We polis are an unforgiving lot.

Mind on the job.

'I understand you knew Miss Keller.'

Wonder who's been dispatched to inform the parents. Hope it's not Bloonsbury himself.

She looks at me, another noisy slurp.

'Well, aye. Not that well, but. Used to get the same bus from town sometimes.'

'And when was the last time?'

'Last night, you know. She seemed happy enough. Well, you know, not great, but then, why should any bastard be that happy? It's a shit life, in't it? Now she's dead. Can't believe it.'

'Where d'you get the bus from?'

'Buchanan Street. I work in a jewellers in the arcade, and she worked in Frasers, something like that. Part time, I think. Saw her about town sometimes, but we weren't that friendly. You know.'

That's good. The automatic distancing. Doesn't want to associate too closely with the victim. A little bit of dishonesty never did anyone any harm, and it means she's less likely to go to pieces on me.

'And did you go out much in the evenings or weekends?'

'Do I go out much? Who d'you think I am? Billy No Mates?'

'Not you.' Jesus. 'Did you go out with Miss Keller?'

'Oh.'

Really?

'Naw, naw, not much. Every now and again, you know, but not often.'

'When was the last time?'

'A couple of weekends ago. I can't remember.'

'Did she say anything on the bus yesterday about what she was going to do last night?'

She looks at me, nodding. Face like a kid who wants to tell the teacher who it was who threw the piece of chalk.

'Aye, that's the thing. She says she was going to the pictures, you know, that wee one along the road. The one that shows all that foreign shite. I was having a right go at her, so I was.'

'She say who she was going with?'

'Aye. Some bloke.'

'Any idea who it might've been?'

'Not sure really, you know. Some guy she's seen a few times. Think he's from around here somewhere, you know, Cam'slang, but I'm not sure.'

'Had you ever seen him?'

Big shake of the head. Drawing back before she gets too close.

'Naw, naw. I joked with her about getting a look at the guy, you know, but I hadn't seen him. Says he was good looking, but you never know, do you? I used to think my Malky was good looking, but look at the bastard now.'

Automatically find myself looking around to see if there's a photo of Malky. She slurps her tea, then her eyes light up and she looks at the TV. Follow her gaze. It's some sad looking guy I've never seen before, and you can tell she's itching to turn the sound up. Time to leave her to

27

it.

'Well, thanks very much, Mrs. Sprott. We'll need you to come to the station later to make a statement.'

'Why? What have I done?'

'You haven't done anything. It's just procedure.' I love that innate trust of the polis. Course, she's right.

'Oh.' Looks back at the TV. Time to go.

I nod at Edwards, he opens the door and out we go, back into the cold of early morning. As we close the door behind us the TV is turned back up, and Mrs. Sprott goes about the business of forgetting everything she knows about Ann Keller.

We stand outside the house and take a look up the street. At least twenty officers milling around doing the thing. Most of them will come up empty, but every now and again you get something like I just did. Put it all together, and you never know. There's a long way to go, and most of it'll be pretty boring. I start to trudge off, head down, wishing for once that I had a cup of tea, rather than a vodka and tonic.

'Why didn't you ask about Malky?' says Edwards, one pace behind.

I stop and look at him, shaking the head.

'Get me a cup of tea, please, Constable?'

He looks chastened and walks off.

Because I'm hungover and I didn't think to, that's why I didn't ask about Malky. But he doesn't need to know that.

6

Almost four-thirty and there's about fifteen of us in the room. What will become the daily roundup, assuming this thing isn't solved inside the first day. Waiting for Bloonsbury to arrive and take charge. He's in with Miller giving her all the latest, and probably getting his balls roasted for not having caught the killer yet.

So, he'll get shredded in there, then after this briefing he'll have to go out and face the hounds of the press, when he'll probably get shredded again. He'll consider this a pleasant interlude.

They've got the photographs on the wall. Before and after, and it's not noticeably the same woman. Sure, we get murder in these parts, although this is Glasgow not Juarez; but not like this. Domestic, casual, accidental, thuggery, we get them every now and again, a few a year. But this; violent, savage, psychotic.

Most of the folks around here are out of their depth. You can tell. They have the look. I wish I was there, out of my depth with them. I may not want to look at those photographs, I may hate the fact that this kind of death has found its way onto our patch, but I've seen worse in the flesh. The bloody, torn and shattered flesh. And every one of those damned photographs takes me back, which is why I'm not looking at them.

Dear old Bloonsbury must be panicking over this one, and God knows what state he's in, given the alcoholic abyss into which he's been plummeting these last few years.

There's some muted conversation, but not much. Not with this on, not with those pictures on the wall. We're all waiting for Bloonsbury so we can go out and get on with it, or go home and try to forget it for the night. Be thankful it wasn't our wife or daughter or whoever that had their entire body slashed to pieces, and hope that it doesn't happen again before we catch the animal who did it.

The domestic stuff keeps intruding there as well. It's inane, but you can't stop it. Still no idea what to get Rebecca for her Christmas. Seeing them tomorrow, although at this rate I might have to cancel. Pizza and presents, and I'll hand over the gift for their mother and hope I get something back. Gone a bit over the top this year. Diamond earrings, just under five hundred quid out of some place in town. Money I can't afford for a present for my ex-wife who's seeing someone else. I don't think I'm trying to get her back, but then why else am I spending the money?

The door opens, and I'm torn from my worsening morosity. DCI Bloonsbury, looking as if he's just been savaged. Think he needs hospitalised. He's a big man, six-five maybe. Back row forward in his day, played a Scotland trial. Nearly made it, although in those days all you got for playing rugby was a lot of sore joints and absurd ears. Well, the way he walks now he certainly got the sore joints. I'm five ten and I could head butt the guy without needing to stretch. He's got the ruddy face of the alcoholic, and looks way beyond fifty-three. The man's a disaster, but somehow, he's been managing to get by the past couple of years.

There was a time last year when he was almost done. His wife had just upped and left him for a plumber from Dundee, taking the kids and everything else of worth in the family. Bloonsbury went over the edge, yet somehow managed to claw his way back. Got a lot of help. He's a bit of a hero round here, for one reason or another. Used to be the star, and people still want to look up to him, even though more and more of us are seeing through him.

So, this was his crowning glory from last year. Just as he was at his lowest ebb, he came up with a beauty. Big murder case out this end of Glasgow. A young woman got one in the neck from some ski-masked fucker with a kitchen knife. The feeling that he was going to be a repeat murderer quickly grew, women all over the city were panicking, and we were looking useless. Bloonsbury was in charge, the investigation seemingly stuck in neutral, and then boom, out of nowhere, the big man put it together, made the breakthrough, and we got the guy. Some demented head-twitcher from the west end who denied it all the way to the joint, but we had him. Enough evidence to put away a thousand murderers.

Bloonsbury was the hero, feted in the papers, got that ugly mug on TV, had all sorts of people queuing up to suck him off. Don't know how he did it, given the state he was in at the time, but it was good to see. Trouble is, of course, he's been getting all the big ones ever since, and not been doing too well. This'll be the last chance, and it's tough not to imagine him hitting the bottle even harder, and maybe, if he's lucky, his liver'll give out and he'll die before he can blow it.

He comes to the front of the room, looking like shit. Stares at us, we stare back. You can see he would rather just be down the pub staring at a full bottle of Glen Ord, or one of these other single malts he occasionally fancies himself as being able to tell the difference between.

'Right then, gentlemen,' he says, ignoring the five women, 'all the facts. What have we got? Herrod?'

Herrod looks to his notebook.

'Victim, Ann Keller. Dark brown hair, twenty-seven, bit of a looker. Had two part-time jobs. Ancillary at the Victoria, sales at Frasers in Buchanan Street. Worked in the shop on Monday, was due in the hospital today.' He pauses, looks through the notes. Try not to let my mind wander, having heard all this stuff already. 'Went to the Classic cinema to see some foreign film.'

Herrod can't distinguish between countries. Never been abroad. There's British, and there's foreign. I talked to him about the Balkans once. But just the once. Knew not to do it again.

'She was due to go with her boyfriend, one Christopher James from Cambuslang, although the usherette

---

31

remembers her as being on her own. He claims to have cancelled the date.'

Bloonsbury blurts in. 'You been speaking to him, Dan?'

'Been in with him most of the afternoon,' says Taylor. 'No alibi for last night. Stayed in, watched telly. Can describe what was on, but that doesn't mean anything. Looks pretty upset. Forensics have been over his flat, we'll see what they come up with. I'm guessing it'll be nothing. Don't think he's our man.'

'Why didn't he go to the pictures?'

'They had a fight. Something to do with a necklace given to her by an ex-boyfriend.'

'Got a name?'

'Looking into it. We'll find him, get him in.'

'Could he have made the story up? Deflect attention, and all that?'

All right, it's a low bar, but this is Bloonsbury a Hell of a lot more switched on than he's been in months. Maybe he's going to go for this one. Wants to be the hero again. Get his name in the papers.

'Don't know. We'll talk to the guy, see what we come up with.'

'Right. Herrod, what else?'

Herrod looks pissed off. I sometimes wonder if he reveres Bloonsbury or hates the sight of him. Or both. Then there are the times when I realise I don't give a shit either way. They deserve each other.

'She leaves the pictures, walks home. Ten-minute walk, she never gets there. Somewhere along the way she's accosted, strangled, stabbed.' Looks at his notebook. 'A hundred and twenty-five times, mostly in the face and chest.' Jesus. Herrod looks at the women, slightly embarrassed, as if they might be delicate. Old fashioned, Herrod. 'He pulled her into a close entrance before he did it, then left the body where he killed her. Found by some poor bastard who lives on the third floor. The deed couldn't have been done more than three or four minutes. The guy checks out, by the way.'

Silence. We're all mad, tough bastards here, but this kind of thing's always going to grab you by the balls, regardless of how many thugs you've arrested. Regardless of how many bodies you've seen decapitated and dumped in a pile in the middle of a forest.

'Why do you suppose he did that?' says Bloonsbury.

'What?'

'Stab her over a hundred times.'

Herrod shrugs. 'I don't fucking know, do I?' he says bluntly. I can't help smiling at that, but quickly wipe it off.

'Aye, right, fine. Any ideas people?' says Bloonsbury looking around the room.

DS Harrison speaks up. An attractive woman, Eileen, and as an extra bonus she's lesbian, making her one of the few women around here that I've not made an idiot of myself over.

'He knew her, hated her, got carried away with an act of vengeance.'

'Maybe,' says Bloonsbury. Never know with the guy if he's being cagey or slow.

I shrug and decide to participate. 'The guy was hardly rational. From the ferocity of the attack, we know he lost it. Lost control. You stab someone over a hundred times, you're not thinking straight. Makes it hard to work out his motivation.'

Bloonsbury sighs, shakes his head. 'Aye, I suppose you're right.' Starts rubbing his eye. The man needs a drink. 'I'll speak to that doctor, what's his name?'

'Arkansas,' volunteers a voice from the floor.

'Aye, right, how could I forget a stupid name like that? All right, anything else? Did the knobs at pathology have anything illuminating to tell us?'

Herrod. 'Aye. Apparently, she'd had sex yesterday afternoon. There were still traces of semen,' and he looks shyly around the women-folk again, 'you know, inside her. Timing-wise, unrelated to the murder. From that we've got male, mid-thirties, blood group AB neg, and that's our lot.'

I tell you, Baird and Balingol are something else. How

33

did they manage to work out that the guy's male just from his semen?

'Ties in with the boyfriend, presumably,' says Bloonsbury, looking at Taylor.

'Aye,' says Taylor. 'Did it in the afternoon, in the toilets in his work in town, he says. It was after that she told him about the present from her ex. They argued, the usual thing. She left without it being resolved whether he'd go to the cinema. He thought about it, decided not to.'

'Right,' says Bloonsbury.

He looks around the room, not sure where else to go with this.

'Right,' he says again, 'this is a sick bastard we've got here. People are going to be shitting their pants, so we need this guy off the streets before Christmas. So, I know we've all got things to do at this time of year, but the quicker we get this out the way, the more time we can spend on enjoying ourselves. So, let's give it everything we've got for the next couple of days.'

Very inspiring.

'Right. We've got descriptions of the lassie going out on the news, phone lines open, and all that. You all know what you're doing, so get out there and get on with it. I've got to go and speak to the papers.'

The meeting starts to break up. All hands on deck. Let's hope there's no more crime in the area for the next few days. Bloonsbury leads the way out the room and then we all start to shuffle after him. Taylor puts his hand on my shoulder.

'I need a drink, Tom. You coming?'

Where better to increase pressure in the investigation than from the pub? I nod and lead the way. The group disperses around the station, each with things to do. Not much conversation. All this is very intense. The thought that at some stage we're going to come face to face with this guy. And if we don't, it's because we'll have fucked it.

Almost out the door when Sergeant Ramsey stops my steady progress towards the first vodka tonic of the day.

'Got something for you, Tom.'

'What?' I don't look impressed.

'Aggravated assault in Westburn. Your show.'

Fuck.

Taylor shrugs. 'See you in a couple of hours, Sergeant. I'll still be there.'

Aye, right.

7

Superintendent Charlotte Miller is forty-nine, and therefore younger than a lot of the chief inspectors at her fingertips. This is, no surprise, a source of friction. Most of these guys are in their early fifties, they're not going anywhere, and they're from the 'women should be in the kitchen, either doing the washing up, or getting taken over the table in a porn video' generation. Confronted with a woman who is a) smarter than them, b) in a position to tell them what to do, c) going places they can't even dream about, and d) much, much better looking, most of them spend their days in a foul mood, dumping on delinquent constables. And sergeants.

Point d) may seem the most trivial and sexist of the lot, but you have to be realistic. If this woman looked like one of those 1970's Czechoslovak shot putters, chewed tobacco and bent iron bars with her teeth, I'm sure they could cope with it a lot better. But she's a dream. I'd have her before any of these strapping, ball-crushing constables that pass through here – even the good-looking ones like Bathurst – but there's no way Miller's going anywhere near the likes of me. It's not because she's married, because faithful she ain't. It's a power thing. She goes for people in power, people that can do things for her. And note that – people. Not just men.

Gorgeous *and* bisexual. Holy crap. Seriously, any time you meet a woman like that, it's like they've been invented. By me. The chances of me, Miller and another gorgeous woman all ending up in bed together might be nil, but at least they're not as nil as they would be if she wasn't bisexual in the first place.

Look, don't sneer. We've all got an imagination, and this is how I choose to exercise mine. What do any of us think about, comforting ourselves to sleep at night in a

Walter Mitty-esque fantasy?

Things did change a little between Miller and I a few months ago. I guess I'd always had the same opinion of her as most of the other men around here – that vague mixture of suspicion, jealousy and lust – then one day I blundered into her office without knocking just as she was changing to go out to an official lunch.

It was late summer. She'd been wearing a white blouse and I'm guessing, a white bra, and I walked in on her as she had both of them off and was standing by her desk in trousers and nothing else. As I entered, she was bending over, but she straightened up, made no attempt to cover herself and looked at me as if she wasn't standing there topless.

It was a weird moment. We stared at each other for a long time; although, obviously, when I say we stared at each other, I mean she looked me in the eye while I stared at her breasts. I knew it was wrong, but by God I couldn't stop. I was keen to look her in the eye, I really was, but all I could do was stare at her breasts, thinking, holy mother of all Jesus, those are the most magnificent breasts I've ever seen in my life, I want those breasts. I couldn't speak, because all I would have said was, *Wow, look at your breasts*, or *Have you seen your breasts, they're amazing* or something equally stupid. So, I stood there, mouth slightly open, staring at her breasts, until she said, 'Sergeant?' and the spell was broken.

I finally managed to look her in the eye, said, 'It can wait,' and left, closing the door behind me.

I remember walking out into the station thinking that it was utterly bizarre that a man – me – who had seen so many breasts in his life, should be so enamoured by any pair of breasts, but I was hooked. Must admit that I've viewed her with a lot more respect since then.

That's probably wrong, isn't it?

She's married to a boring suit called Frank, who sells oatcakes or some shit like that abroad. So the guy's never here, which gives her plenty of time for bridge building.

Met the bloke a couple of times and nearly fell asleep talking to him. One of the camel coat Ibrox brigade, turns up there about once a season and talks as if he knows a shit-tonne about Scottish football, when in truth he doesn't know any more than any other comedian who supports the Rangers. Believe he's got designs on becoming a director, and they're welcome to each other.

It's nearly ten o'clock and me and Taylor are sitting in the pub. I've just arrived, having smoked my fiftieth of the day on the way here. Taylor's been here since about five. Given that, he's remarkably cogent. Probably been making a pint last a few hours, since there was no one here to buy him a round.

The aggravated assault was the usual thing. Domestic, brothers, one of them ended up in hospital, the other's in a holding cell back at the station. They were fighting over a woman, which is no surprise, and she played the innocent, desperately concerned third party throughout. Playing one off against the other, and if any of them should be in the slammer, it's her.

'Your round,' says Taylor, with the detective's eye for detail. I think I could dispute that but choose not to bother. Make my way to the bar, catch the eye of the sultry barperson, Agnes.

'Vodka tonic, and a pint of heavy,' I say, and she nods and goes about her business. It's a quiet night, there's no one else within hearing range and I wonder whether I should go for it. She's wearing a tight white top, displaying adequate amounts of cleavage, and as she bends down to retrieve the tonic from the fridge, I get a good view of her massive buttocks. Very sexy. She stands up, slightly flushed around the chops, not a bad looking girl. Nevertheless, decide against. Go for idle chatter.

'Can you change the tape, love?'

She listens to the music for a second and shrugs.

'It's Christmas,' she says, pouring the pint.

'There's more to Christmas than Band Aid. You must have Bob's Christmas album.'

'Bob who?' she says.

Decide it was just as well I didn't go for it and hand over a twenty-pound note. Then, drinks and change in hand, make my way back to the table. Sit down, suddenly occurs to me it's a few hours nearer Christmas and I still don't have anything for Rebecca. Look at the watch. Have to have something by five o'clock tomorrow evening.

'What do you think of Bloonsbury?' says Taylor, licking the froth from his lips.

'What do I think of him?'

'Aye. Has he still got it? For a big case like this, I mean.'

'I doubt it, but he seemed a bit more switched on this afternoon. But let's face it, the Addison case aside, what's he done in the last five years?'

No answer. There is no answer.

'So why,' I say, 'did she put him on this one?'

Taylor shrugs. 'So's he'll screw up, maybe.'

'Why?'

'It's like James Bond in *The Man With the Golden Gun*.'

'You mean there's an Asian dwarf?'

'No, not the film, the book.'

'Never read it.'

'James Bond's washed up, at a dead end. He's been brainwashed by the Russians. The Secret Service have no more use for him. But, you know, he's James Bond. They can't just pack him off to a desk job. So they send him after Scaramanga, the deadliest assassin in the world. If he kills him then he's proved his worth; if he gets killed, then they don't have the problem of what to do with James Bond.'

'So what happens?'

'What do you mean, what happens? It's James fucking Bond. What d'you think happens?'

'Bloonsbury ain't no James Bond.'

Taylor lifts an eyebrow.

'Damned right he's not. She's sailing him down the river and when he screws up, he's gone.'

Take my first drink. Goddamn. Put in too much tonic. How do I manage to still do that after seven or eight million of them?

'So then what?'

'We get it,' he says, shaking his head. 'Would have been Crow, but now that he's sloped off to his one-bedroomed ruin in Arrochar, we'll get stuck with it. And it'll probably be after he's killed again, and the press are baying for blood. Bloonsbury's won't be enough.'

'So?'

'So, we'd better start thinking about how we're going to get this guy.'

'Oh.' Work. 'So that's what you've been sitting here thinking about, is it?'

'Not just that,' he says, and I'm not sure I want to know what that means. 'Anyway, someone's got to do it, 'cause Jonah's probably face down in a ditch by now.'

'What have you come up with for your five hours ruminations?'

He takes an especially large drink, licks the froth from his lips, lays his hands on the table.

'Fuck all. I was waiting for you.'

Very funny.

'I'm serious,' he says in reply to the look on my face. 'So, what have we got? Some weird bastard who slashes a woman to pieces. Total rage, cutting her up to the extent that she's unrecognisable.'

'Why not just leave it to the profilers?' They have these folk who just sit there all day inventing people. Someone pishes against a wall and they spend three weeks compiling the psychiatric profile of the man, before deciding his brother stuck a carrot up his arse when he was three.

He points his finger at me. I hate it when he does that. 'Because they don't know fuck all, son,' he says.

He's right.

'So why so brutal to the face?'

It's like being at school.

'Personal grudge.' Think about those photographs. 'Deep personal grudge.'

He nods. 'Either against her, or someone who looks like her.' Fits the bill. 'I'll go for the latter. If he knew her, we'll find out about it, but it doesn't feel right.'

'Could be some psycho who sort of knew her. Worshipped her from afar, et cetera. She didn't know anything about it, he makes his approach one night after the cinema, she rejects him, he loses his shit.'

'Maybe, maybe. I don't know. I like the sound of it being some flake with no previous relation to her at all. Completely arbitrary. If she hadn't been there last night, she would never have got it. She was in someone else's place.'

'So, what? We're looking for a guy who's been dumped by a girl with dark brown hair? That could be me.'

'Aye, well you've been dumped by just about every size, hair colour, personality type combination, so I'm not about to drag you in.'

'Thanks.'

'Don't mention it.' He takes another drink. Funny how he's managed to speed up now he's got someone to buy him a round. 'What we need is a description. She was walking along a main road, for fuck's sake, just come out of a busy cinema.'

'There were like ten people at it.'

'Whatever. You'd think the woman in the ticket booth, at least, would be able to remember a few more faces.'

'You can't rely on people.'

'Ain't that the truth,' says Taylor, then with another long pull at his glass he finishes off his pint. 'Buy you another, Hutton,' he adds, to general astonishment.

I nod in surprise. Taylor never buys a round at home. Now, two nights in a row.

Taylor makes his way to the bar, I look around the pub. The usual crew. One or two others from the station, but never too many. Most of them prefer the Whale, and they're welcome to it.

The door to the pub opens, and with a portentous gust of cold wind, in walks Charlotte Miller. Raised eyebrows from the Feds, and then we all pretend we haven't noticed.

Try not to choke on my vodka when she walks over to our table and sits down. I attempt a smile of acknowledgement. Smell her perfume, breathe it in. *Don't imagine her naked...!* She's wearing a fuck-off blue trouser suit and, as usual after fourteen hours in the office, looks as if she just got dressed five minutes ago.

'It's a cold night,' she says, rubbing her hands.

I nod. Look her in the eye. Seems there's a bit of a spark there, as there has been ever since the breasts incident. (In my head it's known as the Breasts Incident.)

'What happened with the assault? Brothers, was it?'

'Yep.' Talk normally. 'We've got one at the station, the other's in hospital.'

'Over a woman?'

'Yep.' She smiles at this and shakes her head.

'You men are all alike,' she says, mundanely.

Taylor returns with the drinks and nearly drops his pint. Makes a quick recovery. Give the guy his due. He's suspicious of her, but she doesn't turn him into a quivering blob of jelly, the way she does some of his contemporaries.

'Dan,' she says. 'Been here long?'

Classic. She'll know exactly how long he's been here. Now me, that would have had me in a tangle of deceit and idiocy, trying to explain why I'd spent so long in the pub. But so what if Bloonsbury had given us his big Jock Stein speech? It was the end of the day and if we had nothing else immediate and wanted to sit in the pub, we could. But I would still be trying to justify myself. Taylor's too cool for that; or past caring.

'About five hours,' he says. 'Can I get you a drink?'

She nods. 'Bruichladdich, neat, thanks.'

He turns back to the bar. She taps her fingers on the table. Long fingers, and I imagine them all over my body. Sometimes I bore even myself with the ridiculous one-tracked-ness of my brain when this woman is around.

'What are you doing for Christmas?' she asks.

'Working.' Stick to one-word answers.

She smiles, almost looks understanding. 'Someone's got to. Frank and I are going to Braemar.'

I nod, unsurprised. Braemar. Of course.

'When are you seeing the children?' she asks.

'Tomorrow evening.' She asks about the children every now and again. I think she learned to do it on a management weekend. One of these things where they pitch twenty people into a bog on Benbecula with a box of matches, a pot noodle and three sheets of toilet paper, and tell them to survive for a fortnight.

'Oh,' she says. Taylor is labouring behind a guy at the bar trying to decide between cheese & onion or chardonnay & pickle flavour. 'You won't be out late, though?'

I think I'm starting to sort of gawp at her. She must know the look. What's she getting at? I don't see this coming at all. She almost sounds nervous, except that it's not a word I could possibly associate with her. I shake my head and say, 'I doubt it.'

She taps her fingers.

'I was wondering if you'd like to come over later. To the house, I mean. Frank's going to Aberdeen on business for the night. Just like him, Christmas Eve, for God's sake, but you know what he's like. Meeting him in Braemar on Thursday morning.'

Various thoughts flash around my head. Vague things about Aberdeen and Frank. Push them to the side. She's inviting me to dinner, at her place, when her husband's going to be out of town. What in the name of Dylan could that be about?

'I think I could manage that.'

She smiles. I could eat that smile. 'Great. I'll speak to you tomorrow.'

Taylor returns, glass in hand, lays it down in front of her. Wonder if he notices how pale I've become.

———

She smiles at him, lifts the glass. 'Cheers,' she says, and before we can make a grab for our drinks, she's downed it in one. Looks at the two of us. Having said what she came to say, and realising she isn't about to get any meaningful conversation, she stands up.

'Right,' she says, 'thanks for the drink, Dan. See you both tomorrow.'

We nod, she turns and walks out, leaving a trace of expensive perfume in the air. We watch her go, then the door is closed behind her and Taylor looks curiously across the table.

A moment, then he says, 'What, Sergeant, was that all about?'

'I'm not sure,' I reply, shaking my head. 'There are dark forces at work that neither of us can possibly hope to understand.'

He rolls his eyes, and takes another long drink.

8

He remembers a frosty November morning. Breakfast in a café in the centre of town, and then a walk through Kelvingrove Park. The sky was clear, the air was cold and crisp. The morning that it started to go wrong.

They had spent the night together; made love in the evening, and then again in the morning, although only after she'd insisted on a trip to the bathroom for mouthwash. She had ordered pancakes, maple syrup and bacon for breakfast; he'd ordered the same. They both drank coffee.

They'd talked about her buying a new computer. He was trying to persuade her to get a Mac, because he had a Mac, and he would have been able to help her out with any problems. She'd said with a smile that it was almost as if he was being co-dependent sometimes. When she'd seen the look on his face, she'd quickly added that she was kidding. Even though he'd known what it meant, he'd Googled *co-dependent* when he'd got home, to find out if there was anything else that she could have meant by it, some way in which she could have offended him that he hadn't already realised.

By then it had already started, they'd already had their first major fight. Walking through the park, hand in hand, the morning as perfect as it could get, sex and breakfast and blue skies and crisp, fresh, clean, sharp air, they had met two of Jo's friends. Alex and Eugenie. Out for a walk on a cold, crisp and fresh November morning. They had stood and chatted, although he had not had much to say. They'd been Jo's friends not his, he considered it just an interruption to the perfection of the morning. And then Alex had suggested they all went for coffee, and the interruption had suddenly blown their day apart. Jo had looked at him, he had silently conveyed his desire to not

---

go for coffee, and then she had accepted.

They sat in the coffee shop for an hour and a half. He said nothing. He had wanted Jo to know how much he didn't want to be there. He'd stared out the window. He'd looked bored. At one point, after the mugs had been cleared away, he'd even put his head on the table. It hadn't seemed rude, not to him. He had merely been expressing himself. He thought it would have been ruder to say something.

When Alex and Eugenie had gone, Jo had torn into him. She didn't use the word co-dependent then. Worse. Much worse. They had argued in the street. People gave them a wide berth.

Later they'd kissed, they'd made up. A few days later, at any rate. They'd had sex again, but it wasn't quite as magical as the mouthwash morning. It was never quite as magical again.

Co-dependent. That was what she'd said. He called it caring and loving, a desire to see that everything was perfect in her life. And she'd called him co-dependent.

Before the end he had bought a PC, so that he could help her out with any PC difficulties she might happen across.

*

Early morning. He stands in the newsagent. Looking for a present for Jo, although he's not sure when he's going to get the chance to give it to her.

He buys presents every now and again. When she comes back, he'll be ready. This one is because he's feeling guilty. Guilty about what he'd done to Jo the previous evening. He'd only wanted to talk to her. Had only wanted to sit down, find out how she'd been doing. It would have been nice to hold her, to run his fingers over her skin, to kiss her; to lie naked with her, to caress her breasts, to eat her, his lips and tongue all over her body; to slam into her, his erection aching and sore, over and over.

Had that been too much to ask? That was all, all he had wanted. Why hadn't she just said yes? It was Jo, he was sure it had been Jo. Why hadn't she just agreed to make love to him, like she had so often in the past?

He looks helplessly along an endless collection of boxes of chocolates. A glorious array of enticing packages, and every one, everything he looks at, reminds him of Jo, and reminds him of that bloodied body. He sees blood spraying into the air, he feels the knife warm and damp in his hands, he feels the soft flesh of the face splay under the force of his stabbing. It all makes him feel vaguely unwell, nauseous, but he decides it's because he hasn't had any breakfast. He wonders if he should go for a cup of tea. Looks at his watch, almost time to get to work. Plate of Cheerios would sort him out.

He can't get the vision of what he did out of his head. It was supposed to give him relief, but he is beginning to accept that maybe it wasn't Jo under that frantic knife. And he still wants to see her, but doesn't want to do to her what he did last night to that woman. That would be...unnecessary.

He looks over the middle row of books, feels a flurry of the heart, a coldness in the blood. Then he realises it's not her, not Jo, the woman with dark brown hair on the other side of the shop. She looks up, notices him staring at her, and looks away. The hair's the same. Maybe a bit shorter, curlier.

He starts to follow as the girl walks slowly out of the shop. Maybe it is Jo. Those eyes, he saw the light in those eyes. Maybe she's had plastic surgery so he wouldn't recognise her. That's the sort of thing women do.

He walks out into the cold, grey morning. Eyes narrowed. Heart beats quickly. She hasn't noticed yet as she walks along the crowded road. Too many people.

Could he do it again? So soon? The previous evening he had lost control and then staggered home to throw up, like a pathetic little child who couldn't take it. Staggered home in shock, throwing up when he walked into the house; and still the thought of it turns his stomach.

Jo steps under the bus shelter and waits. Seven or eight other people there. He follows her and stands at the side. Glances over occasionally, but she doesn't look back. Suffers the churning in his stomach, feels sick every time he thinks of what he did. Could he do it again? This time she catches his eye and he recognises that look. Fear.

Why are they all frightened of him? They don't know what he's going to do. Maybe it isn't fear. Maybe that's what he's looking for it to be. Maybe she's just got indigestion. So he smiles pleasantly and wonders which bus she's going to catch. He looks at his watch. He has to get to work, no point in arousing suspicion. There are too many people about anyway. This isn't a quiet street after dark. Morning rush hour is no time to make advances upon women, even when they ask for it. Gives her another look, which she avoids. Time to go to work.

He turns away from the bus stop, walks across the road and is nearly hit by a taxi. A horn blares.

9

Christmas Eve. Bloody awful morning. Had far too much to drink last night. Sat up until some time after three with Taylor, listening to all his marital difficulties. Wondered at first why he seemed reluctant to go home, then, as the lager took over, he started telling me all about it, and I got what I had managed to avoid at the party on Monday night. The 'my wife's having an affair' speech. It comes to us all, and you hear it so often you become immune – until you're the poor sod in question.

Debbie's all right, but she's a few years younger than him and that's always going to tell in the job. She's a teacher at Cathkin High, a new build on old playing fields up on the hill above Cambuslang. I went there in its previous incarnation, when the only things that were shiny were the razors the pupils used to cut up the drugs. God knows what it's like now they're in a new building the taxpayer'll still be forking out for in fifty years' time. Can't imagine it's any easier for the staff, and apparently she returns home every night with horror stories of student brutality and didactic ineptitude. Combine that with similar tales of wretchedness from Taylor, and you can tell what fun nights they must have in. I kept thinking of the irony of him feeling guilty all year about his fling with DS Murphy, when Debbie has spent most of that time in the arms of the biggest guy in the PE department.

So, I arrive this morning, ten minutes after eight, feeling and looking like shit, having totally forgotten about having to buy a present for Rebecca and a night in with the station god-queen. Saw Alison on my way in – think it's going to be a regular feature – and she nearly wet herself laughing.

Cup of coffee to start the day, then a phone call downstairs. The thug brother had been released with the usual stipulations, and I was happy because it meant I could forget about it for a while. Ten minutes later we got a message from the hospital that brother number two had just unexpectedly died. Brain haemorrhage, as far as they could tell, but they weren't sure. So we have to go and get the first idiot and bring him back in. Up the charge to murder or manslaughter, or whatever. Fortunately, that bit's out of my hands.

The clock has now ticked its way round to just after ten, and the office is in a state of ferment. Seventeen burglaries overnight, three reported rapes, a couple of major assaults, another ten or so minor ones, a shit-tonne of other petty criminal activity, and in the middle of all that some guy walks in and says he saw Ann Keller not far from the cinema, sometime after eleven on Monday night. Several people are wetting themselves with excitement. Bloonsbury presumably, but it's hard to tell. He has looked this morning – if it's possible – worse than me.

I've been delegated a sexual assault case, just so a bad morning can get a little bit worse. Young Asian girl attacked by three teenagers on her way home from a party. Father's going mental. Not at the teenagers – silent fury and a gun to the back of the head for them, should he ever find them – but at the mother for phoning us. There's no justice like your own justice, and you keep yourself to yourself. Anyway, I got packed off with PC Grant to start the ball rolling. Did our stuff to kick off the investigation, and now the girl's downstairs making a statement to a couple of female officers. Fine by me, and now I'm back on the murder case, detailed to follow up various reported sightings of Ann Keller the previous evening.

Most of them are futile – indeed, nearly half are downright impossible, given what we already know of her movements – and the rest are dubious. The only one to make any sort of sense was the bloke who came to the station. Everything he said tied in with what we already knew, and he came up with a description of the guy we're looking for. Assuming, of course, that this bloke isn't him.

These headcases move in mysterious ways. We got a photofit out of it anyway, and that'll be on the news all day. These things never actually look human, but sometimes they get results. Course, I've to spend the rest of the day following up all the other crank calls to see where it gets us, which will be nowhere.

On my way out, I bump into Sergeant Harrison. Experience has taught me to keep mouthwash in the desk drawer, so I'm no longer setting fire to everything upon which I breathe.

She's pinning something on the noticeboard about a police charity evening early in the New Year. I hate those things. Stand and watch her for a second, before realising I'm staring.

'Eileen,' I say.

She turns, smiles.

'Rough night?'

I ignore it. 'I need some advice.'

She sticks in the last drawing pin, checks it's straight, and steps back.

'Don't drink so much, and get to bed earlier.'

'Very funny. What do you know about twelve-year-old girls?'

She smiles. I like Eileen Harrison. Not sure why. Maybe it's because I'm pretty sure there's no chance I'll ever get her into bed.

'Well, I was one once, if that's any help.'

'I need an idea of what to get Rebecca for Christmas.'

'Your daughter?'

'Yep.'

She purses her lips.

'How much money are you spending?'

'Fifty pounds, maybe,' I say, wondering if I'll be judged.

'Is she mature for her age?'

Feel like I'm under investigation. Imagine Eileen Harrison viciously interrogating suspects.

'Not sure. I mean, you can't tell, can you? Who knows

what she's like when I'm not there? She could be doing drugs and boys and all that stuff, for all I know.'

Purses her lips again, looks disapproving. 'You've been in the job too long, Tom. Not all children are baby adults, doing dodgy deals and out for what they can get.'

'But some of them are.'

'Fine. Get her a piece of jewellery. If she's older than her years that'll do her, and if she's not, it'll make her feel mature, and show that you respect her. How's that?'

I look at her; she smiles and turns. Why is it that woman have so much more common sense than men? Must be genetic. We got testosterone, they got common sense and multiple orgasms.

'What kind of jewellery?' I say weakly to Eileen Harrison's back.

She turns, still smiling. Pitying smile, this time.

'Use your imagination, Tom, she's your daughter.' And off she goes to chew the testicles of hardened criminals.

Suitably chastened, I make my way out of the station.

*

Three down, four to go. This is going to be a long day. Sitting in the drab waiting area of a small lawyer's office in Tollcross as a result of a phone call from an Ian Healy, who says he saw our murder victim on Monday night. Sounds a little more plausible than the others, particularly the last one, a seventy-three-year-old man who claimed to have seen her in Woolworths in Rutherglen at half past ten yesterday morning.

I'm sitting beneath the watchful eye of an annoyed PA. Face like a wasp's sting, the typical Glasgow police sceptic. I want to arrest her for something.

The door opens, out steps Mr. Healy, preceded by a small man in tears, who looks suspiciously at me as he walks by.

'Don't worry,' says Healy to him, 'we'll get her back for you.'

The man half turns, gives a watery smile and is gone. There goes an interesting little story, the details of which I couldn't want to know less.

I stand up, take Healy's outstretched hand.

'Detective Sergeant Hutton,' I say. Firm grip, the guy's young and doesn't look like a fool. We're a couple of goals to the good already.

'Come in, Sergeant,' he says, and ushers me past the PA.

Walk in, simple enough office, sit down.

'Sorry about Mr. McKay,' he says. 'Problems with his dog.'

'Ah,' I say. I really don't care about the dog.

'Very weird situation,' says Healy.

'I believe you might've seen Ann Keller on Monday evening?' I say, cutting to the business end.

He nods, looks serious, leans forward. 'Yes. Monday night, on my way home from the pub. It would've been some time not long after eleven.'

'Was she alone?'

He nods, looks even more serious. I hate lawyers. 'Yes. Well, kind of, but that was the thing. There was a guy walking just behind her. I didn't pay that much attention, but I got the impression he was following her, hassling her…'

'So why didn't you say anything? Give her some help?'

He looks taken aback. The question wasn't entirely fair – implied that the woman might not be dead if he'd done something – but it doesn't do any harm to keep them on their toes.

'I don't know. You don't, do you? He wasn't speaking to her or anything. It was just an impression I got. I forgot about it until I saw the news last night.'

'Aye, fine.' Shuffle about in the pocket, produce a photofit picture, pass it across the desk.

He studies it, shakes his head. 'Definitely not.'

Good. That was a picture of Herrod, and the first two I showed it to already identified him as the killer. It'd be

---

53

pretty funny if it was, but unfortunately, he's got a hundred and fifty police witnesses as an alibi.

Pass over another picture. He looks at it, shakes his head again. Pass the third over, the real one this time. He studies it closely, another shake of the head.

'No, not him either. At least, I don't think so.'

I take it back off him, look at it, shove it back in my pocket. These damned pictures are lousy. It could be anybody. It could be this guy sitting across the desk.

'Do you think you'd be able to come down to the station later and make up one of these for the man you saw?'

Slight twitch, hesitation – just enough – then, 'Sure. Not for a couple of hours, but I could do it this afternoon.'

Don't betray your thought. 'That'd be great, thanks Mr. Healy.'

You never know what these headcases are going to do. It takes a mad bastard to invite the police in when you've committed murder, but then it takes a mad bastard to knife a woman over a hundred times.

Five minutes later I'm walking down the stairs, staring at the photofit. It's not right, but it's not a million miles away. And our witness only got a brief look at him, so who knows how accurate the picture is in the first place? There was never enough there to suggest Healy's our man, just a suspicion, and if I'd still been hungover, I would have missed it. There's a lot said for gut feelings, but I usually find they come to nought or make you look like an idiot. Sometimes, though, they pan out and then you look like a genius, so you have to go with them.

Let the guy come into the station and then see what we can make of him. Won't be hard. Find out what pub he was in, who he was with, check it out. Could have asked him in there, but didn't want to give anything away. If the guy suddenly disappears and another fifty murders are committed, I can take the time to feel bad.

Another check of the list. Four down, three to go.

10

Two o'clock – the time I fixed for Healy to pay us a call – came and went without a sign of the guy. Gave him some time to be late and then we all leapt into action. I had communicated my doubts about him to Bloonsbury, so when he didn't show, Jonah went from nought to sixty in the time it takes to down a double shot of a single malt.

Taylor and I went round there. The office had been closed up, but then it was Christmas Eve. Went to his house and he wasn't there, went to the PA's house, found her up to the armpits in Christmas cooking and looking as miserable as before. She told us Healy had left the office not long after twelve for a lunch appointment and that as far as she knew he'd intended going to the station thereafter. Claimed ignorance as to where he was having lunch but the woman's his PA for God's sake, she must've had some idea. Taylor persuaded me not to employ thumbscrews and we left without any further information.

Now nearly five and I've got to get going. Pizza and presents with the children. Found five minutes to disappear into a jewellers this morning, in between interviewing suspects, and got Rebecca a gold chain. Good for women of all ages, according to the girl in the shop. Bit nervous about what their mother is going to think of the diamond earrings. Shall see her briefly when I hand back the kids. Not as nervous as I am about what's to come later in the evening. Dinner with Charlotte Miller.

Walk into Taylor's office to say goodnight. We're all just out of the afternoon meeting, where we had the usual exchange of ideas. Things are moving. Plenty of calls from the public to follow up and now a juicy suspect has hoved into view. Pretty much decided the boyfriend is off the hook. Doesn't have the right look about him. We're checking out a few others from Ann Keller's rollcall of friends and relatives, including the ex who gave her the necklace that caused the fight with the boyfriend, but I still go for it being some psycho who hardly knew her.

Anyway, all we've got at the moment is our lawyer. However, once the initial gut feeling has passed, you have to be sceptical. It can't possibly be this simple. The guy wouldn't just present himself to us, no matter how much of a headcase he is. He probably hasn't turned up at the station because he's been knocked down by a bus, or he simply forgot. Anything. Hasn't stopped Bloonsbury breaking out into assholes and shitting himself with excitement, however.

Taylor looks up from his desk. Tired eyes, puffy face, the man needs a break. That, and vast amounts of alcohol.

'I'm off, sir. Got to go do the good father routine.'

He grunts. His desk is an unruly mass of paper. I've got a feeling that's the way he wants it, to keep him here well into the evening. Debbie must be out with her well-hung gymnastic instructor.

Taylor, the poor bastard. I know what it's all about, and all he has is his job.

'Exchange of presents?' he says, voice weary.

'God knows what they'll have bought me this year.'

He grunts out a laugh, face doesn't change.

'Right. I'm going to stay here for a while. Think Jonah's going to be working late. Two sad bastards together. See if I can help him save his career again.'

'He still ain't James Bond.'

Taylor stares into the morass of paper on his desk. Might be thinking about what I just said, might be thinking about a lot of things. Looks up eventually.

'Whatever. At least he seems to be going for this one. Mind in gear, cut back to one bottle of whisky a day. We'll see. Want me to let you know if we find your man?'

Hold up fingers in a sign of the cross.

'I'm in at eight tomorrow. That'll do me.'

'Oh, aye? What are you doing after you've got rid of the children?'

Can't keep a bit of a smile off my face, but there's no way I'm telling him where I'm going.

'Things to do, Chief Inspector, things to do.'

He grunts again, no hint of a laugh this time.

'Women, eh?' he says, and it pains him to say it. Can see him thinking of Debbie as he opens his mouth.

'Why don't you leave her?' I say, with accompanying instant regret. I don't have the time to get into this discussion at the moment, certainly don't have the inclination. Hold up my hand. 'Sorry, that was way out of order. None of my business. Look, I've got to go. Will I see you tomorrow?'

Rubs his hand across his forehead. Tired, doesn't care, too much on his mind, even if it is only the one thing.

'God knows, Sergeant. Don't know what I'm doing tomorrow. Don't know what she's doing tomorrow.' He looks pathetically up at me and shrugs.

I nod, try an expression of compassion but don't know if it's anywhere near the mark. Shrug.

'Merry Christmas, sir,' I say, and turn away.

'Ho fucking ho,' he says to my back.

Back to the desk. Herrod isn't in the immediate vicinity, which is good, because I can't be doing with any cheap remarks about bunking off early. Last look at all the paper. Hundreds of things to do but nothing that can't wait until tomorrow.

Jacket on, house keys, car keys, phone, head for the door. Goodnights to the few polis still lingering about the office, don't bother trying to kiss any of the women. Pass PC Bathurst on the way out. Smile, wish her a merry Christmas, she sort of winces back at me. Fine. Along the corridor to the top of the stairs. Look out the window to the dark of night. You can see the cold. Hear footsteps behind me and I turn, hoping it's not going to be work. Greeted by Bathurst, all rosy red lips and worried expression.

'Can I talk to you, Sergeant?' she says. Voice low.

'Sure. What's up?'

She glances over her shoulder, bites her lower lip.

'Not here. Can I talk to you later? After work, maybe. Are you doing anything tonight?'

Tonight? Really? The one night of the last three years when I don't have time for PC Bathurst. Still, she does look as if she really wants to talk, which is kind of disappointing.

'Sorry, Evelyn, tonight's not the night.'

She bites the lip again, looks over her shoulder. I run through the course of the evening, wondering where I can make time. I could cut the kids short, I suppose, but hardly even consider being late for Miller. About to open my mouth but manage to stop myself. Damn it, I see little enough of them as it is.

'Really, I can't. Got two things on tonight. Christmas presents for the kids.' And I'm sleeping with the boss. At least, I presume I'm sleeping with the boss. Maybe she's just asking me out there because she wants to interview me for a position with the Grand Lodge of the Knights Templar. Cover myself in tar and get to find out who's got the Holy Grail.

She smiles nervously and nods.

'All right. Maybe some other time,' she says.

'How about tomorrow?' I suggest. 'We could do lunch. No, not lunch, expect I'll be too busy. After work?'

'Sure,' she says after a hesitation. 'It's not urgent, I just need to talk to someone, that's all.'

'You don't have any plans for the evening? No parents or eighteen-year-old strapping boyfriends to see?'

'Parents are in Inverness. I'm going up for New Year. I wasn't really planning to do anything other than watch *Mission Impossible 3* again.'

'I think I can save you from that.'

We stare at each other for a minute. Crosses my mind that she really is young enough to be my daughter, and almost feel paternal. Reminds me of my real daughter.

'Look, sorry, I've got to go.'

She smiles. 'I'll see you tomorrow. And I'm sorry about

the other night. I was rude.'

Don't know what to say to that.

'Right. See you,' I say, and turn out the door, the smell of her still with me. Along with that unwanted interloper, curiosity.

11

Standing on the doorstep of Miller's house. The doorbell has just rung with a comforting lack of affectation. I was expecting it be the *Hallelujah Chorus*, or something equally grandiose and pretentious, but instead it was a fairly close approximation of ding-dong.

Jesus, I'm talking pish. I have to relax. She's only a woman. I've had hundreds of them. No, really. Try not to wonder why I'm here, because that's not going to get me anywhere. Maybe it's just this: I've been thinking about her since I saw her topless, and maybe she's been thinking about me. There's weirder shit than that in life.

Or maybe she wants to talk about my time in Bosnia. She knows a little of the story, and every now and again she makes some comment about how she must learn more about it, it's so interesting, and on and on. Yet, I don't believe she's interested in my part in the Balkan wars any more than I want to go back there.

My part in the Balkan wars, for fuck's sake.

Still in a mild state of excitement after the first meal of the evening. The kids were all over me, after ignoring my instructions and opening the presents there and then. They went down a bomb. I'll have to thank Harrison. Nearly fell out with Andy over the ridiculous fusty moustache he's attempting to grow, but then he's a teenager and he'll do a lot more stupid things than that before he hits twenty.

Anyway, their mother arrives, not just to pick them up, but to sit and have a drink. So there we were, the happy family. I hand over the gift to Peggy, she does the same opening it there in front of me routine, then nearly freaks. In a good way. You could tell the kids loved it. All the while I was wondering what her current partner, Mr. No Personality, would make of it if he were to walk in but then the way the conversation went, I got the impression he'd taken his deficient character back to Paisley and was leaving my family alone.

They all ended up pleading with me to come and spend Christmas dinner, to which I agreed, leaving myself with the quandary of what to do about the delicious Bathurst. Almost asked if I could bring her along, but thought better of it. So I'll check out of work tomorrow at five, and rejoin the family; and if the merchant wanker has just walked out, it looks like I timed my expensive present to perfection. There are two things women never fail to fall for – diamonds and occasional displays of maturity. They work every time, and I managed to pull both off in the same day.

The door opens. Superintendent Charlotte Miller. I stand and stare at her. Her eyes, I'm looking at her eyes. She leans against the door.

'Are you going to come in, Thomas? You look freezing.'

I'm no fashion freak – another plus to my character – so I don't know what you'd call what she's wearing. Sort of pyjamas. And blue.

Walk tentatively into the house, not sure whether I'm going to find anyone else there. Had the sudden thought on the way down here that maybe she was inviting about twenty people from the station and we were all keeping it quiet thinking we'd been specially selected.

I wander into the dining room, low lights, roaring fire, soft music, two place settings at the table. Christmas tree in the corner.

'Can I take your jacket, get you a drink?'

I take my coat off, hand it to her. I've got that weird feeling in the throat you get sometimes when you know you're about to have sex.

'Vodka tonic, please.'

'Sure,' she says, and shimmers out the room.

God. To Hell with the questions as to why I'm here, I can worry about them tomorrow. Plenty of time. Relax and enjoy yourself, Hutton. And it might finally be time to stop feeling guilty about all those lascivious breast-related thoughts.

I start looking at the pictures on the walls. Sailing ships and big seas mostly. I've heard she's a member of the Royal and Northern Yacht Club just around the corner. Doesn't sail, just goes there to hang out with the rest of the local money and to sleep with whatever big stick she can get her hands on. Very admirable.

The mind rambles on. If I had to guess I'd say the music was Mozart, but that's only because I saw *Amadeus* twenty-five years ago.

She comes back into the room, rid of the jacket, and clutching a bucket of ice and a bottle of expensive looking French white. Pitches up at the drinks cabinet and sorts out my v&t. Pours herself some wine.

'No art can compete with life whose sun we cannot look upon,' she says, as I stare at a picture of some old sea battle.

Hmm. That'll be a quote by someone or other then, but it's lost on me, and I'm not especially encouraged to ask her to elaborate.

She hands over the vodka, raises her glass.

'Merry Christmas,' she says.

Raise my glass in reply. 'Yes,' is all I can think to say. I'll have to do better than that.

She wanders over to the comfy seats by the fire, sits down. Her smell is intoxicating. I want to smother her in ice cream and spend hours licking it off. I want to rub chocolate sauce into her breasts and drink vodka from her belly button. I want to swathe her buttocks in cream and thrash them senseless. I want to pour syrup over her pubic hair and vagina, bury my head between her legs and emerge five hours later a sticky, gooey mess.

'Sit down, Thomas, for goodness sake. And relax, you look like you're scared shitless. I'm not going to eat you.'

Damn.

Sit down on the next available seat. Take a long draw from the vodka, which contains a comforting lack of tonic.

Feel the warmth of it descend into my stomach; instantly relaxed.

I sort of smile at her and then stare into the fire. Hypnotic flame. Relaxed by it and by the smells in the air. Charlotte, burning wood, the real Christmas tree. A fantastic, festive, erotic dream.

Feel her looking at me, but keep staring into the fire. She asked me here, she can make the first move. Take another drink from the vodka and realise I've nearly finished it already. Better slow down or I'll be making an idiot of myself.

'We don't talk much,' she says.

I drag my eyes away from the flame. Her lips are moist, her nipples are obvious against the satin. I get that weird feeling at the back of my throat again.

'We're all too scared of you,' I say. Not sure about my candour, but it's out there.

She smiles. Sips her wine. Eyes shine in the light of the fire. 'It's good to get to know one's people a little better.'

I nod. I want to smother her backside in honey, and drink champagne from her ears.

No, wait, that'd be weird.

'I don't know what sort of things you'll have heard about me, Thomas. I'm sure I must have a reputation.'

I've no idea what she wants me to say to that. Well, darling, we all think you're in it for the power, and you'll sleep with anyone who'll help you on your way.

'Well, it's all true,' she says. I finish off the vodka. 'Frank and I have an understanding.' She runs her hand through her hair as she says it. Smiles.

'You sleep around and he doesn't mind?'

She laughs. 'That's about it, although it's not that one-sided. He's spending the night with some Malaysian tart in Gleneagles.'

The face betrays something as she says it.

'Sounds as if it bothers you.'

'Why should it?' Then, 'Well, maybe you're right. It's funny. I do it often enough to him, but sometimes I think

---

he's driven me to it.' Could be about to get the marriage history. Usually, I'd take this opportunity to go to the toilet and hope they'd changed the subject by the time I got back; but this I want to hear. She disappoints.

'Sorry, I won't bore you with that.'

'I don't mind.'

'Some other time. I want to relax and enjoy myself tonight.'

The fire crackles, the music trundles along, all string quartets and harpsichords. There is a semi-uncomfortable silence. I want to break it, but I haven't the faintest idea what to say to her. Stare once again into the depths of the flames, because when I look at her, I'm back in her office on a warm day in late summer, and I can't look her in the eye.

'I think about that day a lot too,' she says. 'I was surprised how much I enjoyed you looking at me.'

I manage to look her in the eye this time. The elephant in the room. I hadn't actually realised it was an elephant, but then maybe that's what elephants are when they're in a room.

What in the name of fuck is going on in my head? Jesus.

She stands, slightly discomfited by my continuing silence and says, 'Get you another drink?'

Beginning to realise that she's as uncomfortable as I am. You get impressions of people and usually it's more extreme than the reality. We're all made from the same mould, that's the cliché I'm pointing to. Some guy might seem like a dick, but he probably won't be too much more of a dick than you are yourself. It's just how he comes across. Same for every cool bastard, every comedian, every Neanderthal. Every foible, every personality trait is magnified beneath the eye of humanity, when underneath we're not really that different. And so it might just be with Charlotte Miller. Strong, sometimes bruising exterior, all the better for climbing up the ladder and putting men in their place; but underneath she's filled with the same insecurities and contradictions as the rest of us.

Here we go. Hutton, the classical goddamned humanist.

We stare at each other, the back of my throat tingles and goes dry. Hand her the glass, our fingers touch. Feels like electricity stabs through me. Decide the signs are right and to go for it. She's only human, same as the rest of us, and she hasn't asked me down here to discuss whether Thistle'll ever get back into the Premier League. Stand up, imagine myself as James Bond – before he got brainwashed by the Russians, or whatever it was that happened to him.

My head is about a foot away from hers. My mouth waters. She smells glorious and I fight the urge for this to start in a frantic passion. I lean forward and kiss her lips – hardly any pressure – and taste the wine in her mouth.

I run my fingers down her neck as we kiss and I feel her shudder, and then down her back and I slip them inside the silky material until my hands are resting on her buttocks. Absolutely beautiful soft skin, perfect shape to be caressed by two desperate, needing, wanting hands. Our kiss becomes more passionate, her arms are round my neck, and I squeeze those fantastic butt cheeks, moulding them, caressing them. God, I'm so hard, so damp, my cock pressed against her. I can't wait to feel her, to slip my hands between her thighs to see if she's as damp as I am, so I move my hand round, feel the touch of her neatly shaved pubic hair, and then run my fingers down over her pussy and ease two fingers quickly inside her. She's soaking, as desperate for it as I am, and at the touch she gasps and thrusts herself against me, her mouth open, her tongue all over me.

*

Five o'clock in the morning, Christmas Day. Driving back into Glasgow. Just spent my best night with a woman in a long time. Got a disgusting warm feeling, which points to me being moderately in love. That's usual, and it'll pass.

No chance of blundering into marriage this time. The best I can hope for is a rematch but even that can hardly be guaranteed. I'm fully aware that the next time I see her it'll be like it never happened, and I'm liable to get my backside handed to me for being lousy at my job. But for the moment I'm content to bask in the glow of post-absolutely phenomenal sex. Body like a twenty-year-old, breasts you could lick ice cream off for weeks without getting fed up, a tongue on her like a knife and a technique honed over decades of experience. Spectacular.

Tongue like a knife? Where did that come from?

Drive through Glasgow, wishing the roads were always this quiet. Haven't given all the other things going on a thought all evening, and now they start to intrude. Bloody murderers, dinner with Peggy and the kids, what to do about Bathurst. Kicking myself for being so stupid as to double date on Christmas Day. Don't know what to do. Overnight Bathurst has dropped from the sexual wish list. Women of my own age or older from now on, and banish all thoughts of young constables twenty years my junior.

Pull up outside the flat just after five-fifteen. Tired, but feeling pretty cool. First night in a long while that I haven't drunk too much, although had I been stopped by a zealous young police constable in the last half hour I would still have been in trouble.

Up the stairs, let myself into the flat. Two and a half hours sleep and then a frantic fifteen-minute rush to get to the station in the morning. At least the roads will be quiet. Wondering whether to tell Taylor about my evening, but knowing I won't.

Walk into the bedroom, yawning. Don't turn on the light. The curtains are open, and the streetlights fill the room with dull orange light and dark shadows. Am in the process of undressing when I notice there's a woman lying on top of the bed. Fully clothed, but undoubtedly a woman.

12

Early Christmas morning. He lies awake. Imagining he hears sleigh bells outside, can see the snow on the ground. Thinking of Christmases past, the presents he never received.

Jo never gave him a present. He'd wondered for a while if that was why she'd dumped him when she had. One week before Christmas. A long time ago now, it seems. Was it last year, or the year before? So much in his head. So much work, so many tortured and difficult lives. So much of an effort not letting everyone in on the secret.

She didn't dump him to avoid buying a present though. That would have been too stupid. She had plenty of money. She dumped him because she was getting plenty of sex elsewhere.

He'd loved her, he'd cared for her. He'd bought her presents, lots of presents. Took a silver necklace along to their first date, let her know right from the start that she was on to a winner. He listened, he always listened. Let her do what she wanted. Let her breathe. Gave her space. He massaged her head when she had a headache, bought her dinner when she was hungry, he sent her flowers every day. Every day.

She had thrown that back at him the last time they talked. As if it wasn't a good thing. She was sleeping with other guys while he was sending her flowers, yet he was the bad guy? She was sleeping with other guys while he was waiting outside her house with a box of chocolates, yet he was the bad guy? She was sleeping with other guys while he was leaving ten romantic messages on her phone every night, yet he was the bad guy?

At first he'd wondered if he'd been the problem, if he'd been the one to blame. Yet that was absurd. The notion was absurd. He had given her everything. Everything. He had given her wildflowers every day. Every damned day. And she'd fucked her way through entire rugby teams worth of men.

He'd been heroic in his romance, while she'd been a slut. She was a slut, one of the sluts, one of those damned sluts who went to bedrooms at parties and took on as many guys as they could get hold of. Yet he'd been the bad guy.

She was at parties, stripped naked – if she even bothered taking the time to remove her clothes – lying on a bed, eating men. Fucking one, while sucking another one off, her hands grabbing at another couple at the same time. That's who she was. A complete slut, men all over her, so many damned men, men beyond counting.

'How does that make me... the fucking... bad guy?'

The words are spoken to an empty room.

She'd moved away. Moved house. He hadn't seen her in so long. Was it a year or two years? The time seemed so long. It dragged. He thought about her every day, yet there was no possibility of ever seeing her again. Unless she decided to come back.

Would she come back? It seemed incredible to him that she had not already regretted leaving. All those men, but what did they ever give her? Sometimes he wondered if something had happened to her. Maybe that was it. Maybe it was the things he'd said when she'd ended the relationship. She'd never admitted the other men, but he could tell he'd been right when he'd accused her. No one looks that guilty unless there's something to be guilty about.

Three o'clock in the morning, the non-stop clock ticking in his brain. Christmas Day. She should be lying beside him; instead, she was probably still at some hangover of a Christmas Eve party. Just her, and all those men.

He'd find her soon enough. These other women, the ones who looked like Jo, but who weren't Jo, they were all the same. They weren't Jo. Sometimes they might as well be her. They weren't Jo.

One minute past three in the morning. The non-stop clock ticking in his brain. He'd find another Jo. He'd find another one.

Jo fucking all those other men, yet he was the bad guy.

'I wasn't co-fucking dependent…'

Fucking Jo.

13

Sitting in the lounge, small lamp burning dimly, coffee all round, the Christmas tree unlit and pathetic in the corner, one man's weak concession to seasonal spirit. On the settee sits Evelyn Bathurst, sleepy eyed, Tesco's own Columbian No.3, black, three sugars, in her hand. Decided she needed to speak to me tonight, thought she'd come and wait for me, so let herself into the flat. Police make the best criminals. I've hit the wall. Need sleep. I'm close on forty-five and massively unfit, not eighteen. If she doesn't get to the point soon, I'm going to fall asleep on her.

'I shouldn't be here. I'm sorry.' For the seventh time.

'It's no problem, Evelyn.' Another large draft of coffee, another cigarette; hope they start kicking in. 'I don't mind. Just take your time, I'm not going anywhere. When you're ready.'

Mr. Compassion. Course, I want to give her a shake and tell her to get on with it, but she's fucked up by something.

Glance at the watch. Almost six o'clock. Crap.

I look at her, the worry lines on her face. At least this'll make it easier to get out of the thing tonight, assuming she actually talks to me in the next two hours. She looks like a young girl sitting there. About to tell her father she's pregnant; or she's dropping out of university, to go and build water pumps for villagers in West Africa. Sitting here like this, I cannot believe I tried to get her into bed.

Whatever. Bite me.

She drains her coffee. Looks at me. I recognise it. This is it. If she's about to tell me she's pregnant or that she's going to drop out of the police to go and build water pumps for villagers in West Africa, I'll be disappointed.

'You have to promise me you won't tell anyone about this,' she starts.

Looks on the point of tears. Better sharpen up.

'I'm not about to tell anyone.'

'If this gets out at the station...,' and she doesn't finish the sentence. Lifts the mug to her mouth, finds it empty.

'I'll get you another cup. You get yourself together and tell me about it when I get back in.'

She nods, wipes her eyes. I take the mug and head for the kitchen.

I stare out of the kitchen window at the cold and empty streets while the kettle boils. Wonder what she's going to say. Start to get a bad feeling, and for the first time I think that maybe I don't want to know what she's just about to tell me. Sometimes ignorance is best.

Make the coffee, take it back in, hand it over and sit down. This time there's no delay. Engages my eyes for a second, takes a deep breath, then she starts talking immediately. Words tumble out in a great rush, sentences tripping over each other.

And immediately I know I was right. I don't want to hear it.

14

Walking into the office, five to eight. Wide awake. Had a shower, still feel dirty. Brought Bathurst in with me and she's gone off to their locker room. She lifted the weight from her shoulders by transferring it to mine and came into work in a better frame of mind than she was in at my flat. Not that I can do anything for her, but I said the right things and she's made her confession. And now I'm stuck with the information.

The light is on in Taylor's office and I stick my head round the door. I'm glad he wasn't part of what I've just heard about. Want to tell him, but know I can't.

'Morning.'

He looks up. Smiles, sort of.

'What were you up to last night, then? Spotted three minutes ago promenading across the carpark with Constable Bathurst.'

God, you can't do anything, can you? I'm about to go on the defensive but decide against. They can think what they like.

I don't smile. Don't feel like it.

'Any news?'

He nods.

'Aye. While you were out shagging last night, some of us were working.'

'Spare me.'

'We got Mr. Healy. Picked him up at a pub in town, steaming out his face, about half ten.'

What was I doing at half past ten? I was deep in the arms of Charlotte Miller. Already seems a long time ago.

'And?'

'He sobered up pretty quick. Got him in a cell overnight. Jonah's coming in to talk to him this morning.'

'And is he going to be sober?' Almost spit the words

out, knowing what I now know about Jonah Bloonsbury. If Taylor notices the tone, he doesn't comment.

'Is he ever? He'll have the run of CID today without Miller in, so who knows what he'll be like?'

'What do you think of our guy?' I ask.

He leans back in his chair, tosses a pen onto the desk. Purses his lips. Shakes his head.

'Don't know, to be honest. I see what you mean about him, but I think he's just a stupid little shit.'

Implied criticism, I shouldn't have been getting everyone excited.

'Right. I wasn't sure. Bloonsbury was the one frothing at the mouth over it. Just a gut feeling.'

He nods. 'Aye, well my gut feeling says it's not him, but Jonah's the one to make the decision. Anyway, we can get a blood sample. That should sort it out.' Another shake of the head. 'Why would a guy invite the polis in?'

'To give us a false description. Lead us astray.'

'Maybe.'

'Anything else?'

'Pretty quiet, so far. The usual crap after the pubs shut last night, but not much for us. That desk of yours looks pretty crowded. Maybe you'd like to see to some of it.'

'Boss,' mock salute, and out the door.

Go to the kitchen to make a cup of coffee before I face the paperwork, most of which has been put off for several weeks. I could work non-stop on it for the next month and not clear it all away. Meet Alison in the kitchen, looking far more cheerful than I care for anyone to look today. She smiles at me; I do my best to respond.

'Merry Christmas,' she says, and gives me an almost lingering kiss on the lips.

'Merry Christmas,' I say back, and the words sound totally different.

She busies herself with the kettle.

'What's the matter with you, you miserable sod? It's Christmas.'

'It certainly doesn't feel like it. What are you doing up

---

here, anyway?'

'Sink's blocked downstairs. They don't want us using the kitchen. And the lift's broken.'

'I know.' Don't feel like making small talk, but I'm here now. No option. The woman did use to be my wife after all. 'So, you're not spending a cosy day with McGovern?'

'Cosy night,' she says. 'We both finish at four, then we're going down to the Creggans' in Strachur for the night. Tomorrow off. What about you?'

Have to think about it. Remember the wonderful family dinner coming up. Hope I'm more in the mood for it when it comes the time.

'Dinner with Peggy and the kids after work.'

She lets out a low whistle. 'Back in favour?'

Shake my head, wait for the kettle to boil.

'Who knows?' I say eventually.

She lets me go first, and I make the coffee as strong as possible. Plenty of sugar, turn to go.

'See you around. Have a nice time tonight,' I say.

'You too. And Tom,' she says, making me turn back, 'get some more sleep. You look awful.'

Thanks.

Back into the office, park my backside at the desk, stare at the mountain of paperwork. Not so much of a mountain, as I don't have a noticeable in-tray, more of a sprawling landscape of hills and forests. Drink coffee, feel depressed. Eventually turn the computer on and wait for it to crawl into life. Try to think of Charlotte Miller and the wonderful evening, but thoughts of what Bathurst told me insist on intruding.

They, whoever they are, say that school days are the happiest days of your life, and I always thought that was some kind of bullshit. But now, I'd give anything to be in the middle of three weeks holiday and be about to open up a barrel load of presents.

Think of Christmases past, and start the trawl through the paperwork. Good Christian men rejoice, with heart and soul and voice...

15

Here's the story from Bathurst, and I've no particular reason to believe she's making it up. No motive, your honour. It dates from just over a year ago, and the big murder case that temporarily saved Bloonsbury's career.

At first I didn't think it was going to amount to much. Another sordid tale of police corruption, no surprise to anyone, and just so long as the media don't get wind of it, no one cares.

Now Bloonsbury's wasn't the only career which was saved from the hangman with that case. There was also the matter of Detective Chief Inspector Gerry Crow, another drunken sod who belonged at a 24/7 AA meeting. It was Bloonsbury's case, but it was so high profile that it was all hands on deck and Crow got in on the act. It was sort of a joint credit thing, although Bloonsbury managed to whip more of the cream from the top. Crow escaped getting kicked into touch and when he did eventually take early retirement five months ago, it was with a good deal more honour than he would've had a year earlier; or than he deserved. The guy got out of jail.

A woman is found lying by the banks of the Clyde, not far from Carmyle. She's been assaulted, butchered with something the Interahamwe might have used in Rwanda in '94, and left to die. She briefly lives to tell the tale, relates the usual story about a guy in a ski mask and all sorts of ridiculous shit, then duly dies a couple of days later. Nevertheless, despite the attacker's weapon of choice, from what we could gather from the victim, it appeared that it'd been an assault that had got a little out of hand.

So, it's not that the press get everything, of course, not until the trial, but suddenly every woman within five miles starts to panic. They ignore it at first, but once the victim dies, the papers pile in there and make it the latest big thing, it being a slow month.

It's Bloonsbury's gig, and right from the start Crow is sniffing around in the background, breathing in Bloonsbury's alcohol fumes for extra sustenance.

Anyway, the press are all in on how dangerous this comedian is, and how every woman in the city really ought to be living in fear. So, every woman in the city starts living in fear because they've been told to, and there's a public outcry about the lack of police success.

Things are going badly, with none of us looking good. A lot of pressure, something needing to be done, and now, whoever it is that solves it is going to be a hero. It's at times like this that the odd officer will resort to fudging a little evidence. Give him some vague idea who he's after and he does the rest himself. It ain't right, but as long as you know you're gunning for the right guy, it ain't wrong either. Trouble is, they haven't a clue who the right guy is. None. They have hair samples and skin samples, and two and a half million blokes in Scotland from whom to choose.

And in the middle of the feeding frenzy, when we're all looking like idiots and reputations are being exploded like the bridge at Mostar, the guy nearly does it again. Same story, different outcome, still no more clues to his identity. This time the victim is some idiot who's out looking for the guy. Some clown who's been watching too many Steven Seagal movies and fancies a pop at the killer. Has been out on the prowl for him every night for two weeks, then finally finds him. Only, it isn't quite on the terms she's anticipated. The guy comes from behind and raps her over the head with a brick before she has the chance to tell the guy she's a black belt in karate. Still, she's marginally more Buffy than Goofy. She manages to get him a good stiff crack in the balls, and the two of them make a tactical retreat.

Course, the press don't care that the woman's a fucking idiot. They love it, and it ends up being us who are queuing up to look stupid.

And then, out of the thick fog of this confusion, comes an arrest. Having done the usual act of desperation of rounding up all the usual suspects, suddenly from that lot, DCI Jonah Bloonsbury has his man, with Crow shuffling along in his wake taking as much of the credit as possible. The murderer is in custody, the streets are safe – these things are relative – and two careers have been saved. All out of nothing. There's a lot of suspicious looks cast between polis, but they've got the conviction, despite the guy denying it all the way. And more importantly, if it isn't him who did it, the real murderer never strikes again.

And then.

This is where Bathurst comes in. She isn't long in the force at the time, determined to become Chief Constable of Strathclyde by the time she's thirty-five, all that crap. But not wet behind the ears, no way. She knows what's going on, knows the sort of things that have to be done.

So, she's thrown into the middle of the investigation, and one night in the Whale she's approached by Bloonsbury, breathing mint and looking sinister. Everyone knows his story, the wife having just walked out, and now desperate for a breakthrough with the case.

He speaks in a hushed voice, gets all cosy and conspiratorial. Tells her that they have their man, but you know how it is, darlin', they just don't have enough to nick him. This is the first she's heard of it, but she's thinking, I'm just a constable, it's not likely that I'm going to know everything that's going on. So she buys it. They need her help, he says, but obviously there can't be too many who know about it. Lists the ones who were going to be in on it and no one else would know. A little evidence doctored, a few things placed where they shouldn't be, the odd clue left lying around, and they'd have their man. If she went along, he would see that it benefited her greatly, and she doesn't need him to tell her that, because it's obvious.

So it doesn't take long, and three quarters of an hour and a couple of whisky sodas later, she's in. Along with Crow, naturally, Sergeant Herrod – no surprise – and young Edwards, who belongs to the *Hang 'Em High* brigade. Five in the gang, and off they ride into the sunset to fight for truth, justice and liberty.

I thought that was going to be the story, and I wasn't at all surprised. That's how these things go. I was beginning to wonder why she'd brought it to me now, because I've seen enough of these over the years to really not care. Blind eye, and all that. Then she brings me up to date.

Monday night, Christmas party. Everyone getting drunk, the usual thing. It was the second one she'd been at, so she knew what to expect, i.e. a queue of drunk guys attempting to get inside that tight white dress of hers; me included. One of the drunk Lotharios was Edwards of course, not long after he had stripped for the benefit of us all. Destined to get nowhere with her, but desperate all the same. He goes for it, giving her all the crap he can think of, subjecting her to a three-quarter hour rambling monologue. Starts talking about their great breakthrough case of the previous year, starts telling her things she never knew. She had been a bit drunk herself to start, but this kind of thing sobers you up quickly enough.

Bloonsbury and Crow had been in on it all along. Not just stitching up the guy, but the whole damned thing. The murder, everything. The sick, demented bastard who committed the two attacks was Crow himself, with Bloonsbury's full knowledge. He carried out the first assault in an intended series, but of course got a bit carried away with himself, probably because he'd found his true vocation in life. Murdered the girl. Then they let the hysteria build, feeding morsels to the scavengers every day to sustain and cultivate the frenzy, then timed the second attack to perfection, so that when things were at their wildest, when the heat was at its fiercest, they stepped in and picked up their man.

Jesus, no wonder he protested his innocence. The guy didn't have a clue, but they must've had their eye on him right from the start. I don't know how they did it, but they knew they had a guy who wouldn't have an alibi for either of the two nights. They must've planned it for weeks. All right, they had taken the guy from the list of usual suspects, so it wasn't as if they got a complete innocent. Justice is justice, however.

Stitching guys up, when you know you're doing it to the right person, that's one thing. Doing it to someone when you're not sure, but you need a break, well, you can understand it. Pretty stupid, and it can backfire, but we've all done it. But this? Committing the crime, so you can solve it and take the credit? Holy. Fucking. Shit.

Surprised? No way. Crow was a sick man, and Bloonsbury was just pathetic and desperate. Don't know what Herrod or Edwards were up to, but then Edwards told her there was a bit of infighting after the first assault turned to murder.

So that's the story, and as she was telling me all this my mind wasn't working particularly quickly. I took it at face value, still vaguely curious as to why she thought she had to tell me everything. Then she dumps it on me, the thought that had occurred to her, the seed that had been sown and which was growing into a monster of a beanstalk.

She was sickened on Monday night, and went home questioning herself and what she had allowed herself to get drawn into. Then Tuesday morning dawns in a siren's wail of frantic activity. She gets down to it, the same as the rest of us. Then sometime during the day it hits her, a massive punch in the stomach. Maybe it's a repeat performance. Maybe it's another set-up. Bloonsbury was getting himself drunk in front of us all, but who knows what Crow is doing these days? Hitting the bottle in the backwoods, certainly, but it's not as if we can account for his movements. So, maybe he's committed the crime in cahoots with Bloonsbury, and after another murder or two they're going to go through their tried and trusted stitching up routine.

So, that's the story. All true, except the last bit which is speculation. The first lot is bad enough, and I'm clinging to the hope that the second lot is Bathurst's overactive imagination. I think I managed to persuade her as such, but it's got me thinking. Can't get a fix on a logical, clear argument. Not surprising. There are too many questions. What would be in it for Crow? Maybe it's nothing to do with Crow, and Bloonsbury's got someone else to do the dirty work this time. But what could Jonah Bloonsbury give anyone as payment for that kind of thing? All his money is in alcohol. Herrod, Edwards, they couldn't possibly condone this. The first was an assault that went wrong. What happened on Monday night was miles beyond that.

I don't know. I need to get away from it all, think clearly. I need to persuade myself that they had nothing to do with Monday night. The knowledge of the previous case is bad enough, without being lumbered with all this. I want to talk to Taylor, and I'll need to if they're involved with this murder. But if they're not – and there's no reason to assume they commit every crime around here for their own ends – then I know Taylor won't want to know about it. I certainly don't.

I need vodka tonic, and lots of it.

And to Hell with the tonic.

16

Made a decision. Going to go up to Arrochar and speak to Crow. Haven't the faintest idea what I'm going to say to him, but I know if I don't follow this up it's just going to eat away at me. After that, I don't know. Depends a lot on what he says, although I'm not sure how I'll raise the subject. Just have to wing it. Leave it until tomorrow, however. Tonight I've got dinner with my happy family and I'm not going to let it get in the way of that. A problem put off to another day is a problem solved.

Lunchtime, sitting in Taylor's office, chewing the fat. I mean that literally, having purchased a sandwich from the canteen. Taylor's preoccupied, presumably thinking of that wife of his.

'Ever hear of Crow?' I toss into the afternoon.

He looks up.

'Drunken Gerry?' Shakes his head, distasteful look on his face, as we all have when we think of Crow. 'Nah, and I don't want to either. I think Jonah went to see him last month or something. Said his place was a shit-tip.'

I take another bite into the rubber of my sandwich, another swig of coffee to mask the taste.

'Why d'you ask?'

Can tell from the tone of voice he doesn't care, making the question easier to avoid.

'Just wondered.'

Taylor grunts and resumes his morose reflections. Decide to plunge into the middle of them.

'So, what you doing tonight?'

He looks round, shrugs. 'Cosy Christmas dinner at home with the wife and the in-laws. Mum, dad, Betty, that idiot Anthony and all fifteen of their idiot children, or however many it is they have now. I lost count.'

'You going to make it?'

'Don't know. They're waiting 'til six and if I'm not in, they'll get on with dinner. And you can see how busy I am, so I'm not sure. Might just be held up at the station.' He puts his hands behind his head and stares at the ceiling.

Sound thinking. I've never met Anthony and the children, but I've heard enough about them.

I'd been on the verge of asking for an update on his marital status, but decide against. It's Christmas Day and I've already got enough on my mind without being burdened with all his troubles.

Yes, very Christian of me.

Another foray into the midst of the sandwich, followed by instant regret. Catch a whiff of alcohol in the air, look up to see Detective Chief Inspector Jonah Bloonsbury standing in the doorway. His nose glows effervescently red in the midst of a dour face. Fresh from interviewing our prime suspect.

'Good work, Tom,' he says, 'but it's not him. I see what you were thinking, though.'

Aye, right. Don't care, having already had the thought myself. Gut instinct goes wrong again. Might have to do something about that, but not sure how you improve your guts. Bisodol, maybe.

'You let him go?' asks Taylor, a man who still possesses guts of steel.

'Aye. It just wasn't right, you know. And it turned out the bastard was up to his arse in alibis.'

Look up. No way.

'You're kidding?'

Shakes his head. 'Produced a couple of names, checked out. Think he was taking the piss when he was talking to you, stupid bastard. Last thing he did was threaten to sue, so I pointed out to him that that might not be a very good idea. Think he got my meaning.'

'Blood test?' says Taylor. Tone of voice that says he couldn't care less.

Bloonsbury shakes his head.

'No point,' he says. 'He's not our man, and if I start

drawing blood from the bastard then we will get a lawsuit.
You know what these lawyers are like. Anyway, says he
was serious about the description he gave us, so we'll
check it out. He's doing a photofit just now. Probably be
totally different from the other one we've got. Maybe we
should pick up that first bastard who came in.'

'You can't go arresting everyone who tries to help us,
Jonah,' says Taylor. 'Bad for business.'

Bloonsbury grunts, get a whiff of J&B.

'Aye, whatever. I'm going to get something to eat. Any
of you want anything?'

I hold up the worst sandwich on planet earth and Taylor
shakes his head. Bloonsbury grunts again and wanders off.
Glad he didn't stay much longer.

Plunge into the sandwich again, come up with meat.

'Seems a bit odd,' I say, 'don't you think? The lawyer
suddenly coming up with alibis, I mean.'

'Who knows? Lawyers, they'll do what they want. If it
makes the police look stupid, they don't care.'

'But to spend a night in a cell for nothing.'

'Probably got his reasons. Trying to get away from his
girlfriend. Anything. More likely, fully intending to sue.
And if that's the case, I'll bet he won't be put off by an idle
threat from Jonah. Bloody lawyers. Not much business, so
they go looking for it themselves.'

'Still got a bad smell to it.'

'That was Jonah's breath. Forget it, Tom.'

What am I doing worrying about it, anyway?

Briefly wonder where this leaves the tentative theory
about Bloonsbury being behind the whole thing. The
further I get from the conversation with Bathurst, the more
disinclined I am to believe it.

'Where now?' I say to Taylor.

He sighs heavily and leans even further back in his
seat.

'Fuck knows,' he says.

*

Four-fifteen, daily roundup. The investigation has almost ground to a halt. All those of whom we were suspicious check out. The boyfriend, ex-boyfriend, anyone who has volunteered information, the family, the neighbours. We've got a hold of everyone that ever so much as kissed her and come up empty. A brick wall. And that's one of the problems with this job. We could at some point have spoken to the guy who wielded the knife, and just didn't recognise him.

Bloonsbury seems even more depressed than normal. I'm trying to remember what he was like during the last murder case, because if Bathurst's right, then he knew all along he was going to solve the crime. Any worry or exasperation on his part would've been feigned. All I can remember is the guy holding off the drink, and making us all suffer with him. Seen to be not drinking would be part of the plan, the anguish it caused him a genuine consequence.

This time, however, you can tell the difference. You can smell it on his breath, on his clothes and his skin, you can see it in his face – the man has not decided to hold off from the booze. Jonah Bloonsbury; legend. Not even good for an Elvis impersonation at the Christmas night out anymore. And that's what he's become. Elvis. Wasted, bloated, permanently smashed out of his face. Clinging to the songs of the past, but become a bitter caricature. In years to come people are going to be doing Jonah Bloonsbury impersonations around here. But at the moment, he's the one doing it.

But what should I care? I've been unimpressed since I started working with him, and now I know he's as much of a criminal as the scum we've been hauling in here all these years. He deserves what's coming to him. I have a vision of him in three years' time, or three months', sitting on Argyll Street under the rail bridge into Central Station. A scab on his nose from where he drunkenly fell into the gutter, a dirty beard and wearing the same clothes he now wears; hat on the ground, growling at passers-by to give him some change for methylated spirits or brake fluid, or whatever it is that the jakes are drinking these days.

He's standing with his back to us, looking at the pictures of Ann Keller which still adorn the walls, and which will continue to do so until we catch our man, or until they are pushed aside by new photographs of new victims – the real fear and possibility. He turns, looking bloody awful, slumps against the edge of the desk. A liquid lunch.

'Sergeant Harrison, give us what we've got.'

Herrod's got the day off, hanging out with Bernadette, the kids, and most of her family. Wonderful Christmastime. Bet he's just itching to come into work, but she won't let him.

Wonder how Miller is getting on with her dull husband in Braemar. The thought of her gives me a warm feeling – *hardened cop turns to mush over woman in authority* – as it has most of the day.

Mind on the job. Sergeant Harrison.

'We don't have much, to be honest. All avenues of enquiry have so far led to a dead end. We have had a big response from the public. Several people saw her at the cinema, and we can be pretty sure she was alone. We've had two sightings of her walking along the street, post-cinema, two descriptions of a man either talking to her or walking close behind. The descriptions don't match, however.'

'Conclusion?' says Bloonsbury, butting in. The voice displays no interest.

Harrison shrugs. Here's a woman who enjoys her job but would rather be elsewhere.

'It was dark, too brief a passing glance. Somebody passes you by in the street, you've no reason to remember them, the mind is not going to have very good recall.'

Bloonsbury grunts. He was hoping for some illumination on whether one of them was lying, preferably the first one since he's already decided our lawyer friend is innocent. Harrison is right, however. These things are a stretch at the best of times.

'So,' says Harrison, 'we're struggling with any witnesses from Monday night. We've spoken to her boyfriend, with whom she had a fight on Monday during the day, and to seventeen ex-boyfriends or lovers.' Seventeen? Hey, my kind of girl. 'Everyone checks out. Small family, but they all seem genuinely upset. There's nothing there to suggest a motive from any of them.'

'Again, conclusion?' says Bloonsbury. Wonder if he's even listening to her.

'Either her killer was someone who barely knew her, or did not know her at all,' she says. 'Or we've missed something in all our interviews,' she adds, not a concept to bet against.

Bloonsbury nods, sort of mumbles to himself – increasing the impression that the man is losing it. A low mutter, the words undistinguishable. Perhaps considering the possibility that he was the one to miss something. A drunk faced with his own fallibility – what else should he do but mutter? Or perhaps he curses the rest of us.

'Right, then. That seems to be about it… Anyone else got anything to say?' he says, looks around. 'Hutton?'

Crap.

'He carries a grudge beyond rational thought, either against her or someone who looks like her. If it's the latter, we're in deep shit, because he's going to be bloody hard to find. Who knows how much Ann Keller looked like the object of his hate? It could be any guy out there. Any damned guy.'

'A bit of profile, no clues, no substance,' says Bloonsbury, darkly. 'That's all we've got. Anyone else?'

Most of us stare at the floor. There's nothing else to say. Christmas Day and we're sitting here with those pictures looking down upon us, if a cadaver with no eyes can look. None of us want to be here.

Bloonsbury sighs, heavy breath, you can smell the drink. Even at the back where I'm sitting with Taylor – a silent, preoccupied Taylor, other things on his mind.

86

'Right, people, bugger off. Away home and enjoy your Christmas if you can,' and the words sound especially bitter from Bloonsbury's mouth, as we all know he has no home, no family, to which to go. 'We're going to have to start afresh tomorrow. Go over all the family and boyfriends again, see if we can come up with anything. If it was one of them, I want to know about it. If it wasn't...' and the words trail off.

If it's just some guy who chanced upon her and went about his business, then we're in trouble. Another clue might not come our way until the next woman with dark brown hair he chances upon ends up mutilated in a ditch.

17

His thoughts are never linear. Back and forth, back and forth. Mostly he thinks about the first time. The best time. When it was still fresh and pure, before there'd been any arguments, before she'd started seeing all those others behind his back. He'd been at her house looking at old photographs. They'd been friends, although he already wanted more. Just hadn't been sure how she'd felt about it.

The photographs had been of a holiday she'd taken with friends in Greece. A lot of monuments – which was why she was showing them to him – and then in the middle of ancient Greek architecture there had been one of her and her two friends topless by the swimming pool. She'd been embarrassed, she'd quickly moved on. They'd looked at the photos for another minute or two together, and then she'd put the book away and offered to make another cup of tea.

As she'd stood with her back to him, he had realized. She wasn't embarrassed at all. She hadn't forgotten about the topless photograph. It was her way, her way of letting him know, of gauging his interest. And he had sat there and said nothing.

He stood behind her, silently. She was talking, but he wasn't listening. Then softly he kissed the back of her neck. She shuddered at his touch. Then his hands were upon her.

That was what he liked to remember. That moment. That first touch. Her shudder, her body tensing, and then the moment when she gave into him and relaxed, the moment he ran his hand over her breast and realized how hard her nipples had become.

That moment was so magical, so perfect. Yet it rarely stays that way in his head, the vision quickly sours.

Fucking Jo.

What was she doing sitting topless by a swimming pool

in Greece? How many men had been there? How many had stared at her breasts? How many had she accommodated in the evening, how many had licked and sucked and bitten those breasts? And how many men had she lured with the innocent photograph collection once she'd come home?

She couldn't even stay sweet in his memories. Everything soured with Jo. Everything. That was why he'd had to kill her, that was why he would have to kill her again, that was why he would have to go on killing her until she was actually dead.

*

The imitation log fire flames away in the middle of the room; the tree sparkles in the corner, green and red; the lights are low, dark shadows haunting the warm colours; candles flicker, glinting in Peggy's diamond earrings; Nat King Cole sings Mel Torme (we've already had Bob's Christmas album, and weirdly she refused to have it on again); there's a scent of spices, and in the air there's a feeling of Christmas. Large dinner, safely washed away with a bottle of 2008 South African red. We're sitting on the floor, backs against the sofa, staring into the fire. Holding hands. Warning shots are being fired, but they're obscured by the Christmas haze.

Arrived only a little late, and was immediately swamped by ex-wife and children, still glowing from yesterday's feel-good dinner experience. Spent half an hour looking at all the different presents, noticing that there was nothing from the suit from Paisley. Let it pass without comment, however. Masses of food, all good-natured, and a damn sight better atmosphere than we managed most of the Christmases we were still together. I may have detected a concerted family plan to win back the parent formerly known as Dad, but let's not jump to any conclusions. I am a lousy detective, after all.

And so, we come to the crux of the evening. The kids

are packed off to their rooms, quite happily for once, to play with their iCraps and all the other modern garbage that we didn't have when I was a kid, while Peggy and I sit with our backs to the sofa watching the flames. I think I know where this is leading, but sometimes these things don't always end there. She squeezes my fingers and I decide it's time to ask the question which has remained unasked these last couple of days.

'Out with it,' is how I broach the subject.

She smiles. 'I love it when you talk to me as if I was a suspect.' Kisses me on the cheek. 'What are you talking about?'

'Brian.' The merchant wanker was called Brian.

'Oh.' The smile disappears and she looks vaguely detached. Chews her lip, which I know means she's about to tell me something she'd rather have kept to herself. Wonder if she's murdered Brian, and his body rots beneath us in the cellar.

'He left me for some twenty-year-old hairdresser.'

I don't quite manage to hold in the laugh, at the tone of voice as much as at the fact of it. She tries to look serious, but starts laughing as well. I always loved that laugh. The first thing that attracted me to her, leading me away from the acidic arms of Jean Fryar.

'What's the story?'

She sighs. 'That tells it all, doesn't it? It'd be nice to have always intended to invite you for dinner, but this time last week I still thought it would be me and Brian.'

'He dropped you the week before Christmas?'

She gives me a look. 'Must you say drop? You make me sound like a footballer.'

'Who was she?'

'Don't know, don't care. Can honestly say I've had bigger disappointments in life.' Another squeeze of the hand. 'It really was a lot nicer having you round, and the kids were a lot happier too.'

Well, of course. The kids would've been happier having Hannibal Lecter over for dinner.

90

'Don't know what you saw in him in the first place.'

The answer is on her lips, and I know what it is, but she bites it back. Neither the time nor place. It wasn't as if she immediately married someone else when we split, the way one idiotic half of the partnership did.

'What about you?' she says, neatly changing the course of the discussion. 'Married any constables lately, or are you just slowly working your way through the station in a deliberate passage of sexual frenzy?'

Very funny. The tone is such that I let her away with the marriage jibe. The question has me thinking of Charlotte Miller, however. Decide that I'll refrain from telling Peggy about her, but don't acknowledge to myself the consequences of it. If Miller had been some casual sexual partner, I would've told her, but it was more than that. Or at least, that's how I've blown it up in my head.

'Nothing much. Struck out with a twenty-year-old constable at the party on Monday night.'

'You like them older these days?'

'Piss off.'

She laughs again, grabs the nearest wine bottle and fills up the glasses. She leans against me, her head resting on my shoulder.

'But, I mean, there's no one special at the moment? It's so long since I've seen you.'

Someone special. Well, I've decided the Superintendent is special.

'Dan, he's special,' I say. Hide behind terrible humour, the male way to deal with awkward questions.

'You know what I mean.'

Am almost on the point of owning up to these new feelings for the boss, but decide not to be an idiot. Peggy has met Charlotte Miller, so she'll wet herself laughing if I tell her what I'm thinking. It would also be goodbye to the night's entertainment.

Shallow, Hutton, very shallow.

'No, no one special,' I say.

Feel her head burrow a little further into my shoulder.

'The kids have missed you,' she says, letting the words fall out into the warm Christmas atmosphere.

What is she saying?

Damn, it's obvious what she's saying and wasn't this what I wanted? Massively expensive Christmas present, remember?

That was before last night.

Forget last night, you moron!

'A week ago, you were snuggling up to Brian.'

Her hand rests on my stomach. A finger finds its way through my shirt, starts drawing circles on my skin.

'I know. I can't describe it. It's not like I miss him. I mean, the guy was, I don't know... something...'

'Boring as fuck?'

'I suppose you're right,' she says, laughing. 'Boring as fuck.' Another long pause. 'It's just been really nice having you around these last couple of days.'

She looks up at me, and I don't even hesitate before the inevitable happens. Lean down and kiss her warmly on the lips, feel her tongue immediately in my mouth. She always kissed like a goddess, Peggy, and three years of kissing a sea-anemone hasn't dulled her abilities.

Finally manage to expunge the thoughts of last night and give in to the moment. Let her dominate, which was always what she liked to do. And when it begins, it's at a hundred miles an hour, and just keeps getting faster.

18

There's no snow, it's not even cold. Christmas Day, grey and mild, given way to dark and bleak evening, moisture in the air, relentless drizzle threatening. And what a night for Jo to be out. Why should she be out on her own on Christmas Day?

He had caught her eye in the bar. She'd smiled and hadn't flinched, so there was a chance she was interested. Or curious. Must be some explanation. On her own at a table, eyes wide, drinking white wine, looking around the bar. Dark brown hair, nice smile. Not at all like Jo really, but there was something similar. He wanted to go and speak to her, but couldn't bring himself. Nervous around women, even now.

She had finished her drink, and now was walking slowly towards the bus stop. Won't find many buses today.

He walks ten paces behind, wondering whether he should make his move. What does he have in mind? He's not sure, and whenever he thinks of Jo under his bloody knife, he winces. How many times would he have to kill her for it to make a difference?

In an occasional moment of clarity he knows that not all women with dark brown hair are Jo, but the moments pass.

The woman stops ahead of him and turns. She looks at him, he slows his pace, stops five yards away.

'Well, are you just going to follow us all night, or are you actually going to talk to us?'

He stares. This isn't Jo. The mouth is too big, the eyes too wide, the voice is different – wrong accent. Sweet Jo. Doesn't really know what to say. Much easier to talk with a sharp instrument.

'What's your name then, pal?'

Should he tell her the truth?

'Ed,' he says, with hesitation.

'He speaks,' she says. 'That your real name?'

He feels intimidated. Maybe this is Jo. It's like he has this giant ball of sludge or fudge or mud or something in the middle of his brain, preventing him from thinking clearly. 'No… it's not,' he says eventually.

She's standing beside a close into an old tenement and nods at the door. A dirty grey building, damp and depressing under the orange glow of the streetlights. The door has a voice entry system, but the lock is broken.

'You want to come up?' she says.

She's inviting him in… He doesn't say anything, can't, and as she enters the close, he follows her in. The beat of his heart quickens.

Up the stairs. She smiles to herself, and wonders how much money he'll have in his pocket. She imagines she recognises the type. Rip them off and they're too embarrassed to come back and trouble you about it. You can always tell the quiet, pathetic, easy ones a mile away.

'You don't say much,' she says, opening the door.

He swallows. He has to find some confidence, has to stop feeling like an awkward child. A woman has asked him into her flat. It's not Jo. She's not Jo. Maybe this could be someone other than Jo. He could move on. Forget about her. Forget Jo. Maybe he can forget Jo. Stop thinking about Jo.

'You didn't ask me up here to talk,' he says with a good deal more confidence than he feels.

The doorway leads straight into a large sitting room, sparsely furnished. Old TV in the corner, a settee and matching seat, picture of Wallace and Gromit on the wall.

'D'you like a drink?' she says.

'What's your name?' he asks.

'Margaret,' she replies, but he hears Jo. Because of the mess in his head. Because of the giant ball of sludge. He shakes his head as if that might clear it; she notices the strange movement and has the first pang of doubt. No messing around, slip him the powder, take his money, bundle him out.

'A drink?' she repeats.

'Just water,' he says, and watches her walk through to the small kitchen.

'Take your jacket off,' she says. He wonders what to do with the knife in the inside pocket. He doesn't need it yet. Maybe he won't need it at all. This isn't Jo. He leaves the jacket on a chair by the door. Maybe he shouldn't use the knife. It's not Jo. Relax, enjoy himself. The woman wants sex, give her what she's after.

She comes back into the room. She has removed her coat, and is holding a glass of water in one hand, white wine in the other. She hands him the water. He stares at her breasts. Large breasts, cleavage showing, a cheap pink t-shirt.

'Like what you see?' she asks, taking a drink of wine. It has been open too long, cheap to start with. She swallows it anyway, does not let the taste, bitter like lemon, show on her face.

He holds the water, but doesn't drink it. He seems mesmerised by her chest, and she straightens her back to emphasise it. She reaches forward, holds his hand – which is a little too clammy – brings it up to her right breast and leaves it there. His fingers take a grip, tentatively squeeze. She suddenly feels horrible, and wants him out of her house. Is beginning to recognise the personality type she has attracted tonight. How can she be so wrong when reading these men? When she brought them back to her place, she had to be certain she had the quiet, pathetic ones. The ones who wouldn't cause trouble. Not the nutters. Not the ones who would overreact.

She sees it in his eyes, knows what she's got here.

He presses on her breast. It's been a long time since he touched a woman's breast. This one is bigger than Jo's. Much bigger. This isn't Jo. The size of the breast confuses him, but excites him at the same time. His mouth is watering. He is erect.

'Sorry,' he says, voice measured, surgically detaching

95

his hand from her breast. 'I'll have to go to the bathroom.'

'Right.' Thank God. 'Through that door there,' she says. 'First on your left.'

He starts to walk away, remembers the knife, but there's nothing he can do that would not be obvious. He gives her a strange look, then walks from the room.

This is an odd guy; she decides to not waste time thinking about it. There is a jacket to be searched. She picks it up, is about to put her hand into the outside pocket, when she notices what's inside. Just the butt of the knife, that's all she sees, but it is enough. She drops the jacket back onto the chair.

If this guy had been a hard man or a ned – the fact that she would not have invited him back in the first place notwithstanding – she could have understood him carrying a knife. Might even have expected it. But not this man. Nothing hard about him, and the threat is all psychological. He is strange, troubling. Possessed of something other than sanity.

She stands up, no time to think, and makes her decision.

He stands in the bathroom, looking at himself in the mirror. Trying to imagine he's someone he's not, but doesn't know who he wants to be. Lover. Killer. Both. He wants to be someone with confidence. Jo crushed him, made him feel so small. He'd been a different person before Jo. She'd ruined him. It was time to get the old man back, the old confidence. Once he had confidence, it didn't matter, didn't matter what he did. He could kill with confidence and he could make love with confidence. He could go out there, right now, and he could hold her, and he could see what he felt like doing right at that moment.

She had asked him back, she had been attracted to him, she had been drawn in by him. Why not make the most of it?

A final look in the mirror – into confident eyes – then he heads back out into the hall. Expecting her to still be standing in the sitting room, but she is gone.

'Margaret?' he calls out. The front door is closed, her wine lies on the small table beside the glass of water. 'Margaret?' again. No reply.

He checks the kitchen. Has the thought that perhaps she has gone into the bedroom and awaits him, naked, prostrate, ready and beckoning. Desperate.

He walks over to his jacket and picks it up, realising as he does so that it's not as neatly hung as he'd left it. He finds the knife, searches the other pockets for his wallet. Nothing has been taken, but if she went through his jacket, she knows about the knife. Shit. He looks round.

'Jo?' he shouts.

He lifts the knife and runs into the bedroom. He flicks the switch, the unclean room is bathed in harsh light. He notices the giant poster of Manhattan on the wall, but Jo is not there. Runs back out into the hall, then goes through every room in the house, every possible hiding place. It is a small flat; it doesn't take him long.

She's gone.

He seethes. This has tipped the balance between all those personalities raging inside. He stands in the middle of the lounge, and pointlessly looks at his watch. He must have been in the bathroom for at least three or four minutes. How far could she have gone?

Far enough.

There is no possibility that he can wait for her to return. She could have gone for the evening, and in his rage he kicks at one of the seats. Picks up a vase and throws it at Wallace and Gromit. Catches Gromit on the ear. He picks up the small table and breaks the legs of it on the floor.

Suddenly he explodes in an orgy of violent rage, room to room, breaking and smashing. Massive destruction. He swears as he does it, curses Jo for bringing him to this. Sees her face when he looks in the mirror, smashes his fist into the glass. His hand comes away bloody, but he doesn't notice the pain. Picks up a lamp in both hands, the clay breaks beneath his grip, such is his wrath. Attacks the mattress with the knife, stabbing violently, eyes closed, furious slashing. The mattress becomes Jo, her face wielding to the strength and vicious fury of his attack. He's screaming at it, screaming at Jo as he tears her apart, the knife ripping through her flesh, every muscle twitching and firing and blazing, Jo's face being slashed to bloody pieces. Sometimes the words *fucking Jo* form in amongst the screams, but mostly it is a wordless howl of rage.

There is a knock at the door.

He stops. A piece of glass from a picture frame tinkles to the ground, a light, friendly sound. A sound like Christmas. He stands in the still of the bedroom, breathing heavily, sweat on his face. It is near dark, the lights having yielded to his fury, the flat dimly illuminated by the streetlamps outside.

Gentle tapping at the door again. Insistent. He is curious. It is not the knock of an angry neighbour. It insinuates itself into the room. Still he does not move, listening to the beating of his heart, pondering what to do.

The quiet knock at the door continues, his curiosity triumphs over trepidation. He walks back through the hall and sitting room to the door. Is the visitor still on the other side? Imagines he can sense them, feel them breathe. It is a man. Some other lover of Jo's perhaps.

He turns the handle, the lock clicks, the door opens. He looks out into the dark, surprise registering on his face. He knows this man, doesn't understand. Backs off, but leaves the door open. His visitor smiles, walks into the room. Closes the door behind him, the click of the lock the only sound.

19

It's a typical Boxing Day. Grey, cloudy skies, the threat of rain, mild and miserable, not even a chill in the air.

Driving along the Loch Lomond road on the way to Arrochar. The loch looks bleak and humourless, the surrounding hills lost in the low cloud. In the winter it can be unutterably depressing, and in the summer, when it looks good, half a million people swarm from Glasgow to check it out. There's usually about one day in late March when it's worthwhile.

Other things on my mind. Great sex with Peggy. Then we sat up in bed for a couple of hours, reading Calvin & Hobbes. A perfect evening, which finished up with the expected result – she asked me back. Not in a direct, unsubtle, come on back Tom, kind of a way, but the suggestion is out there, hanging, waiting for me to pluck it out of the air. And I'm at a loss.

Two days ago I would've jumped at it. Now, because of a night with Charlotte Miller – another man's wife, a woman completely out of my league – I hesitate. I'm being an idiot, but I can't do anything about it. I know I'm not about to lure Charlotte away from her boring suit of a husband, but there exists the possibility that I end up in her bed again. Go back into the bosom of the family and that door is closed.

I was nervous going into work this morning. Waiting to see what her reaction would be towards me, waiting for a sign. As it was, she never showed up. Things were pretty quiet, and at shortly after ten I made my excuses and set out for the unclean hole that will be ex-DCI's Crow's abode.

So, general confusion on the women-front – no change there – and I try to think about what to say to Crow. But I can't. No idea how to confront him.

Drive into Tarbet, dull and empty, and up the hill past the Black Sheep. Its doors optimistically open, two sad cars parked out front.

Know I can't just come down here for a chat, that I have to force something from Crow. Also know he'll be a reluctant interrogatee. Why should he be anything else? If Edwards was telling Bathurst the truth, Crow isn't going to go volunteering the information to a member of the force who wasn't part of their gang. Have also considered the possibility that Edwards was bullshitting, in the mistaken hope that he would impress Bathurst – he was drunk, after all, and desperate. Consequently, I know I can't barge in there and start smacking Crow about.

Down the hill, turn the corner, past the hotel and into the village, such as it is. Loch Long looks as grey and dull as Lomond, the mountains on the other side completely obscured above a few hundred feet. Keep wondering what I'm going to do with any information I come up with; keep wondering how I'm going to tell Peggy that I'm not coming back; wonder if I should go back anyway, or what part Charlotte Miller will play in the decision.

Round the head of the loch, up a small side street, pull up in front of the house. Mind on the job, but I can smell Charlotte Miller. Taste her.

Crow's old Vauxhall is parked outside, still in need of massive bodywork repair. There's a spit of rain in the air. Feels colder down here, beneath the hills.

Mobile rings just as I'm getting out the car. Herrod. I'm not answering that. Throw it onto the passenger seat, pull my jacket tighter and go to the door, ring the bell. Can hear the faint sound of a television. Creaking floorboard, then a second later the door opens.

Crow stands before me. He breathes, I nearly choke on the fumes. He never went in for spirits. Beer man, and a bottle of wine if he felt like it. His face is a disaster, and he looks like every jake you ever passed in the centre of town.

The smell from the house isn't too fine, and I'm not sure

I want to get invited in. Wonder how long his pension will keep him in this, before he gets kicked out and ends up where he belongs.

'Hutton?' he says, unpleasantly. 'What?'

'Thought I might have a word, Chief Inspector.' Show respect, even though I can think of no one less deserving.

'Jonah sent you on an errand?' he grumbles. 'Let you in on the secret. Herrod told him to piss off, I expect. Need someone to do their dirty work after last month. Well, you can tell him to fuck… off.'

He begins to close the door.

'This has nothing to do with Jonah. I don't know what you're talking about.'

He stops. A half-truth – I haven't the faintest idea what that was all about. I can worry about it later.

'What is it, then?'

'Christmas. Thought I'd just come and see you, see how you're getting on.' An absolute garbage shitstorm. Serves me right for not giving it more thought on the way down here.

He steps back from the door, ushers me in.

'Load of shite, Hutton, but you might as well come in since you're here.'

He walks down the short hall and into the room with the TV playing. I close the front door behind me.

The room is a tip. Empty wine bottles, beer cans, dinner plates, microwave oven-ready meal containers. Crow's wife left him ten years ago, taking all four of their children with her. He moved into this place just after that, and some of this stuff looks as if it's been sitting here since then.

He slumps into his favourite chair – the one surrounded by the greatest amount of detritus – and stares at the television. A *Morcambe and Wise* re-run. At least, you have to assume it's a re-run. The BBC'll do anything to try and get an audience.

'Have a seat,' he says, and gestures to an old settee. I sit on the edge, clearing junk out of the way.

'Here,' he says, and tosses me an unopened can of warm McEwan's. Seriously.

'Thanks.' Rather drink my own urine, but I try not to offend. Open it, take the merest sip and put it on the coffee table with all the other crap.

I really don't know what to say – beginning to feel stupid – so sit and watch the TV. Eric and Ernie are in bed together. Jesus, the '70s...

'Well, what is it Hutton?' he says. 'You didn't come down here to drink my fucking Export.'

Ain't that the truth?

Consider subtlety, but that's not really an option. It would've required some prior thought. Might as well just get to it.

'Heard a rumour,' I say.

He looks at me, a flicker of interest.

'Oh, aye?'

'About you and Bloonsbury stitching up your man over the murder trial last year.'

He nods, takes a loud slurp from the can.

'What about it?'

What about it? I don't know.

'Did you do it?'

'What?'

'Plant evidence? Incriminate him, because you didn't have enough to put him away?'

He looks me full in the eye. Contempt.

'What's this, Hutton? You working for some polis commission? You on a crusade against injustice? Fighting on behalf of the wrongfully imprisoned Fucking Headcase Killer One?'

'What did you mean about Bloonsbury needing someone to do his dirty work after last month?'

He barks out a laugh, chokes on a swallow of McEwan's, washes it away with another loud slurp from the can.

'Listen, Wee Man, why don't you just fuck off? You obviously don't know fuck all, so take a hike. You're out your depth, Wee Man, out your fucking depth.'

I don't know about that, but really, what *am* I doing here? Waste of fucking time.

I stand up to go. This is getting me nowhere and I'm not going to tell him everything I know. And what difference does it make if he did murder that woman last year? Really?

As crusaders for truth go, I'm utterly useless.

One last question, because I don't care what he thinks about me asking it.

'You have anything to do with the murder the other night?'

He looks up at me, but there's nothing in those eyes. No giveaway, no hint.

'The fuck you talking about?'

'Ann Keller. She was murdered in Cambuslang on Monday night.'

He shakes his head, rolls his eyes. Plenty of drink, no acting. Nothing to do with it. Gut instinct.

'Wee Man, the only times I've left this seat in the last five month is to go for a shite, and to open the door to you. Now fuck off. And excuse me if I don't see you out.'

Look down at him. Had enough. The stench, everything, is leaving a bad taste in my mouth. And I hate getting called Wee Man, particularly by drunken old fucks who're about a foot shorter than me.

I see myself to the front door, step out into the rain. It feels clean and cold, and the grey day seems a lot fresher than it was ten minutes ago.

20

Bosnia, late summer '94. I was sitting by the side of the road. It had been raining, but the sun had just come out and the heat was making steam rise from what tarmac there was left on the surface. I hadn't slept in a couple of nights, but at some point in the Balkan summer that seemed to have begun in March, my body had become used to it.

Sleep was when bad things happened. When you lay still the world around you changed. You went to sleep in a bed in a small room in a quiet house in a nondescript village, and woke up to find you'd been surrounded by armoured vehicles, or that there were soldiers from God only knew what side, going from house to house. Your body got to learn that not sleeping was bad, but that sleep itself could be much worse.

I had a bottle of water in my hands. I'd dropped my backpack on the ground behind me and lain my camera on a large stone, set back from the road. I hadn't taken a photograph in five days. There were a couple of editors back in London wondering what I was doing, but I wasn't thinking about them anymore.

There was a kid walking towards me along the road, dragging a tired old doll alongside. I could see that she was crying before I could hear her. A kid walking alone in the middle of a forest, miles away from the nearest town. Jesus, I couldn't have wanted to know her story less. At the very least it would have been a great photo, but I was through with that. I was only picking up my camera again to move it from one shithole to another.

She got closer, walking in my direction, but she had no interest in me. She possibly couldn't even see me. She was walking along a road, and I doubt she had the faintest idea where she was going. The tears had made lines through the dirt on her face, her mouth was open in a frozen grimace. I think I knew as soon as I saw her that it wasn't a doll she was pulling along beside her. It had a weight that a doll would never have had.

The thing that really got me about the fact she was dragging a baby beside her along a potholed road, was that she was holding it by one ankle. The baby was wearing some rudimentary all-in-one, which was dirty and torn; the other leg hung limply, the shoulders and head bumped silently along the ground with the arms. The baby's face was looking at me as the kid approached. It was a face that had been dragged through the dirt for many miles.

The girl walked past me in silence, never noticing I was there. Lost in her own disaster. It didn't even cross my mind to ask if she wanted help, as if the fact that she was ignoring my presence absolved me from having to provide any assistance.

I didn't move, but watched her all the way down the road, until she had disappeared out of sight behind the trees. The last sight I had was of the baby, its head bouncing out of a pothole.

I stared into the trees across the road. There was silence. No birds. The birds had got the fuck out of Dodge as soon as the war had started. They had more sense than the rest of us. Even the insects appeared to have given this place a rest.

The kid might have gone, but the baby's face was emblazoned in the back of my eyes. At some stage I realised that my face was wet with tears.

Some time later I heard the low rumble of a truck, coming from the same direction as the kid. The day was so quiet that I could hear the truck for some time before it appeared, slowly negotiating its way around the holes in the road. It was an open-topped green 4 tonne military vehicle with no plates. There were two guys in the cab at the front, seven or eight slouched unhappily in the back. Hot, dirty, miserable. Croatians, leaning on guns, or slumped over, their elbows resting on their knees. Most of them looked at me as they drove past. They didn't stop.

I wondered for a while what they did when they came across the kid in the road. The kid with the baby. Maybe they slowed down.

*

Walk back into the office just after lunch, having helped myself to a Little Chef all day breakfast on my way home. Herrod called five times while I was out, but I let the phone ring out each time. Not in the mood.

Can tell something's happened. Herrod's there, talking agitatedly to someone on the phone. There are a few more constables about the station than there should be on Boxing Day, and they all look as if they've got something to do. One of them calls over that Taylor wants to see me, then scurries off. The door to Miller's office is open and I can hear her speaking to what is obviously an inferior. Recognise the tone. It all connects with the press hanging around outside the front door. The place is in a state of controlled excitement. Wonder if we've got our man, and where General Bloonsbury is amidst the turmoil.

Herrod slams down the phone as I walk past.

'The fuck have you been?' he growls, and I've a mind to tell him what I was doing. Ignore him. He gets up, and walks quickly out the office.

'I'm getting your mobile surgically attached to your arse,' he grumbles as he goes.

Another constable buzzes past, catch the faint trace of alcohol. Walk into Taylor's office, expecting to find him feverishly arresting criminals. He's leaning back in his chair, feet up on his desk, a cup of tea in his hand. Looks as if he's just enjoyed a nice bit of lunch. An oasis of calm. Pull up the seat across the desk but don't go so far as to put my feet up.

'Can I take it I missed something?'

He takes a drink from his tea, places the cup back on the desk, puts his hands behind his head.

'Where've you been, Sergeant?'

'Pursuing an independent line of inquiry.'

He nods. Trusts me enough to know he'll find out about it when I'm ready to tell him. Although, in this case, who knows when that's going to be?

'We think our man had another go last night. Followed a woman back to her flat in Rutherglen, she asked him in...' raises his eyebrows as he says it, and he's right. Don't these people read the papers? 'She starts thinking there's something a bit weird about him. He goes to the toilet, she looks in his jacket, discovers a knife. This lady, for some reason, doesn't know anything about the murder on Monday night. But she does know she's got a potential nutjob in her bathroom, so she gets out. Goes to a friend's house. The friend is a bit more switched on, shows her our first photofit in the paper, and she thinks it's him. Waits until this morning...'

'What?'

He shrugs. 'That's the helpful public for you. Anyway, she gets one of us to go back to her flat with her, just in case he's lying in wait. Long gone of course, but not before he's ripped the shit out the joint. She's still downstairs, don't think she's finished wetting her underwear yet.'

'Fuck...'

'Anyway, we've got a bit of a better description out of it, but who knows? It's a distinct third photo we've got now, anyway, rather than an evolution of the first or second. These people are just useless. The lot of them.'

Takes his feet down, drums his fingers on the desk. 'Useless,' he repeats. 'Still, he blew it, and we should be a step closer.'

'So, how come you're sitting here with your feet up while everyone else is in ferment?'

'Thinking. Got to think in this job, Hutton, I've told you before. That's why you're still a sergeant.'

One of the many reasons.

'Where's Bloonsbury?'

'Still down there. Got the crew going house to house

and the SOCOs going over the flat. Jonah's in charge, and bloody miserable that the guy got away. Has this theory that now he's blown one, the guy'll back off and disappear and we'll never get him.'

'What d'you think?'

'I think he'll show his hand. These headcases can't keep their knives to themselves. Bloonsbury's too busy wallowing in J&B to be positive about anything. Had a pickled napper for the last ten years. Still don't know how in God's name he solved that murder case last year.'

Used to wonder about that myself. Now might just be time to tell Taylor, but I hold back. I have to know more, and I haven't the faintest idea how I'm going to find it. CID just doesn't train you well enough in investigation.

Change the subject.

'How'd you get on last night?'

He snorts, shakes his head.

'Awful. Just awful. In-laws were as bad as usual, then Debbie gets a call about half nine and was on the phone for… well, you know…'

'King Dong?'

That one hurt, hold my hand up in apology.

'Yes,' he says, eventually, 'King Dong. I ended up coming in here, didn't go home until about three.'

'Get anything done?'

'Worked like a dog. Took my mind off it.' Indicates the desk, and there's a lot less paperwork lying around than usual. 'You should try it some time.'

Ignore that remark. 'What are you going to do?'

'About Debbie? No idea. Don't know why she doesn't just leave.'

'Maybe he doesn't want to take her in.'

'Aye, maybe.' Nods, purses his lips. Looks resigned and miserable. 'Suppose that's what she's doing. Trying to get me to leave, so she can have the place to herself.'

'Why don't you talk to her about it?'

Shakes his head and I realise I'm out of my depth with this. I'm no counsellor. I've always just accepted my marriage break-ups with resignation. It's not like I haven't realised why they were happening.

'We haven't talked in years, Tom,' he says.

He looks terrible and I wish I hadn't reminded him of it. We'd been doing fine, and the juxtaposition of that with my own Christmas Day – my marriage going in the opposite direction, if I want it to – makes me feel guilty.

Change the subject again.

'So, what have you been thinking?'

He sits back, toys with his tea. Think I've got his mind on to it just in time.

'Just wondering if it's worthwhile trying to flush him out.'

'How are you going to do that?'

'Bait. This one last night saw him in a pub. He didn't speak to her there, but followed her when she left. Follows the pattern of Monday, where we think he followed her out of the cinema.'

'Don't know that for sure.'

'But it's likely. Anyway, the guy is going for girls with dark brown hair and he's working in our area. We've already checked out the pub from last night, spoken to the staff that were on, a few of the regulars. No one can remember him. Not a known face around town.'

'But we have to know the public places he's likely to frequent.'

'Come on,' says Taylor, 'we're talking about Rutherglen and Cambuslang, not New York. There ain't that many pubs, especially given how many have closed down the last few years. We've got to think about the way he's worked so far, decide which are his likeliest haunts, see if we can set a trap. So that's what I was doing. Thinking.'

Very commendable. More than Bloonsbury will have been doing. More than me too, with my romantic preoccupations.

Focus.

'How many officers with dark brown hair have we got?'

'Three, maybe another couple who could pass. I'm sure

we could manage to get wigs from somewhere, however,' he says, voice condescending. I deserve it. Of course we could get wigs. It's time I switched the personal stuff off and actually thought about this.

It's the usual flawed bunch riding into the sunset for justice and liberty: Bloonsbury soiled with alcohol; Herrod drunk with the desire to arrest anyone – in this case probably everybody in Glasgow over the age of twelve with a penis; the cuckolded Taylor, consumed by doubt and depression by the actions of his wife; and me, for all I'm worth.

Someone's got to be doing some clear thinking and I can't leave it all to Taylor.

'We could even get a few of you young constables and sergeants dressed up as women,' he says, smiling. 'I see you in red, or pink maybe. Pink stretch cycling shorts, wonderbra and a hairnet.'

'Fuck off.'

Smell the perfume first, then look up. Charlotte Miller stands in the doorway, arms folded, looking down on us both. Wonder how long she's been there, because Taylor wouldn't automatically have deferred to her.

'Interrupt a serious debate, did I, gentlemen?'

'What can we do for you?' asks Taylor.

'Some work would be nice, or d'you think you can do your jobs without ever getting up off your backside?'

'The job's getting done,' is all he says. Cool, better than I would be if I was here on my own.

'See that it does,' she says, and the voice is just the way you'd expect it to be. Sharper than a pint of freshly squeezed lemon juice. 'Nice of you to come in, Sergeant. Where have you been all morning?'

'Something to follow up.'

'You want to share it with me?'

It's absurd, but there's just something about her makes me feel like I'm at school. Despite everything.

But here we are. She doesn't usually keep track of my movements. I slept with her, and now she's going to treat me like dirt for the rest of my life.

'It's a little awkward,' is all I can say.

She gives me the dog shit look.

'Perhaps then you'd like to come into my office and explain it to me,' and before the words are out of her mouth, she's turned on her heels and gone. I look at Taylor, he smiles, then laughs.

'What'd you do to deserve that?'

Shake my head – I'm not about to tell him that either – then get to my feet.

'So where were you this morning?'

Breathe heavily. 'Tell you later,' I lie, and walk out.

Walking through the office I start to wonder if she's asking me in there so she can jump me across the desk.

Get to her office, step through the open door, close it behind me. She's sitting at her desk, reading a file. I can feel a strange sensation of arousal. I can smell her, and it makes me nervous. Wish I could feel more in control, as I picture her standing topless beside her desk.

She lifts her head. The eyes tell it. I'm not in here on any romantic expedition.

'Now, Sergeant, where you were this morning?'

Curse silently to myself.

'I was pursuing an independent line of inquiry,' I say. Sounds lame this time.

'And are you going to keep this independent line of inquiry to yourself?' She says the words 'independent line of inquiry' with mockery.

No idea what to say, no intention of telling her what I was doing. I'm not protecting anyone – well, maybe Bathurst – because I don't care about most of these people. I just can't go mouthing off about this when I don't know yet whether any of it's true. There's also the possibility that Charlotte Miller already knows all that there is to know.

'Could it possibly be related to our ongoing murder inquiry?'

'I don't know.' Find the voice, at last, if not many

words. 'However, I don't think it is,' I weakly add, under the weight of the stare.

'Very well, Sergeant, if you must keep these things to yourself. However, can I remind you that this is a very public inquiry, and everyone is demanding quick results. The Chief Constable more than anyone. We work under tight enough constraints as is it, without being able to afford the time for senior Detective Sergeants to swan off for four hours on a whim. Do we understand each other?'

I nod. Nothing to say. She has most definitely managed to dampen my ardour.

'That will be all then, Sergeant,' she says, and I know when I've been dismissed. Turn to go. Get a quick look at a picture of her in uniform on the wall. Looks severe. Seductive, but severe.

'Thomas?' she says to my back. Almost at the door, I turn round. Harsh, then the sudden use of the first name. The usual management technique.

There's a smile on her face – of sorts – which I naturally can't read.

'I hope we can be mature enough to keep these things separate from our private life.'

Our private life? Decent.

'Sure.' Nothing else to say. She's in charge, in so many ways.

She hesitates, as if she's unsure. Shyness in someone else, you might think.

'Frank's away to Italy at the weekend,' she says. Missing another game at Ibrox. What kind of fan is he? 'I was wondering if we could do something?'

'Of course,' I say again, and manage what I hope is a smile. Be cool and calm, and I quickly make my exit before I betray myself.

Stand outside her door and ward off the curious looks from one or two constables and non-uniform staff in the office. Immediately excited at the prospect of spending more time with her, immediately guilty at what Peggy and the kids would think if they knew. Due to phone her this evening, and I know they'll want to see me at the weekend.

Already thinking about my excuses as I make my way back through the office. Crack open a fresh packet of Marlboro's, nip outside, and smoke three of them before returning to address the mountain on my desk.

21

Nearly nine o'clock, still in the office. As always when there's some big murder inquiry on, there's even more crime than usual. I got farmed off to deal with an aggravated assault and an attempted bank robbery. Seriously. A bank robbery, for fuck's sake. Suspects were apprehended in both instances.

In the first case it was a wife turning on her husband – after fifteen years of abuse, she said. It was a shitshow, an uncomfortable, horrible, domestic shitshow.

Meanwhile, the bank robbery was the comic relief. Rank amateurs. Even so, they would probably still have managed to get away with the fifteen quid they'd nicked if they'd remembered to fill the getaway car with petrol.

Found time for a brief word with Bathurst. Curious about that remark of Crow's when I first arrived. Bumped into her downstairs, on her way home at the end of her day. I was wondering if she'd told me everything there was to tell. People rarely do.

'Went to see Crow this morning,' I said.

She looked frightened straight off. Saw it in the eyes, heard it in the voice.

'What did you say? You didn't mention me?'

'Don't worry.'

'Why did you tell him you were there?'

Didn't know what to say to that, and I wasn't going to admit to being such a clown.

'Just asked him a few questions. Suppose he might've worked it out, but his brain must be so pickled it's hard to tell whether he's capable of clear thinking. Look, I really don't think he or Bloonsbury had anything to do with Monday night. Don't worry about that, all this is nothing to do with what happened last year.' She nodded slowly – unconvinced. 'There was something else he said. About having had dealings with Bloonsbury and Herrod last month. You know about that?'

She looked even more worried. Puzzled.

'He assumed at first that was why I was there.'

Kept shaking her head. Bit one of her nails.

'Look, I don't know,' I said. 'I'll dig around, but I have to be careful. Don't want people getting suspicious.' Then I suggested a way out for us both. It would need a lot of courage from her and nothing from me, but it wasn't me that created the situation in the first place. 'You could go to Miller, tell her everything. You're going to look bad, but if it's bothering you that much...'

'I can't,' she said. Scared.

'She's not as bad as she seems.' Personal experience – get her in bed and she's a kitten. *Kitten?* Jesus, you really are from the 1950s. 'If this is going to bug you, if it's going to make you not want to be on the force, then you've got to get it out there.'

'It'll be the end of my career.'

I wondered if I could deny it, but I couldn't. If she wasn't kicked out for her part in it, who would want to work with her after she'd done this?

'Depends how much you want your career. Cause if you do, you're just going to have to forget it, get on with your life. It was over a year ago – you've done all right so far. You'll have to let it go. Believe me, Monday night had nothing to do with those guys, so you've either got to accept what you were part of and forget about it, or get it out and face the consequences.'

She kept shaking her head. It was a big discussion and warranted a Hell of a lot more time, but I didn't have it.

'Look, I've got to go. Think about what I've said. Don't do anything yet and we'll talk at the weekend.'

She smiled weakly at that and nodded. Not sure, of course, if I'll have the time to see her.

That was it, and we went our ways. We're both in work tomorrow and we can take it from there.

Had a brief interview with Charlotte as she disappeared

---

for the evening. Wants to go away tomorrow evening, spend the night in some hotel somewhere. Said she had a place in mind. I didn't fight it, and as I stood in her office having the brief discussion on the subject, I just wanted to leap over the desk and rip her clothes off.

Not long after that the expected phone call from Peggy came through. Juggled enough women in my time to sound cool about it. Even so, like a complete idiot, I couldn't bring myself to say definitely no about tomorrow night.

So, just after nine on a Friday night, up to my eyes in paperwork, and I can't concentrate on a single line of it. Charlotte, Peggy and Evelyn Bathurst keep intruding into the thought process. Mostly Charlotte.

As far as I know, she's spending the evening alone. Very tempted to go down there when I've finished at the office. Utterly succumbing to infatuation and there's only one road to go down once you start feeling like this; there's only one thing that's going to happen. You're going to make an idiot of yourself.

I'm forty-four for fuck's sake. Bit of a slow starter, but after Bosnia I had all those women and by God, I don't believe I made an idiot of myself with any of them. Too messed up. There may have been several who were angry, certainly several that were hurt, and my behaviour would be considered reprehensible in many quarters, yet I never made a fool of myself. Now, however, we're right smack in the middle of the biggest murder inquiry we've ever had in this patch, and I'm acting like a lovesick clown. Jesus.

The quicker I fall flat on my face – get dumped by Miller and screw up with Peggy, ending up with no one but two-bit no-hopers, my equals in life, snagged in the pub on a Saturday night – the quicker I can get on with things. So, if I go to see Miller tonight, I'll either get put in my place, not before time and just what I'm needing, or else I'll get into her bed for the night and plummet deeper into the abyss.

First, however, I've got to get this work done. Jesus,

who joins the police to do paperwork?

Finish off the cup of tea at my right hand, sit back in the seat, stare at the ceiling. Begin contemplating getting out of here, doing all the crap tomorrow. Ponder what my reception will be in Helensburgh, because no matter how wrong it is to do it, I know I'm not going to be able to stop myself going down there. Uninvited.

*

Of course – because it's the way of things for there to be copious amounts of shit dropped onto the path of life from an enormous height – however bad I imagine I might end up feeling when I get there, it doesn't even begin to wipe the arse of how it actually works out. Not a damned patch.

22

Evelyn Bathurst looks not unlike Jo.

She parks the car on the road at the bottom of the garden of the large house in Helensburgh, steps out into the rain. Stares at the lights in the house fifty yards away along the driveway, wonders about what she is doing. Shivers, pulls her jacket closer around her.

She locks the car door. Her own car under repair – faulty brakes – she has borrowed the car from Constable Forsyth, on duty through the night. Forsyth believes that she may repay the favour sometime.

Bathurst will not get the chance.

She swings back the gate, feels the beating of her heart. Looks at her watch, wonders if the Superintendent will be at home. A Friday night, not long after ten o'clock. Whatever it is that Miller does, she will find this an unwelcome interruption, with unwelcome information.

Takes a deep breath, tries to calm herself; begins the long walk up the driveway. She has somewhere else to go, someone else to whom she could talk – not that she was going to mention that to Thomas Hutton – but she has decided to come here first. Perhaps she'll move on later. Perhaps not.

Should she have listened to Hutton? But it wasn't Hutton talking, it was her conscience. She had been meaning to do the same thing for the past year. Slowly the desire had worn off. The months will do that to you. But now it was back, born of fear, guilt and self-loathing for what she had been a part of. There was no need to confide in Hutton any further. What he had said earlier in the station had been all that she'd been needing to hear.

Her ponderous steps take her nearer to the house, her stomach crawls with nerves. She wonders if she is about to be dismissed, in the manner she has heard Miller dismiss so many officers in the past. Not as bad as she seems, Hutton had said, and she hopes it is true.

She automatically rings the bell, without a clear thought in her head; moves back from the second step so that she is outwith the meagre protection of the front of the house. The rain soaks her head. She shivers again in the cold. Throat dry, nervous fingers.

The door opens, catching her unaware. She stares into the dim light of the house, feels the rush of warmth. Charlotte Miller stands in front of her. Doesn't recognise Bathurst at first. Miller wears a long, blue silk pyjama top, her legs are bare. Bathurst looks at her skin, smooth and gold in the dim light from behind.

'Constable Bathurst?' she says, surprise in her voice coming with sudden recognition.

Bathurst nods, says nothing. No words. They stare at each other for a few seconds, before either awakes to the other. Miller shakes her head, feels the cold, summons her inside and closes the door behind her.

Bathurst stands in the hall, looking around. Unaware of what her husband does for a living, she wonders what Miller earns as a superintendent to afford such opulence.

'I'm sorry to bother you on a Friday night,' she begins, but Miller stops her with a shake of the head.

'Don't be silly, Evelyn. Take your coat off and I'll get a towel. How long were you standing out there?'

Bathurst thinks of stepping out of the car, seems like an hour ago. Doesn't answer, removes her coat, Miller ushers her into the sitting room.

'I've just got a quick phone call to make, then I'll get the towel,' she says.

She disappears. Evelyn Bathurst stands in the middle of the room, suddenly warm, aware of the dampness of her hair.

*

There was nothing special about the story of the kid

119

walking along the road, bumping the head of a dead baby in the potholes. Yep, it sounds special. It sounds absolutely fucking horrendous. It sounds like the kind of thing that doesn't happen every day. But that's just what people think nowadays, because most of the population haven't spent time in a war zone.

Previous generations were always going to war. That's what they did. Everyone went to war, everyone got used to it, learned to live with all the awfulness of what you see, what you live through. You got home, you coped. If you didn't cope, they locked you up, or you hit your wife, or you drank yourself into oblivion, or you became the guy stuck away in the corner of the village that everyone told their kids to stay away from.

These days, it's all about coping. Society is about the individual. It didn't use to be. It used to be about society functioning as a whole, and if that meant that individuals got fucked over to enable society to function, then so be it. These days individuals have the right not to get fucked over. Very thoughtful of society to put the individual first, except, inevitably, with the kind of juxtaposition that the grey, nuanced areas of life spit out, it plays its part in society falling apart.

So, everybody hurts and everybody cries and everybody has a story to tell, and this is just mine. Except I don't want to tell it; I don't want to talk. The story is so shit, how I came to be sitting at the side of that road in the first place, that if I have to think about it, if someone was ever going to force me to think about it, then Jesus, I won't just cry, I won't just go quietly mental...

There was nothing special about the kid and the baby with its head bouncing off the road, except it was the only story I told to the psychiatrist I saw a month after I got back from the Balkans.

I sat down, she asked me a couple of questions, I cut her off and told her the bouncing baby's head story, and then before I'd got to the end – although, of course, it's a story that doesn't really have an end – I got up and walked out. I didn't want to tell her any more, and if I wasn't going to talk to her then there was no point in being there.

As I talked, I stared at her throat. She had an unusually large Adam's apple for a woman, and I just stared at it the whole time curious about her gender, wondering if the Adam's apple wasn't actually all that big, and that maybe I was exaggerating it in some bizarre attempt to distract myself.

I never saw her again. Looking back, I struggle to visualise her Adam's apple.

*

Not much after six a.m. The rain still falls in a steady drizzle, as Constable Bathurst arrives at the station, leaving Forsyth's Peugeot in the car park, the keys in the exhaust. He will be off duty in a couple of hours. From there she will walk home, a ten-minute promenade through wet, deserted streets in the early morning.

As she steps out onto the street and rounds the first corner, someone sees her, sees her dark brown hair dully reflect the orange street lamps, but she does not see him. She walks on, the dull ache in her leg muscles heightened from sitting in the car.

She thinks about Charlotte Miller, has vague thoughts of Thomas Hutton, but thinks not of the problems with which she stepped out that evening. Wonders whether to have coffee when she gets home, or whether she should go straight to bed.

She will, however, never get to choose.

23

Having a weird dream where Peggy and Charlotte are naked together on a huge front lawn somewhere, singing Aerosmith – *Crazy* – when the phone rings. It plagues the dream for a while, before I'm plucked from the fantasy into the cold early morning. Still dark outside, cold in the bed. First thing I think of is driving down to see Charlotte last night, and getting my rude awakening. Constable Forsyth's Peugeot 307 sitting outside her front gate. Forsyth. *Forsyth?* So I sat there feeling like a fucking idiot, before turning around and heading back home. Resisted the pull of the vodka bottle, went straight to bed. I cannot believe she went for Forsyth. Course, I can't believe she went for me either, but at least I'm not some spotty constable for whom shaving is a distant dream. At least we'd had some sort of thing going on since the curious incident of the breasts in the lunchtime. But Forsyth?

Look at the clock while my hand makes its tortuous way out from under the covers, on the long journey to the phone. Not yet seven o'clock.

'Yeah?' I mutter down the phone.

'You need to get in.'

*

Dawn's grey light begins to show behind the tenement buildings. The rain has stopped, the cold does not seem so cold. The small area at the bottom of the park where the body was found is log-jammed with police; the entire park is cordoned off from the public. The Saturday between Christmas and New Year, and not too many people have crawled out of bed. A few anoraks with their dogs stand around and watch the police activity, such as it is.

And what are any of us doing, these too many chiefs and too many Indians? The SOCOs are doing their business, while the remainder of us stand, magnificently impotent, in monstrous misery and anger.

The body of Evelyn Bathurst has already been removed.

The first officer at the scene did not recognise her, her face having been dealt with in the same manner as Anne Keller five days ago. Multiple stab wounds, so that she was utterly disfigured. The body was identified by the ID card in her inside pocket. Strangely, it wasn't until then that the constable on duty had to throw up.

The gang's all here, each and every one of us looking sick. What makes it worse? That she was one of us? Or is it just that it's happened again, the killer has struck once more? He's back, and he's not going away until we catch him.

Bloonsbury is still drunk from last night. Very fetching he looks in his desolation and inebriation. Taylor at least has managed to sober up, just looks hungover – the same as that idiot Herrod. And Charlotte Miller stands alone. Even saw her shed a tear. Haven't seen her at the scene of a crime since she got here, but this is different. This is a combination of all our worst nightmares.

Tried speaking to her a few minutes ago, got nowhere. She looks in shock, but you would have to be built of granite not to be moved by this.

'And when he was home, there lay his uncle smitten on the head, and his father pierced through the heart, and his mother cloven through the midst.'

That was what she said, those her only words. Her voice was small, and like all intellectuals who cannot speak the truth of their emotions, she hid behind a literary reference. She does, at least, look genuinely distraught.

Forsyth walked past her not long after and they didn't even look at each other. And what were they up to no more than a few hours ago? Why would a Superintendent have a constable back to her house? There can be only one reason, and it's the same one that took me there on Christmas Eve. Makes me wonder why she's asked me away for this evening.

Now, however, tonight in a hotel looks extremely unlikely and if I don't spend the entire evening at the station, I can be glad of the fact that I did not dismiss Peggy's invitation. Yet these are trivial considerations at the moment. They would be, even if this latest murder had not been one of us, and a popular member of the force at that.

I've got my back to a tree, the tenth smoke of the day in my hand, my mind all over the place. I'm going to have to talk to Taylor, no doubt. Who is there for me to betray, now that the only one of the gang of five whom I would have protected has been killed?

Sequence of events. Monday night – Anne Keller is murdered, and at the same time Edwards is telling Bathurst of last year's great conspiracy. Two days later Bathurst fills me in on the full story. Doesn't want me to tell anyone else, so I have to presume she hasn't. I go to see Crow, he looks dumb about Monday night – and gut instinct says he's telling the truth – although there is something about Herrod and Bloonsbury, as if the conspiracy is still active in some way. Our killer tries to strike again, this time unsuccessfully, and the potential victim gets a good look at him. Bit of a vague description of course, since all these people are idiots, but it certainly isn't anything like Crow. The guts continue to say that he had nothing to do with the murder. I speak to Bathurst, advise her to go to Miller, and the next episode in the story is the one where she gets murdered.

So, was she killed by the same man who killed Keller – the same m.o. as far as anyone can tell at this stage – or was she murdered in copycat to keep her quiet, in which case, how did they know she was about to play the whistleblower? Could I have alerted them by my pointless trip to see Crow? That's the thing that consumes me the most. Was I to blame for her death?

God, it's a horrible thought. But the gut feeling says that Bathurst was just another victim in the line. Dark brown hair, walking alone through the streets in the middle of the night, she fits the mould of the victims.

But then there's that other gut feeling, the one which says there's no such thing as coincidence. If she's dead now, it's because of her knowledge of what happened last year. And if somehow they know she told me...

Get the shivers, feels like a hand at my neck. Light another cigarette as the cold morning continues its painful appearance. Another media crew pull up and I wonder how Bloonsbury's going to handle them in his state.

Taylor appears, looking hellish, much the same as the rest of us.

'You all right, Sergeant?' he says.

Cigarette in the mouth, I nod. Why is he asking me?

'I mean,' he says, 'you two, you had something going, didn't you?'

Aye, right enough. He thought I spent the night with her leading into Christmas Day.

'Nothing but another in a long line of rejections for me, sir,' I say, and the cigarette tastes awful. Serves me right for smoking more than a half packet before breakfast.

'Oh,' he says, and looks disinterested. Doesn't believe me, which is fine.

'This is a fucking mess,' he says, looking around at the commotion. And a Hell of a bigger mess than he supposes.

'Telling me,' I say. Crush the cigarette underfoot, determine not to have another until I've eaten something. 'I need to talk to you, sir.'

'Yeah, sure, whenever. Not now, though. Someone's going to have to talk to the press. Jonah's in no fit state.'

'Still fucked from last night.'

'Still fucked from Monday night,' says Taylor – in one of our old jokes – as he walks off to talk to the gathering herd of TV, hungry for the story for the morning news. Nothing people like better with their Cornflakes than a bloody mutilation.

*

Been a long day. Our battered husband woke up and wants
to press charges. Had to go and speak to him, and having
found the wife unlikeable and hard to believe, he was just
as bad. Perfect for each other, except that one of them is a
brutal, lying bastard. Or perhaps, as occurred to me at
some point during the day, they're both brutal bastards and
they're both telling the truth about the other's brutality. Got
a feeling it's going to be like Michael Douglas and
Kathleen Turner in *War of the Roses,* and they'd save us all
a lot of trouble if they just went off somewhere and fell
from a chandelier together.

The shit has hit the fan, of course. The Chief Constable
showed up, acting like he owned the place – I missed him
fortunately, the guy's a moron – dragged back from his
'winter retreat' – that's what he called it – and not too
happy about it. As it is the need of authority to dump on
the next most senior in the firing line, Miller got it in the
neck, and everyone expected her to come firing thereafter.
Didn't happen, however. She got them all together –
missed this as well, at the hospital – and gave them some
concerned talk, considerate, subdued, about the need for a
quick result, not only for the benefit of the public, but for
our own good. Stressed the need for good, honest work, to
do the job well and not try anything that could backfire.

Good police chatter, but not at all like Charlotte.
Usually she's in amongst us like an Uruk-hai with a
chainsaw. Never been around her when she's lost one of
her people before, so you don't know what she'll be like.

Mirrors the entire mood of the station. Everyone's the
same – subdued, miserable, determined. We've got to get
the guy, there's going to be no messing about and every
other crime that gets committed along the way is even
more of an irritant than usual.

At some point in the afternoon Mrs. Bathurst showed
up from Inverness, all tears and anger. Never wanted her

daughter to be in the police in the first place. Once she'd got her anger off her chest she broke down, and Charlotte spent a lot of time with her. Another surprise.

Two calls from Peggy, which I ignored. Ended up texting back that I'd call her later when I had time. About tonight, there's just no way. It's going to be a long evening and I'm just not in the mood for any happy families. She's got to realise it, though, and if she doesn't then we're no further forward than we were three years ago.

Into Taylor's office, finally, at some time after six. Been wanting to talk to him all day and been growing more frustrated at the delays which have piled up, at the rubbish which keeps getting in the way. Had hoped to make the late afternoon brief, but missed that as well, thanks to another aggravated assault in Rutherglen Main Street. Don't know what's happening down there.

Find Taylor staring at the wall, his usual position. Thinking. Shut the door behind me, pull up a seat across the desk.

'Got some bad news for you, Tom,' he says.

Really? Taylor looks bloody terrible. Hope the bad news isn't going to be about him, that really it's bad news for him, not me.

'What?'

'Thistle lost two-one at Raith.'

'You're kidding?'

'Morton won, so did Ross, so you're down to ninth.'

'Fuck.'

'Winning one-nil, let in two goals in the last five minutes.'

Bloody Thistle, bloody useless. Should start supporting one of those crappy wee teams in League Two; you know the ones who draw a crowd of six and get pumped every week.

'I don't care anymore,' I say, in a voice that suggests otherwise. 'I'm an East Stirling fan these days.'

'They got beat, 'n all.'

'Funny.'

———

He laughs, but it's not a day for laughing and it dies on his face.

Time for work. Got a small knot in my stomach.

'What have I missed?'

He lets out a long breath, runs a hand through his hair. God, he looks tired. He needs a break and when I think about it, I can't remember the last time he had more than a day off.

'Same m.o. as before,' he begins. 'Exactly. Almost the same number of stab wounds, 'cept a hundred and twenty-seven this time. Got some skin samples and they've already checked out. It's the same guy. Strangled her first, but didn't kill her, then laid into her with the knife.' Feel sick, try to be dispassionate about it but this is Evelyn Bathurst. 'Mostly to the face and abdomen again, and some around the crotch.' Lets out another long breath. 'Only other thing, and I don't know what to make of this, they found evidence of her having had sex. But there was no semen involved. She'd been penetrated but with, you know, a dildo or a vibrator. There were small bite marks, small bruises. He hasn't got proof yet, hasn't found anything else to sample so far, but Baird's guessing she'd had lesbian sex.' He looks at me for the first time since he started talking. 'Did you know that about her?'

Shake my head. Have that instant egotistical thought – this explains why she rejected my advances! Feel guilty for even thinking it.

'No one seems to know what she did last night. You any ideas?'

Already been asked, of course. Shake my head again.

'So, who knows where she was? Time of death was around six this morning. Couldn't have been dead longer than about ten minutes when she was discovered. Apart from that, God knows. Yeah, and one of the constables – Forsyth, I think – gave her a loan of his car, but he says he's no idea where she went with it. He was on duty all night and she brought it back and left it. You all right?'

Aw, Jesus Fuck. Feel that hand on my guts, squeezing,

twisting.

What does that mean? Look away from Taylor, stare at the floor, fumble with a pack of cigarettes, try to gather my thoughts. It was Bathurst who was with Miller last night, not Forsyth. She went down there to tell her about the gang of five, and then what? *They had sex?* That doesn't make sense. And after she tells her, she gets killed.

Coincidence again? It can't be. Too many coincidences. So, what? Miller is in on it and she followed Bathurst back up here and took care of her? No way. The same killer as the last time. A man, definitely a man. Maybe she phoned Crow, got him to do it.

'Sergeant, you want to share this with me?' he says, and I suppose I owe it to him. But I can't tell him about Miller. Not yet.

Where do we go from here? Crow, it leads back to Crow. The guy reeks of more than just alcohol. He was the one who murdered the woman last year, he's the one capable of the crime. Ignore the gut feeling, because there's definitely something going on with him and Bloonsbury, something more recent.

'Where's Jonah?' I ask.

'What?'

He stares curiously at me. He's right. My thoughts are all over the place. Where's Bloonsbury in all this? He's been too drunk all week to know any better. During the last murder case he was off the drink, you could tell he meant it, he had an eye for the crime – even though I didn't know how much of an eye at the time – but now he doesn't have a clue what's going on. He's lost.

Crow was slime, you could see him doing this to someone, a fellow officer, anyone. But Bloonsbury is just a lush. A sad, pathetic lush on a downward spiral.

'Jonah?'

'Think he's gone to talk to some friends of Bathurst's. Not on the force. Ain't going to help, but he's desperate. Word is, and it's got to be coming, Miller's about to kick him off the case. Don't know though.'

Then what? Us, probably.

'Want to go for a drive?'

'Where?'

'Arrochar. See Crow.'

He leans forward onto the desk. Looks sharper.

'Crow? What has Crow got to do with it?'

Stand up, start to take a cigarette out the packet.

'Come on, I'll tell you on the way.'

24

Driving along the banks of Loch Lomond by the time I finish telling Taylor of the last few days. Nothing excluded, except the bit about me turning up in Helensburgh last night and seeing Forsyth's car parked outside Miller's house. That, and the sex.

He's listened carefully, asked the occasional question, knuckles growing gradually whiter as we've gone on. When we got into the car we were listening to Dylan, as usual, but Bob got hoofed pretty quickly. *I Dreamed I Saw St Augustine* still plays silently in my head, although these days I find I forget the words.

Just past Luss when I wrap up. He breathes deeply, shakes his head. I've finished with me telling Bathurst yesterday evening that she should go and see Miller, and left it at that. First thing he says:

'We need to know where Bathurst went last night. You sure you've no idea?'

I've watched enough people lying to know how easy it is to get caught out. Shake my head, say 'no' in as positive a voice as I can manage.

'Well, if it was something to do with this conspiracy of yours, then why would she need the car? Not for Jonah. She could get a train easily enough. Herrod's a bit further away, but the same applies. That leaves Crow or Miller.'

Hadn't really thought this through, because I already know what she did. Didn't think about how easily he might be able to come to the conclusion.

'She could've got a train to see Miller. It's only Crow lives off a rail route.'

'Aye,' he says, 'but you said she was scared the other day. If she really thinks Crow's the murderer, would she go charging down there on a Friday night?'

Fair point – it was the last place she would've gone.

'But Miller, that's far more likely. And if she went quite late, then she would know the trains might well be off by the time she got back. And...'

He moves to the right and accelerates past a slow-moving truck, the car groaning all the way. I'm not thinking straight, but I should know what he's about to say.

'And what?'

He raises his eyebrows.

'Baird said she thought Bathurst had had lesbian sex.'

It's where he's going, so I might as well go along with it. Not look like an idiot.

'And we know Miller has a certain reputation.'

'Exactamundo,' he says. 'For God's sake. Is there anyone in that station she hasn't slept with other than you and me?'

Almost leave too long a gap, almost damned by silence.

'She couldn't have shagged Jonah surely?'

He smiles bitterly.

'You're kidding me?' I say, a little revolted. 'She slept with Jonah? He can still get a hard on?'

He laughs. 'I doubt it. It was years ago, when Miller was a detective sergeant, and Jonah Bloonsbury was Jonah Bloonsbury. Still wallowing in all the crap that got him started. At the time he helped her along the way.'

Stuck in slow moving traffic, little chance of getting past. Where are all these people going on a lousy Saturday night?

'Anyway,' he says, and the laugh is gone, 'it doesn't make sense. Bathurst goes down there to reveal some great police conspiracy and Miller gets her into bed. And God, it couldn't have been Miller who killed her afterwards.'

'Maybe it wasn't Miller she slept with,' I say, and I can feel the words choke in my throat – lying to the boss. 'Maybe she borrowed the car to go and see some girlfriend, something like that.'

He nods. 'Aye, maybe. Certainly makes more sense. But if that was it, it was someone she kept quiet about, cause no one at the station knows anything about it.'

'Wouldn't you?'

Lets out a long sigh, says, 'Aye', and descends into silence.

We approach Tarbet, glad to see all the slow traffic continue along the Lomond road while we turn off.

'Did you know already?' I ask as we pass the Black Sheep, the ubiquitous two cars sitting out front.

'Know what?'

'What I just told you. That they stitched the guy up, not the bit about Crow.'

'Not the specifics. Same as you, same as the rest of us. I knew they'd stitched him, but I didn't know exactly how, and I assumed they still had the right guy. Not the rest of it, though.' Thank God for that.

'And what about this? You think Crow's the killer?'

'Don't know. Is he capable of it? Of course he is. But any identification we've had of the guy this week, none of it's indicated Crow. And you said yourself about the way he acted when you went to see him. He'd no idea why you were there. And at least there was little artifice to Crow. The man was an open book.'

True. Might as well have had *cunt* tattooed on his forehead.

'What about Jonah?'

Down into Arrochar, a few lights dotted around the head of Loch Long.

Shakes his head again. 'Just don't see it, Sergeant. The man's wasted. This week, he's no idea what he's doing. His career's disappearing down the toilet. He's about to get presented with his cheque and a pension, and in three months it'll all be gone. We'll see him hanging out on the streets of Glasgow.' Slows down as we come to Crow's house. 'He ain't pulling any rabbits out the hat this time.'

He turns off the engine and we step out into the wet, dark of evening. The house looks deserted, no sound from within, no lights. That old car of his has gone. We stand and look at the house, feel the light drizzle in my hair. Taylor leads the way up the garden path, says:

'Think we've missed him.'

He rings the bell, and we stand out in the cold and wait. Look out over the loch, dark and dead in the night, a few lights away along its banks. Can hear the water lapping quietly on the shore, fifty yards away. Shiver.

Taylor rings the bell again, shouts in through the letterbox.

'Gerry! You in there Gerry?'

Nothing. He tries the door but it's locked.

'How's your shoulder, sergeant?' he says.

My shoulder's fine, thank you. I'll use the sole of my right boot if you don't mind. He steps back. I'm about to kick at the lock when the door of the adjoining house opens. Old guy appears, looking suspicious, annoyed about his Saturday night being disturbed.

He stares at us, doesn't look happy. Taylor produces his badge, but it's dark and from the way the guy's squinting, he could have brought out a parking ticket and he wouldn't have noticed the difference.

'Detective Chief Inspector Taylor, this is Detective Sergeant Hutton. We're looking for Gerry Crow,' he says.

The old man stares warily, grunts after a while.

'Well, you'll no' find him,' he says.

'Why not?' asks Taylor, taking a step closer.

'He's pissed off.' – A voice comes from within: 'Would you close the fucking door, it's freezing in here!' – 'Called me up, says he was going away for a few days, asked me to look after the place. Cheeky bastard. Look at it.'

'When was this?'

'Close the fucking door, ya eejit!'

'When was what?' says the old guy.

'When did he call you?'

'I don't know, do I? Fuck's sake, you think I log every one of my phone calls?'

Taylor continues, patient, understanding. I admire that in him.

'Well, was it this morning, yesterday? When?'

The old guy looks over his shoulder, sees something on

the television.

'Look, I'm going to have to go. I think it was this morning, all right?'

'And did you see him go?'

'Naw, naw. I told you, he phoned. Now, are you finished?'

Taylor nods, the old guy turns away.

'He didn't leave you a key, did he?' he asks as the door begins to close, and gets the negative reply as it slams shut.

He turns and looks at me.

'Don't you just love the public sometimes?'

'Think we should arrest him?' I say.

'Bad hair?'

'Aye.'

He smiles then says, 'Door.'

Haven't had to do this in a while. Usually there's some strapping young constable not long out of Kicking the Door Down School on hand to do the job for you.

Boot to the door, as high up and close to the lock as possible. First kick and the whole thing creaks, and suddenly I'm not surprised because I remember what a shit-tip the entire house is. Second kick and the door smashes open, the lock flying backwards up the hall.

'Feet of steel, or rotting door frame?' he says.

'Very funny.'

He leads the way – no need for subterfuge – and puts on the hall light. You can smell the alcohol, the decay, and we split up and go room to room, through everything.

There are no surprises. The house looks much as it had done the previous day, certainly smells the same. Empty beer cans or wine bottles in every room. Liked a cheap German by the looks of things. The walls are bare and sad. Some of the drawers in the bedroom have been left open, a few clothes scattered about. Either someone else has been here searching – an incomplete search – or, more likely, Crow hurriedly packed a bag and grabbed a few stinking clothes before he went. Although it might be that he lived with drawers open and clothes strewn about his bedroom in any case.

Find a couple of hundred porn magazines under his mattress. That's really sad. That's where you keep them when you still live with your parents, but when you're a middle-aged man living on your own? Why not just have them lying out on the bedside cabinet? Habit, presumably. He's kept them under his mattress for forty years. There were a couple of them off-the-shelf from the newsagent, but most of them were a lot more disgusting. Sick Scandinavian things, with animals and women being used in ways that go far beyond the usual extent of women being used in pornography; the more we search his house, the sicker we realise he was.

In a cabinet in another room, Taylor finds the wholly expected and utterly massive DVD collection. Most of them are in unmarked boxes but we don't bother to check them out. He must have picked up most of this stuff from company hauls. We have warehouses jumping with this kind of crap, as well as a variety of other illegal products, and there are plenty of our number who'll use these places like a supermarket.

No sign of a computer anywhere. Try to think if I'd seen one the previous day but I didn't notice. Crow was a simple man, whose familiarity and comfort with technology didn't really extend much beyond the TV remote and the ring pull on a beer can, so it's quite possible he lived a life with his head buried in the non-tech sand.

It's not a big house; half an hour and it's done. I need a shower, feel grim. We stand in the middle of the sitting room. Depressed. Morbid. This guy was one of us.

'You surprised?' says Taylor.

'No, but it's horrible. Jesus, the man's a slime. If he ever comes back and he's not the one committing murder, I want to get him for something.'

Taylor nods, looks around, thinking.

'He isn't coming back though, is he?'

Rhetorical question. There's no way he's coming back.

'You're right.'

'So, what do you think?' he says, and he starts moving towards the front door as he says it. 'What does this make Crow? A murderer?'

I nod as we step out into the cold darkness of night – the breeze off the loch feels refreshing, after the sleaze and stench of the house – and I close the door behind me. It shuts, but only just.

'Aye, I think this makes him an anything.'

We get into the car and sit and stare into the darkness. The windscreen is smeared with rain and it's like the fuzz in front of us stopping us from getting a clear view of the situation.

'What now?' I ask.

'Not sure. But I think we should just keep this to ourselves for the moment. If Crow killed Bathurst, does that mean Jonah was in on it?'

'He must be. There were things done to the body that the press never got hold of from the first murder.'

'This is bad. Bloody Jonah. But then, maybe not him. Maybe it was Miller. We don't know she wasn't in on the Addison case. Or maybe, Crow had nothing whatsoever to do with Bathurst dying. Maybe he's just gone off somewhere. The guy's retired, he can go where he wants. Maybe he went to see some of those children of his,' he says, then shakes his head again. 'All right, no way he did that, but who knows? All the evidence points to last night's killer being the same as Monday night's killer, and all the other evidence points to that not having been Crow.'

Take a deep breath. A neat summation and basically we haven't a clue where to go next.

'Either way,' he says, 'we keep this to ourselves for the moment, and hope no fourteen-year-old delinquents decide to break into the place and find all that crap.'

He starts the engine, gets the heater going full blast then turns the car round and heads back towards Loch Lomond.

Arrive back at the station some time just before ten. The thought of spending a night in a hotel with Miller had long since vanished, but was then suddenly reactivated by a text from her asking me to ring her at home when I was done for the day. Decided not to do that while sitting in the car with Taylor. Pathetically, my heart has been thumping faster ever since.

There's a light on in Bloonsbury's office, Taylor goes in to speak to him. The great man is head down on the desk, grunting in his sleep. An empty bottle of White & McKay sits openly at his right arm.

Taylor lifts it, places it in the bin, then turns out the light as he closes the door behind him.

25

On the doorstep in Helensburgh, where I was three nights ago. Made a brief call to Miller and she asked me down. Don't know what the Hell I'm doing here. Half expecting to find Crow waiting behind the door with a knife. Was tempted to tell Taylor before I left, but I couldn't. Kept my mouth shut, like a bloody idiot. Walking into the demon's lair, completely defenceless. It's the sort of thing you watch people do in the movies, and you think, *what are you doing, you fucking moron? Get back up!*

But I could hardly come screaming down here with that, could I? The demon's lair? It could just be that I'm the biggest and stupidest arse on the planet. So what if Bathurst and Miller had sex? Under other circumstances I'd have been watching the video.

The door opens and Miller invites me in. Dressed similarly to the other night, but a different colour scheme. She smiles, doesn't speak, looks nervous. Closes the door behind me and ushers me into the sitting room. The fire still burns, the Christmas tree still shines, but they look incongruous now.

Half waiting for the appearance of Crow but my guts are telling me it won't happen. Stand by the warmth of the fire, wonder where Frank is, but don't really care. Remember Italy as I hear her pouring drinks behind, then she is beside me and I've got a vodka tonic in my hand.

We stare into the fire. Think I'm going to let her do most of the talking. Need a cigarette.

'Mind if I smoke?'

She shakes her head. Produce the packet, shake one loose and light up. Feels good tonight, probably because I haven't smoked many in the last couple of hours.

'We are all busy in this world building Towers of Babel; and the child of our imaginations is always a changeling when it comes from nurse.'

That's all she says. I've heard that one before; we all have. It's her favourite line, and she gives it to all the new recruits. Can't imagine that it means much to most of them, but it sounds good, and I know what she's thinking. She would have said those words to Evelyn Bathurst, and what Towers can she build now?

'Did you know her well?' she says.

Stare deep into the fire. It's the first time I've slowed down all day. Take a longer drink from the glass than I intended. Feels as good as the cigarette, the alcohol burns its way down, the chill hits my stomach.

After the shock of the start of the day, it's gradually turned into just another murder. You have to stay focused on these things, can't let them get to you, yet your brain can still occasionally kick into overdrive. A warm fire, vodka tonic in your hand and a woman who might be implicated in the murder standing next to you.

Your back was turned. The glass could be poisoned...

Calm the fuck down, man, calm the fuck down.

'No, not really. Not any better than the rest of us.'

'No,' she says, and the voice is small and strange.

'When was the last time you spoke to her?' she asks, after another long silence in the crackle of the fire.

Take a second large swallow of the vodka, have nearly drained the glass already. Does she know I told Bathurst to come and talk to her? Does she know what I know and that I know it? I could run rings round myself. I have to trust her, because why else am I here?

'Last night, about five. She was just on her way out.'

'How did she seem?'

'I don't know. Like normal, I suppose.'

I may have decided to trust her, but I'm not telling her a thing.

'She didn't say anything about what she was doing last night?' The eyes flicker at me, I wonder if she knows that I'm in possession of the facts.

Shake my head, drain the glass.

'No. Said she was going out some place, but nothing specific.'

Out of sight her hand slips into mine, her fingers squeeze. Her touch electrifies and bemuses at the same time. Lift my glass without thinking, the ice cubes clink down to my mouth, with the dregs of tonic. I need another one.

When she speaks again the voice is even smaller than before; the words stab out.

'I heard you went into work together on Christmas Day,' she says. How the Hell did she hear that? 'How was that, Thomas? You spent the night with me.'

I can almost feel my flesh crawl. She sounds like a spurned lover, a young woman lost in the deep fathoms of a relationship she doesn't understand. But this is Charlotte Miller, I can't believe she's hurt.

I look at her, and the first tear has started to trickle down her face. Oh, for fuck's sake. Can't be real. Is there no certainty in life?

Her head rests on my shoulder, a tear drops onto the back of my hand. She's either toying with me or getting genuinely emotional. Either way, I'm so far out of my depth I could've been shit-slammed into the middle of the Pacific.

It may not have lasted between Peggy and I, but it lasted forever by my standards, and all because she was never too emotional. I stopped feeling emotions many years ago. I don't like emotions, especially in other people. I want to exist in another world, a hundred years ago, when everyone had stiff upper lips and just put up with shit and no one ever cried.

'I think I'd better go.'

Cheap, but fuck it, I didn't come here for her to go full Jeremy Kyle. I'm kidding myself anyway.

The hand squeezes a little tighter, something approaching a sob escapes her lips. This is the woman who rules the station with an iron hand in an iron glove.

'Stay with me, tonight,' she says, her voice cracking as

she speaks, and it feels like a hand squeezing my stomach. Why does she need me to stay the night?

Fuck's sake, she's not going to kill me in her bed. Get a grip!

I don't reply but I know the answer. She looks up at me and her face is streaked with tears, her eyes red. I'm getting sucked in and if she's playing me, I'm falling into the trap. Blinded by her air of vulnerability, the sexuality of it – which may be as much blinded by deception, no matter how aware I think myself to be.

She stretches a little, I lower my head, and our lips meet. I can taste the tears, her tongue gently probes my mouth.

We kiss for a long time in front of the fire, until her tears have dried, then we go to her bedroom and this time the lovemaking is more tender and infinitely more intimate than before.

26

It is a cold morning, winter finally seeming to have arrived, after an eternal autumn of mild and wet weather. The clouds are low, the threat of snow in the air. The night before has been busy, the usual Saturday fracas, enhanced by the time of year. Burglary, assaults, stabbings, so much of it enhanced by alcohol. The station buzzes, more crime to be dealt with than anyone has time for. In the middle of two murder enquiries, Detective Sergeant Herrod is landed with an assault from the night before; all the while he ponders the state of his Chief Inspector. The night asleep at his desk, bundled into a taxi and sent home a couple of hours previously. A man to inspire loathing and the distant memory of respect.

Herrod hates every minute of the work that he does, loves it at the same time. The perfect conduit for his rampant ill-humour, the perfect outlet for his paranoia, a brilliant excuse to escape his home and his wife.

Nearly noon and he wonders about Hutton – yet to appear this morning. A Sunday perhaps, but this is no time for a day of rest. Taylor is at his desk, thinking as usual, but no Hutton, and he hopes he is not out investigating a lead. Hates the idea that it might be Taylor and Hutton who solve the murders.

Has had a vague thought as to why Evelyn Bathurst might have been killed, but refuses to believe it, refuses to think about it. Sometimes he is aware of his own paranoia. There is always another reason.

The phone rings as he is in the middle of putting together his report on the attempted assault, and he scowls at the ring. *If this is some other piece of shite...*

'Herrod,' he growls down the phone.

There is a slight hesitation, a small voice.

'Sergeant Herrod?' A woman he does not recognise.

Sounds like a callbox.

A callbox? Where did she find one of those?

'Aye, I said that already.'

More hesitation. Bloody women.

'What is it, Hen, I'm busy?'

'I was told to speak to you. It's about these murders,' she blurts out.

Herrod's eyebrows raise a fraction. Could be something, could be nothing. She does sound nervous, however.

'All right, Hen. Take your time. What's your name?'

She doesn't answer, doesn't want to tell him. He controls the desire to shout down the phone. Something he's used to doing with the public.

'I can't help you if you don't tell me your name, Hen,' he says.

'I'm scared.'

He tries to lower his voice and sound compassionate, although he knows it's beyond him.

'Where are you phoning from?'

'Not Glasgow,' she says, after a few seconds. 'I don't really want to say.'

Herrod rolls his eyes. Here we go, he thinks. No name, no address. Are you on Planet Earth, he wants to ask.

'All right, you don't have to tell me that either, just tell me why you're phoning.' On the verge of hanging up.

'I went out with a man in Glasgow. About a year ago. Just a few times.' She stops, he wonders if she might be crying. 'Maybe a bit more than that. We… I guess we were an item, but it was one of those things. It just kind of happened, even though I didn't want it to.'

Herrod holds the phone in front of his face and looks at it. Oh my God. She's phoning up to complain about her relationship. Wonderful. One step from dialling 999 to report the washing tablet not dissolving in the dishwasher.

'Yes?' says Herrod. This is almost laughable, and he has that weird sense of humour that kicks in briefly before he completely loses the head.

'Maybe three months all in, including a bit of... off and on.'

She doesn't say anything else, not immediately. More money gets put into the machine. Herrod taps his fingers on the desk. Lightening up. What the Hell, might as well spend a day on the phone listening to someone's relationship issues.

'Take your time,' he says again, feeling absurdly pleased with himself that he's actually managed to be nice to someone.

He can hear her breathing. He looks around the station. Everyone else seems to be sensibly occupied. Why is it just him?

'He was just... strange. We were friends for a while. We met at an evening Spanish class at the university. You know, one of those things you sign up for and go to once or twice. Friends, that was all really, that was all I thought. Then one day he comes on to me, really strong. Really pushing it....'

More hesitation. Herrod cannot help himself.

'And you shagged him?'

She blurts out a rueful laugh.

'And you got pregnant?' Herrod has seen the shows.

'Nothing like that. No. No. It just sort of happened, and the sex was all right. You know. I'm not... you know, I don't want you to think... We had sex. That's all.'

The sex was all right, thinks Herrod. Typical woman, so judgemental. At least, they have been in his experience.

He holds the phone away from him and stares at it again. Gives it a withering look and brings it back in.

'Go on,' he says. 'I've got all day. No, I have...'

'It just got... very quickly, very quickly... in fact, looking back, even before it began, it was weird. He was weird. Obsessive. We fought, almost from the start. It was stupid of me to let it last as long as I did, but I couldn't face the big fight at the end. He was just everywhere, buying me presents, over-protective, smothering me. He smothered me.'

'But not literally, because you're on the phone,' said Herrod.

He could sense her staring at the phone, nonplussed by his quick-witted chatter.

'No,' she said, uncertainly. 'I didn't mean it literally.'

'All right,' says Herrod. 'And your point is, caller?' Feels like he's Alan Green on Radio 5, taking some endless call where the caller refuses to ever come to the rub.

'It was just freaky in the end. I ended it a couple of times, he started hassling me. It got...' She shivers. She has tried not to think about it in over a year and mostly she's been successful. The news of the last week had forced it once more uncomfortably into her head. 'He was always there, he was always phoning. I'd get home from work and he'd have let himself in. He'd be there, waiting for me, dinner made, wine on the table. Jesus...'

The words *Jesus made dinner for you?* are on his lips, but the time for sarcasm is past. However slowly, she is finally getting to the point.

'We had a big fight one day, another one, another one... I said everything I was thinking. Everything. I said insults that I hadn't even been thinking. The size of his penis, his breath, his... God, everything. Sense of humour... as if he had one of those.'

Her words are coming more quickly, the feelings are being dredged up as before. Anger and fear, loathing, desperation.

'Jesus...' she mutters down the phone.

'What happened?'

'There were just a couple of days of it,' she says quickly. 'I changed the locks, then I saw him standing outside my house. Watching. I got up in the middle of the night and he was still there. He turned up at my work. Really. He just creeped me out. Then he swiftly got to the death threats.'

'Did you call the police?'

She snorts down the phone.

'Oh yes. Like you lot gave a fuck, ' she says, bitterness bursting out.

'Well why the fuck are you calling the police now?' says Herrod, his disdain given free reign.

'Because I thought you needed help,' she snaps.

Herrod scowls at the phone. Briefly it's a toss up on who will hang up on the other.

'What did you do?' says Herrod.

'I just left. Just as well that I was in a position to. Was renting my flat, job was shit. I went to live in Dundee, stayed with a pal for a while. Got my own place now. Put a lot of stuff on Facebook, made him think I was somewhere else. I heard he kept looking for me.'

'It's a tragic story,' says Herrod. The tone of his voice is awful. Horrible cynicism, deserving that she hangs up.

'Well it is now,' she says sharply.

'What d'you mean?'

'The guy was a freak,' she says. 'I mean… I don't know why he was obsessed with me. Really. Who knows why any of that shit ever matters, why anyone falls for anyone else?'

'Cut out the… I don't know, the philosophical mumbo jumbo, and just tell me why in the name of fuck you're calling.'

Another pause. She wants to hang up, but she needs the call. She's thinking about it too much, thinking about him too much. She needs to transfer those thoughts, get them off her chest, out of her conscience.

'I looked at his Facebook account a while back, which really messed me up on the trying not to think about him front. He was friends with all these women… they looked like me, same hair colour, same sort of age. It was just creepy. He was writing the weirdest shit. I looked again last night because I'd started thinking about it again. That shit just got weirder and scarier, until a couple of weeks ago and then it stopped.'

'And?'

'And… I was wondering if that weird shit had begun to

manifest itself in different ways. More dangerous ways…'

'And?'

Herrod wonders if his life will end sitting here, talking to this woman on this phone.

'Those two women who were murdered in Glasgow. They look like me… I look like them.'

Herrod shakes his head. Jesus. *Hitler, My Part In His Downfall*. She was probably recording the conversation and it would be on YouTube in a few minutes.

'You think these murders are happening because of you?' he says.

'Yes,' she replies quickly.

'Well, OK…' he says. It was possible. After all, her description of the ex-boyfriend being a scary, murderous freak, pretty much tied in with their total knowledge of the killer. 'Go on. Do you have a name for me?'

It would be cool, he suddenly thinks, if this was the breakthrough, no matter how idiotic it sounds. Every case has one. And he's the one on the phone – Bloonsbury is asleep, Hutton's out somewhere doing God knows what, Taylor is staring at the ceiling.

'I don't want him to find out I phoned. You have to promise.'

He nods down the phone. 'Your secret, such as it is, is safe with me.'

Another long hesitation. He hears her swallow, imagines her chewing her lower lip.

'Healy,' she says, the word rushed. 'His name was Ian Healy. He was a lawyer in Tollcross, somewhere around there.'

Herrod closes his eyes. Oh my God! Out of the blue. She has got to be kidding? This can't be for real. His fists clench. He looks around the office – it's busy with people going about their business. No one knows what he knows.

'Ian Healy?' he says, voice lower. 'You're sure about that?'

'Yes.'

Herrod could kiss her. The lawyer Hutton had brought

in, and whom he and Taylor and Bloonsbury had all been happy to dismiss. Bloonsbury had even spoken to the guy for about an hour, and come up with nothing. The man had to be permanently pickled. Ian Healy. He would go round and get him now. No reason for the guy to be suspicious, and it will be him that has the collar.

Life is sweet. Out of nowhere, life is sweet.

'Now, we can bring this man in, but you have to give me your name and a telephone number where I can reach you,' he says. He keeps his voice low, tries to sound reassuring, tries not to betray his excitement.

'Can I not call you back?' she says, and Herrod shakes his head. But it doesn't matter.

'It'd be better if you gave me the number,' he says.

'I'm sorry,' she says, 'I'm frightened. I'll call you tomorrow,' and the phone clicks off.

'Stupid arse,' says Herrod, but there is a smile on his face, and he taps his fingers happily on the desk. Absurd, totally absurd, but sometimes these things are.

Taylor appears from his office.

'Just found out someone else you don't like is dead?' he says.

Herrod shakes his head, and mumbles. Taylor can take a fuck to himself, he thinks.

'Where's Jonah?' asks Taylor

'No idea,' says Herrod, lying. I'm not telling you he's home in bed, still drunk out of his face from last night.

Taylor mumbles something himself, and walks back into his office. Herrod smiles. He hadn't got her details, but she'd call again. He had the feeling. Now, however, there were more important things to do. He would go and interview Ian Healy, then bring the guy in.

He knows he should not go alone, but that's the way he prefers to work. Particularly on something as big as this, where all the credit will be his. Sees his name in lights.

As he lifts his jacket, an earlier thought – how did the woman know to ask for him? – slips his mind.

'Got a few calls to make,' he shouts through the open

---

office door at Taylor, who mutters, 'You don't have to tell me what you're doing,' in reply. Then Herrod is gone.

Shit. Woke up at almost twelve o'clock. Not hungover for once, which left me disorientated for a start, compounded by being in someone else's bed. The curtains were open, the grey light of another dull day filled the room. Got up and stumbled around – wasn't until I looked out the window at the leaden Firth of Clyde that I remembered I was in Helensburgh. Charlotte was gone, to work presumably. So, I had a wander round. Took my time. Kept expecting to bump into a butler or a maid.

Should've been in the office all day, of course, given the circumstances, but since I was already late, I thought I might as well make the most of it. Had a shower, made myself some bacon and eggs and a strong cup of coffee, left just after one.

As I was walking down the drive to my car, who should walk in but Frank. Strangely, I had a moment's guilt about the fact that I hadn't washed up after breakfast, rather than the fact that I'd banged his wife. We nodded at each other. The guy must have known why I was there.

'Charlotte at home?' he asked.

I looked over my shoulder, then back to him.

'Nope,' I replied.

You could see him thinking, hear the question in his head. Well, what the fuck are you doing here then?

'Well, good day, Sergeant,' was all he said.

'Frank,' I said, nodding, and we passed each other by.

And so it is that I arrive in the station at not much before two. Herrod's nowhere to be seen and there's the usual scurrying activity from youthful constables. The door to Charlotte's office is closed, which means she's in town.

Been awake for two hours and have so far managed to keep my mind completely clear of everything that's been going on; that way leads to confusion and worry.

My phone had been switched off all night, had a few texts waiting for me when I finally turned it on over breakfast. A couple of *where the Hell are you*'s from the station, and a couple from Peggy. Should have called her last night. Back in the doghouse, and maybe it's where I want to be.

Notice there's a MacBook sitting on my desk that isn't normally there. Walk into Taylor's office. For once he's attending to paperwork. Looks up, isn't impressed.

'Really, Sergeant? One of our number was murdered yesterday.'

Immediately feel like an idiot. No lie, no inept justification comes to mind, so I just don't answer.

'Right, got something for you to do. We've got Evelyn's computer in. A delicate hand is required. Go through it, read *everything*. If you need some help from the techies, then get to it. She was a girl of her times. Facebook, Bebo, Twitter, Google+, Blogger, Fucko, Wanko and all that modern shit that the kids do. You probably won't need the account passwords going in from her own laptop.' He gestures back out to my desk. 'Read it all, see if there's anything there. Anything about Crow, you know, and the other thing.'

Obviously, I don't look impressed.

'And you can take that fucking look off your face. If you hadn't been so late, you'd be finished by now.'

'Right.'

Start to walk back to the desk.

'And if you find anything, you know, compromising, about her or anyone else at the station, forget it.'

I nod, stop in the doorway, turn back.

'Where's the great crime fighting duo?' I ask. 'How come Herrod hasn't got hold of it?' Herrod would love this.

He shakes his head.

'Haven't a clue where Jonah is. Might be out there somewhere, but I suspect he's at home and not answering his phone because he's in his usual position.'

'And the laptop?'

'Fortunately, I got my hands on it first. You've got it because we know what Herrod would be like.'

I nod, and plod back to my desk.

And so it is that I spend the next five hours in the private world of Evelyn Bathurst. One of the standards of detective work – spending hours at a time going over the mundane, hoping to find one small fact to help you along. At first I thought it might be quite interesting, but inevitably it proved otherwise.

Taylor was indeed right, the girl had truly embraced the modern era. Facebook, Bebo, Twitter, Google+, Blogger, Fucko and Wanko. And the rest. There was me thinking that perhaps there might have been gravitas beneath that stunning exterior, but by God, does anyone look good when the full weight of their collective consciousness is vomited forth on social media? How many times can one person write LOL and still retain any level of intellectual dignity?

And, of course, while she might have been a little too open and honest in the world of private matters, when spewing forth out into the Internet, she made sure she never mentioned her police work. In fact, most of the creeps that would've befriended her on these sites probably never even knew what she did for a living.

Every now and again there was a reference from which one could draw a conclusion about it relating to the Addison case, or some such, but nothing concrete.

So what do I have after five hours in her world? Nothing. Well, I did get to see some photos of her naked that were lurking in the bowels of the computer, but under the circumstances, even a filthy bastard like me wasn't getting turned on.

And that's that for dear young Evelyn. A life that will be forever immortalised on the Internet. Or, at least, until social order breaks down and the very fabric of society collapses. Which might not be so far away. If we're lucky.

By the time I'm done it's long been dark outside, well

past seven o'clock. There's been a change of shift, but there's still the same crap going on. Charlotte emerged about three and walked on by. Acknowledged my presence and that was it. She looked tired, and I don't think it's only because of what we did last night. Still haven't phoned Peggy, although I've been meaning to most of the day. For her part, my phone hasn't rung either.

Walk back into Taylor's office. He's been gone most of the afternoon, only came back about half an hour ago. Spent the time since then staring at the ceiling.

Plant myself in the seat, uninvited. He looks at me, eyebrows raised in question. Shake my head.

'Nothing.'

'Huh,' he says.

Lies his head back, lets out a heavy sigh.

'There has to be something, Sergeant. There has to be something we're not getting. The same person killed Ann Keller and Evelyn Bathurst. So which is it? Was Bathurst's murder coincidental with her involvement with the Addison case – or was it connected, in which case Keller's murder must also be connected.'

'I.e. Crow,' I say.

'Exactamundo.'

And maybe Charlotte, but that I keep to myself.

'I wish I could think straight,' he says. He's not alone.

'What'd you do this afternoon?'

Shakes his head, stares at the floor.

'Went home, went round to Jonah's place.'

'And?'

His eyes are glued to a piece of dirt on the carpet, his mind glued to something else. About to get further revelations on his marriage, I suspect. Brace myself, but I should be willing to hear them.

'I could do without all this shit at the moment,' he says.

'What's happened?'

'Jonah's just a mess. Jesus.'

'You go in? Share a bottle of Teachers?'

'Wouldn't let me in. Opened the door after I'd been

ringing the bell for about five minutes, just stood there breathing fumes. God. This is it for him, Sergeant. There're going to be no sudden revelations this time, no great victory from the jaws of defeat.'

'Unless he's behind it all like last time.'

Shakes his head, laughs bitterly.

'Not a chance. Look at the guy. I've always admired him, and he did use to be the star everyone took him for. I know he was past it by the time you met him, but the guy was up there. But it's been at least ten years now since he did any good work... at least ten years. And if all that about the Addison case is true, well the guy's just sold his soul to Hell. The quicker he gets there the better.'

'If he keeps on drinking...'

'You think? I know for a fact he was told by his doctor three years ago – three fucking years – that if he didn't cut out the whisky altogether, not just cut down, he'd be dead in three months. Well, it's been a long three months.'

'So, d'you think you'll get landed with it?' I ask.

He lets out a low whistle.

'Well, that's what I thought, but...'

'But what?'

Raises his eyebrows.

'Heard a rumour,' he says.

'Aye?'

'Miller's thinking of taking over the investigation herself.'

'You're kidding?'

'Just what I heard. I think Jonah's out, but the word is she's hacked off at the lack of progress and wants to take charge.'

'She can't do that!'

'She's queen. She can do what she wants. She can clean the toilets if she chooses.'

That wasn't what I meant. I know she has the authority, but Jesus, she had sex with Bathurst a couple of hours before the girl was murdered. She could be involved, for fuck's sake, how can she lead the investigation?

A cover up. Pretty obvious really. So it seems.

'Fuck,' is all I say, shaking my head.

'Yeah,' says Taylor. 'And Debbie left,' he adds as an afterthought.

'What?'

'She left. Confounded all the critics by moving in with her young man. So, I'm a middle-aged bachelor again.'

'Shit. You all right?'

He stares at the floor, puffs out his cheeks, lets the air out slowly.

'Don't know.'

'Want to go for a drink?'

He nods.

'Love to,' he says, and gets out of the chair. Takes a look at some of the papers on his desk, murmurs something under his breath and heads towards the door, putting the light off as he goes.

'Any idea where Herrod went? He's been away all afternoon,' I say, following in his wake.

'Nope. Lying dead in a ditch somewhere, if we're lucky.'

*

But Herrod does not lie dead in a ditch. He hangs dead on a wall, impaled by an ornamental sword through the lower chest cavity, his feet dangling three inches off the ground. The drip of blood from his mouth has long ago stopped, the pool on the floor disturbed by the scurrying feet of rats.

28

The only solace he has is the solace of pain.

The pain of hurt; the pain of rejection; the pain of humiliation. The pain of defeat.

Can't stop thinking about Jo. Consumes his thoughts. Bloody Jo. Face tortured, agonizing smile. Jo shouting at him. Jo telling him to fuck off. Jo slamming the door. Jo getting upset. Jo turning down presents. Jo turning her back. Jo running away, disappearing, so that he never knew where to find her. Jo walking out on her life just so that she could avoid him. The man who loved her, who would give her anything.

He wants to take himself somewhere, somewhere within his imagination. A city; big, brassy, loud; where the action is. Just him and Jo hitting the clubs, hitting the night spots. Drinking, gambling, dancing. Making love.

How many times had they had sex? He forgets now. Too long ago. The actual number is gone, lost beneath exaggeration and self-deceit, beneath the most glorious memories of Jo's face during orgasm. Her mouth contorted, that look that almost spoke of pain but was in fact the most incredible pleasure.

However, his dreams never work out. From the prison of his mind, he can't sort out the fantasy. Can't construct it. Like a sixties tower block, it looks good for five seconds, then begins to crumble and crack.

He'll never see Jo again and, if he does, she won't be interested. Not Jo. Jo with her knee-length boots, Jo with her knowing smile, Jo with her G-string and the Celtic tattoo on her thigh and the neatly shaved public hair and her face contorted in pleasure during orgasm. And his fantasies disintegrate into a sordid mess; him and Jo alone in a dark stinking room, getting nowhere, doing nothing.

Eventually he will be purged. Eventually she will

---

understand. She will be at one with him, and the hurt she inflicted upon him. Maybe then she will smile at him and they will be one. She will love him again, the way she loved him before.

She never told him. That still hurts, perhaps just as much as the fact that she left. She never said she loved him, despite the number of opportunities he gave her, despite repeatedly expressing his love for her.

That is one of the many things he does not understand.

29

Another day, another hangover. Four hours in the pub with Taylor, by the end of which I had persuaded him that he really didn't want to be married to Debbie anymore anyway. Did my bit for his peace of mind, although whether he'll still be happy about it this morning I doubt. He looked awful when I saw him, but he wasn't in long before he left again. Away to speak to a couple of friends of Ann Keller's. A great believer in re-covering old ground. You always learn something new.

Bloonsbury is in his office, doing God knows what. Door closed, hitting the sauce more than likely. Miller called for him about half an hour ago, dismissed him ten minutes later. He came out looking an angry man, but then he always looks like an angry man.

Herrod has disappeared. Took a call yesterday morning and went out, no one knows where. May be dead in a ditch after all. The station is certainly a more pleasant place to be without him, however. Hopefully he's accepted an expensive transfer offer from elsewhere. Haven't seen a paper this morning; it could be on the back page – *Herrod in Shock £35M Deal With Old Trafford.*

Meanwhile, I've been landed with the detritus of the weekend – muggings, rape, robbery. It's all showing how desperately undermanned we are. Dire straits. There's just far too much going on, and when we could do with all hands on deck for the murder enquiries, officers are continually getting pulled away on more mundane crime.

Writing up the report on a break-in at a newsagent's at the bottom end of Cambuslang Main Street when Miller appears from her office. Approaches, looking around her as she does so.

'I'll need everything you've got on the Keller and Bathurst cases, Sergeant. Everything. Notes, random thoughts, vague ideas.' She stares at me, and I suppose I must be giving her a look. 'I've taken over from Detective Chief Inspector Bloonsbury. I'll be leading the investigation. I want everything you've got as soon as possible.'

She can't do this.

'Where's Dan?' she asks.

'Speaking to a friend of Anne Keller's.'

'And Sgt Herrod?'

Shake my head.

'Tell them both I want to see them when they get in.'

Another second of her harsh, defensive stare, then she turns away. She stops as she passes the closed door to Bloonsbury's office, perhaps considers going in. Walks on, into her own office. Closes the door behind her.

Well, Jesus, Taylor was right. The criminals have taken over the asylum; the suspect has taken over the investigation. Except, she's nobody's suspect except mine.

Head in the palm of my hand, eyes open. Ignoring the noise of the office going on around me. Certainly, no bloody thought for the newsagent robbery. They got away with several thousand cigarettes and a bunch of pornos. God, maybe this was Crow 'n' all.

Forget Crow. What am I going to do about Charlotte Miller? She's the last person to have seen Bathurst, she slept with her; then maybe an hour later, Bathurst is dead. And Charlotte Miller isn't telling anyone about it.

But do I really believe she had something to do with it? If she didn't, then is there anything wrong with her leading the damned thing? If the two of them were intimate, then maybe she'll be switched on to it – certainly a damn sight more switched on than Jonah.

I stand up, decision made, even though I've no idea where it's come from. She can't do it. She's got thirty officers trying to discover where Evelyn Bathurst was on the night she died, and whose bed it was she lay in.

Knock on the door, don't wait to be invited in. Walk in, head up, full of aggression. Can't think of the right words,

---

160

so I just come out with the first ones that are there.

'What the fuck are you doing?'

Nice start. Suddenly have the image of me sitting on an inter-city train; first class ticket, eating one of these brie and black grape sandwiches, ice-cold v&t, on my way up north for a holiday.

'Sergeant?'

One word, but what a voice. A coiled snake. You can hear it in those two syllables, the anger just waiting to explode. No one talks to Superintendent Miller like that. I'm going to just have to go for it. All guns.

'You slept with Evelyn on Friday night.'

Her shoulders straighten. Face tightens.

'What?' is all she says. The anger's gone, she no longer sounds as if she's about to machine gun me. A little surprised, maybe, that's all.

'You slept with Evelyn. Half the damned force is trying to find out who her lover was on Friday night, and it's you.'

I let the words sink in. I can't read her at all, which is pretty much how it's always been.

'What makes you think that?'

I'd imagined her crumbling before the shock and awe of my all-out, up-front attack, but these are not the words of a woman who's crumbled. This is a woman taking her time, assessing the situation, the extent of the damage.

'I've known all along,' I say, which is a lousy answer, and not one likely to put her under any pressure. Her face relaxes.

Crap.

'What are you going to do?' she asks. There's almost a smile there, or maybe I'm just imagining it because I've seen brutal bastards up close and you can always tell when they're about to smile. Just before they bury the knife in your eye socket.

So, what should I do? I should tell Taylor, and I should tell anyone who wants to listen. Maybe it doesn't mean she had anything to do with the murder, but it's certainly pertinent to the investigation.

I stand there looking stupid. Have lost all that sparkling fire I had when I first got in here, forty-five seconds ago, once again proving to be not even remotely as cool as I like to think I am.

Show some balls, Hutton, for fuck's sake.

'You need to put Dan in charge.'

Her mind is working and it's disconcerting to know that it's a Hell of a lot sharper than mine. Having careered in here in the hope of establishing some sort of command, I'm now being completely reactive.

I could just turn and walk out. Get on a train. Go and live in the Highlands, in a forest by a river. Eat rabbits.

'And if I don't?'

I was hoping she wasn't going to ask that.

'Just do it, Charlotte. I don't know what was going on between you and Evelyn, but you're too close. And if it ever gets out, you're screwed, especially if you take over the investigation. It looks like you've got something to hide.'

'And what do you think? Do you think I've got something to hide?'

'I don't know.'

I feel like Partick Thistle playing Barcelona. Before the game starts you talk yourself into it being eleven against eleven and anything can happen, and you go out all guns blazing and maybe you even get a goal in the first two minutes, and you think, fuck yeah, we can do this; then, half an hour in, you're losing seventeen-one.

'Do you know why Evelyn came to see me?'

I get swallowed up by those eyes. Try to think clearly. What's this about? Does she want to know how much I know, and when I knew it? I'm lost.

'No idea.'

A long pause.

'Did you know she was coming before she came?'

She's fishing. I'm such an idiot that if I let her fish, she'll catch something before too long.

'How, when, it doesn't matter. I know, that's all. Are

162

you going to put Dan on it, or not?'

'If I do, what will you tell him? What if he instructs you to spend all your time looking for Bathurst's female lover? What then?'

She gives me the shivers, for a hundred different reasons. Time to go.

'Just do it.'

If in doubt, resort to Nike marketing blurb. After all, nothing is impossible.

Give her my best look of steel. Try to be hard. Really, I'd be better off not trying anything, just being myself. A messed up miserable fucker who wants to run away. So I turn on my heels and walk out before she can see through it – although I'm probably about five minutes too late for that.

Close the door behind me, feel the relief. Have no idea what I'm going to do if she decides to go for a test of wills by completely ignoring me. All I can do is hope she gives in and lets Taylor get on with it. Otherwise...

As I cross the open plan, the legendary Jonah Bloonsbury emerges from his office. Looks awful, but that's no surprise. Facing up to the fact that his career has finally disappeared round the u-bend. Some men look good on the back of four or five days stubble – me for instance – and some men just look terrible.

He stops to talk to me as our paths cross. Looks broken. Shoulders hunched; clothes pretty much the same ones he's been wearing for the past week; eyes bloody red, might have been pierced with a knife; ruddy face, bulbous nose of the alcoholic, combined with the hollow cheeks of someone who hasn't eaten anything for months; thinning hair, matted, dirty. We get druggies in here who look better than he does.

'The bitch tell you what she's done?' he says. Words trip over each other on their way out of his mouth. Can smell the whisky. Stale and fresh at the same time.

'Yep.'

He slumps against a desk. Herrod's desk, as it happens.

Head collapses onto the top of his chest, and then he appears to notice that Herrod isn't there.

'Any idea where this arsehole is?'

'If we're lucky, he's been transferred,' I say.

'Who'd have him?'

Aye, well, right enough.

'Got a smoke, Hutton?'

Go to my desk and dig out the packet of Marlboro's. Remove two, light up, and then hand him the other and the lighter. As usual, get a look or two from the odd constable, but no one says anything. It shakes pathetically in his hand, flame flickering, and he takes several seconds to find the end of the cigarette. Wish I'd done it for him.

'What you going to do now?' I ask.

He doesn't answer immediately; starts coughing up a variety of revolting substances from his lungs the second the smoke hits the net. A young PC I don't recognise walks by, looks at Jonah as if he's scum. Perhaps assuming he's on the other side of the great law and order fence. Which he probably is.

'She wants us to resign.'

'And?'

Coughs some more as he tries again with the cigarette.

'No chance. I'm here 'til they get rid of me.'

He looks up at me, points the cigarette.

'I fucked her before, you know. Long time ago, but I did it.'

Back in the glory days, when Jonah Bloonsbury was worth it.

'Now look at her. She's fucking me...'

Don't know what to say to him. You're not the only one, big man.

He stands up, attempts to straighten his shoulders.

'Well, I'm not resigning for any bastard. Especially not her. Hasn't heard the last of Jonah Bloonsbury.'

The phone rings behind me, just as he starts to walk off. Saves me from further discourse – not that I was going to say anything else to him anyway.

'If that's for me, tell them I'm away getting pished,' he says, and stumbles out of the office, bumping into PC Forsyth as he goes.

If it's for you, they'll already know you're getting pished.

Lift the phone. 'Hutton.'

'Thomas?'

Peggy. Damn. Had to happen sometime. Couldn't keep avoiding her for the rest of my life. Especially not if I want to marry her again.

'Hey, how are you?'

'I'm all right, Thomas. I tried to get you all weekend. What were you doing?'

Sounds annoyed. Here we go again. The same old story. Except, this time she's got a point. Wait, she always had a point.

'I'm sorry, but you must have seen the news. Saturday morning...'

'Yes, of course.'

'It's been bedlam. I'm on the case, and I keep getting landed with all the other crap that's going.'

'I understand, but you weren't there all Saturday night, were you? Or Sunday morning? What were you doing Thomas? You must've slept. You could have slept here. You could have called. You never replied to my texts.'

She's got me by the balls. Peggy's not one of those high-strung, neurotic types who disappears into insecurity as soon as you mention another woman's name or appear home fifteen seconds late for your dinner. The only reason she's annoyed at me for not showing on Saturday night is because she knows. I can feel it. So, I'm going to have to put a lot more effort into lying.

'Look, Dan's been sending me out on all sorts of stuff. Just haven't stopped.'

'He didn't know where you were on Sunday morning. Thought you were with me.'

Backed up against a wall. Gun at my head.

'The children were looking forward to it, Thomas. You

could have called.'

She pauses, but I've no idea what to say. She knows nothing, and yet I feel as if I've been well and truly caught with my pants down.

'Look, I know we're not back together or anything, but Christmas Day... you know. I just thought... well, if there's someone else you could at least tell me.'

Stand fast. Balls out. Lie big time.

'Honestly, there's not. I was following up something that even Dan doesn't know about. This whole murder thing's getting freaky.' Can't believe I used the word 'honestly'. A sure give-away. 'Can I see you tonight? I'll tell you all about it.'

'Is there any point?'

'Honestly, there's a lot going on, Peggy.' Stop saying *honestly*, you fucking moron. 'I'll come over tonight when I can get away.'

She hesitates, but I've got her.

'All right,' she says. 'I'll wait up.'

'Good. I'll try not to be late.'

'Like I said, I'll wait up.'

Right. The phone goes dead. Put the receiver back down. Feel like I've just got out of jail, but that I'll probably be going back in later on tonight. If I ever get there.

Start going into my feelings on the whole thing. It was her who left me for another man. She divorced me. We had sex for a night, and then wham, I'm under obligation again.

Suppose she's right. It was me that coughed up the diamond earrings. A few days ago I thought I was still in love with her. One infatuation later, and what? I don't know. I should be still in love with her, but I may be too much of a Muppet for that.

Love, for crying out loud. Who am I kidding?

Bloonsbury reappears. Smell him before I see him. He stumbles past the desk, leaning on anything he can.

'Can't believe I forgot my booze,' he says, heading back

towards his office.

Can't believe he's got a bottle in there that's not empty.

30

So, that was it. I got back from Bosnia and talked to a psychiatrist for ten minutes. Haven't talked to anyone since. I don't want it to be about me. Ever. Doesn't matter what 'it' is, it's not about me.

I know it's good to talk, and I know the only way I'm ever going to escape the awfulness of the memories I've carried around since then is to let it all out, but I don't think it's ever going to happen.

I used to think, when I'd come home – after I'd walked out on the professional psych-woman – that I'd find a woman to confide in. A lover. Always found women easy to talk to. And there'd be these women that I'd sleep with or do whatever with, and not once did I ever think, yep, I can talk to you. Not once.

I thought, romantically maybe… is this romantic?… that there'd be someone out there, and I'd know instinctively that she was the one and that I'd want to talk to her, and it would just all come out in a rush, and I'd probably end up crying like some reality TV contestant. There'd be one, and I'd know.

Well, I damn well knew it wasn't Jean Fryar. God, we never talked about anything, other than her and what she needed and what I was giving her and how I could make her life less awful.

Peggy, however, she was different. Right from the start, I thought, this is it. This is the woman I'll talk to. This is the woman with whom I'll sit down, and she'll be my counsellor and I'll be able to get all that crap out of my head. I'll spew it all forth, and she'll sit there and take it in, and it won't be in my head anymore because I'll have got rid of it, it'll be in her head, but it won't bother her the way it bothered me because it won't actually have happened to her, so it'll be like off-loading an illness to someone who can't get it. Peggy was the one, and I was going to tell her tomorrow.

Yep, roll out the Beatles song. Tomorrow never comes.

Never. I'd sit there, thinking *OK, this is it, this is it, now. Right now. Right fucking now. Say something!*

I never said. And she knew. She knew there was a lot of stuff in there, and she waited for me to tell her. It hung over us. We wouldn't really be a couple until I'd shared. And so we were never really a couple. Despite twelve years of marriage.

She's still waiting. And now, it's not so much going to be about diamond earrings, it's not so much about me lying about my whereabouts – although obviously it would be if she knew I'd been sleeping with the boss – it's about me living in a war zone for two and a half years, it's about me being mentally shot and never telling her about it. And the diamond earrings... you know what they were saying? They were saying, *all right, it's time for number seven to come in. I'm here, I'm back, and this time I'm talking. Honestly.*

Honestly, for fuck's sake.

*

Two hours later and just about finished that report on the newsagent robbery. Paperwork. It's not that I'm sitting on it; I keep getting interrupted. The usual crap of any given Monday. I've had enough. Need a holiday from all this. Murder, pointless little criminal investigations, Peggy, Charlotte. I need a break from it all.

Taylor arrives. Walks past me, then stops, takes a second, turns round.

'What is it with you sergeants?'

I glance at Herrod's desk. I don't equate, on any level, the fact that I was late for work yesterday with the fact that Herrod has been missing for twenty-four hours. He's an idiot, and I – despite the occasional opinion to the contrary – am not. Vaguely resent being the same rank as him, although sadly neither of us is going anywhere.

'You turn up when you feel like it, Herrod's God knows where, and now Eileen Harrison calls in sick. Did you know that? Did you know she'd pulled a sicky?'

I've got nothing. One of those occasions when it's best to let him spout. Authority has to spout off every now and again or else it loses its grip on the reality that it's an authority.

'We've got work coming out our arse... I couldn't care less if she's got a tumour in her neck, which she broke falling down the stairs after she had a heart attack. Get the fuck in here, for fuck's sake...'

He's still staring at me like I'm the bad guy. I've been in here since eight this morning, and I'm saying nothing. Admit that I'm a little surprised, as I do think Eileen Harrison is the type of ball-breaking workaholic that would come to the station regardless of being a heart-ravaged, broken-necked cancer victim.

Maybe I should call her.

That thought comes into my head, and then I think, for fuck's sake, leave it alone.

Taylor is still looking at me like I'm the five-day-old leftovers of a chicken vindaloo when Charlotte Miller appears in front of us.

'Gentlemen.'

Having walked in on a lot of anger which doesn't immediately dissipate, she chooses to ignore it.

'I'd like to see you in my office, Chief Inspector,' she says to Taylor, then turns away.

Taylor watches her go, and then gives me a look before he follows her.

'She's probably going to make me a Sergeant so there's someone to actually do all that Sergeant work you lot don't seem to care about.'

He walks off; I watch him go. The phone rings, and I answer with very low levels of enthusiasm.

'Tom?' says Ramsey at the front desk. Just what I need. Another theft of Winnie The Pooh masks in Rutherglen.

'Stuart,' I say, with no enthusiasm.

'Got a woman down here wants to talk to Herrod. It's about the Keller and Bathurst murders. Said she spoke to Herrod on the phone yesterday morning.'

Awooga! They said Herrod disappeared after taking a call.

'Can you show her to one of the rooms? I'll be down in a minute.'

'No bother.'

Phone down, drum my fingers on the table. Got a weird tingle. It's a police thing. Gut instinct. About to get a breakthrough.

Won't go leaping into the midst of the Taylor-Miller conflab just yet. Wait and see if my guts are in order for a change.

31

OK, guts appear to be mostly in the right place.

Just had a visit from Josephine Johnson. Twenty-six, attractive, dark brown hair. Something of the Uma Thurman about her.

She called Herrod yesterday because she thought an ex-boyfriend of hers might be the bloke we're looking for. Didn't give Herrod her name or a number because she was scared. Tried to call him again today, couldn't get him. Something made her change her mind, she decided to come in and cough up the beans.

Started talking about how she saw this guy for a while, and the whole thing was a bit weird. Got a lot of detail before I got the name. To be honest, I wasn't pushing for the name because I presumed it was going to be someone we didn't know. Why wouldn't it be? It was just going to be any old name, and the detail, the story behind her belief that this bloke could be a serial killer, was going to be much more important. Then, of course, it turned out to be someone we do know. Someone we brought in for interview, then let go.

Ian Healy.

So I left her sitting there with a cup of tea and a PC for company, grabbed Taylor and made big feet for Healy's office. Taylor had just emerged from Charlotte Miller looking moderately apprehensive. Just been put in charge of the whole murder inquiry, which is a relief, for me if not for him.

We could have come out like the damned cavalry. Guns, back-up, the whole bit. But it's not Taylor's way. Doesn't want to go tramping all over town if we're going to look stupid. There's no such thing as coincidence in crime – apart from when it happens. Ian Healy might be our man; he might not.

Now we're on the road between Healy's office and his home, having come up empty. His PA sat there playing the fool. Said she had no idea where he was, and if she knew and wasn't saying or if she didn't know and she was worried, she hid it perfectly. Police resentment to a tee.

Short drive to Healy's place somewhere in Parkhead. Taylor hits the London road. Not too much traffic – no need for any flashing blue lights. Briefly reaches ninety-five in the outside lane. He's pissed off.

'How long did Jonah interview this guy?' he says.

'Don't know,' I reply. 'An hour, maybe more. Not sure.'

'I mean, what in God's name was the man doing? He's supposed to be a fucking detective. How can you interview a murderer for half the damned day and then decide he's not your guy? God, you fingered him after two seconds in his office. Jonah spends all morning talking to the bastard and doesn't even bother getting a sample.'

'Come on. I let it pass. You said yourself you didn't think this was it.'

'Fuck it,' he says angrily. 'I spoke to the bloke for three minutes. Jonah practically bought him lunch.'

'He couldn't pick the murderer out of a line-up of four nuns and a blood-covered guy with a chainsaw. He's finished.'

I might be giving too much credit to the nuns.

'Dead right he's finished. Dead right.'

Another nail in Bloonsbury's coffin. Haven't even been thinking about nails in Herrod's coffin. If Healy's our man, there's a chance Herrod's dead. And for all that he's an open sore on the arse of humanity, you never want to see this happen to one of your own.

Up into a side street, then we're parked in front of Healy's tenement. No messing about. Up the stairs, third floor. Start to slow down as we reach the top. Walk more quietly as we near the door. Green paint, slowly peeling.

Deep breath. Look at each other. Nervous. This could be it, this could be nothing. Wish we'd brought guns. Taylor rings the bell, we stand and wait.

'We should be armed,' I say.

'Don't.'

Tries the doorbell again, gives in to the inevitable.

'Right then, John Wayne,' he says. *John Wayne?* Calm down, grandad. 'Do your sergeant thing and kick the door in.'

Marvellous. Over fifteen years on the force and it's all I'm good for. Decide to have a go at something I saw in a movie once. Try the door handle.

With a click that echoes down the corridor, the door opens. Nice and easy. Give Taylor a look and he scowls in return.

Swing the door open, step inside. Taylor in front. Immediately feel it. The darkness, the silence. The curtains are drawn. Not a sound. Not even the faint hum of a fridge or central heating. Scary.

Taylor hits the light switch. Nothing. The electrics are out or the light bulb's gone. Either way, we're walking into a darkened house with every possibility of a psychotic killer hiding behind a door.

'We should've brought guns,' I mutter. He ignores me, starts walking slowly into the flat.

Leave the door open to let in some light. As we take the first few tentative steps, begin to notice the smell. Off milk. Not some rancid pungent stench. Just a hint of it.

The hairs start to spring up on the back of my neck. On my arms. Feel the shiver. A tightness in the chest. I hate this. Walking into the unknown. Who knows what kind of man Healy really is? If he leaps out brandishing a knife, fine, you get into a fight. Take care of it. It's the creeping around in the dark that's the problem. That's the fear. Waiting. For the shock.

I follow Taylor into a room. In the pale light from the door, I can see the settee, the TV in the corner. Light behind the curtains. Taylor walks over and opens them, and the grey light of another bloody cold and miserable Glasgow afternoon comes flooding in.

Look around the room, quickly behind the door; half

expecting Healy to be there with an axe. Got to get a grip.

It's a sad depressing little room. Horrible 80's furniture; 15" flatscreen TV; drab wallpaper, drab paintings; brown carpet; bin overflowing with rubbish; chipped coffee table, covered with magazines and photographs.

We go to look at them at the same time. Porn mags, photography mags – which pretty much look the same from the cover – newspaper supplements. They each have a picture of a woman with dark brown hair on the cover. They could be Josephine Johnson. They could be Ann Keller. They could be Evelyn Bathurst.

We look at each other. It's coming together. We have our killer. No doubt. I can feel it. If only we'd had the sense to break the door down when we first came to check on the guy.

Back out into the hall. Look into the bathroom, try the switch again, still nothing. We can see it fine, however, in the light from the other room. A nasty little room, unpleasant aroma. Move on.

Skin crawls! Feel it stretch and strangle, a noise from another room. Faint but distinct. A slight movement and then there's silence again. We are not alone.

Look at each other, walk slowly back out into the hall. Muscles tense. Every sense heightened. That smell getting stronger. Waiting for the attack. Small flat, only two rooms left. Kitchen and bedroom. Kitchen first, glance in. Can barely make it out in the dark. Large room, but plain. The fridge door is open, emits no light. A bottle of milk lies smashed on the floor. So much for the smell.

Bedroom. This is it. No light from the other room penetrates in here. We stand unsure in the doorway.

'Anyone there?' says Taylor. Silence. 'Healy?'

We wait. Nothing. Look at each other, barely make his expression out in the dark.

'Aw, fuck this,' he says after a few seconds. Walks quickly into the room, me behind. Straight to the curtains, starts to drag them open. Something scampers from underneath the bed, past our feet. Fuck! Heart jumps. Fists clenched. Realise it's a fucking cat. Look to the door as the curtains open and light pours in. No cat. It's a rat. Big and grey and ugly. Fucking huge.

Finally see it out the corner of my eye. Turn round. Big rat to keep my attention off this. Taylor's already staring, face set hard. On the wall beside the bed. Bloody; pale; dead. Detective Sergeant Herrod impaled through the stomach with an ornamental sword, suspended on the wall. The blood has long since stopped dripping. His mouth is open, blood congealed on his lips, his eyes stare blankly back at us. The weapon missed the tie, a subdued silk M&S job he must have got for Christmas. It hangs free, some of the blood from his mouth having dripped upon it. Squares of beige and blue, black marks streaked across. A new design. Shoes are gone. Herrod's feet in dirty white socks.

We stand and stare for some time. Drinking it in. A police officer impaled on a bedroom wall. Try to get a grip on my train of thought. What it means for the murder inquiry. What it means for the station. The second officer down in two days. Think of Bernadette; bitter, she'll enjoy it in a perverse way. We stand and stare, as if expecting something to happen.

'Keep waiting for him to tell us to fuck off and mind our own business,' says Taylor.

32

Early evening roundup. A bit later than usual as a result of the day's events. First one with Taylor in charge. Bloonsbury's back in the office having heard about Herrod, but he's staying out of our way. Sitting silently in his room with a bottle at his right hand. Don't know why Charlotte doesn't just send him on his way. The guy is on duty and embarrassing himself and everyone who has to come into contact with him.

Beginning to think Miller might be as far off the rails as he is, that maybe she's losing it. Two of her officers have been killed in the last couple of days, she's got a murder inquiry exploding out of her control, and she's lost. Saw her for a few seconds on her way to talk to the press. Her earlier self-assurance was gone. Pale, shocked, almost broken. She's still not returned, which is perhaps why she hasn't got hold of Jonah yet.

The door closes, the gang's mostly here. Taylor stands in front, done this loads of times. Never this big, though. Never for the killer of two officers. Hard to fathom the feeling in the room. It wasn't as if any of us liked Herrod, the man was too personality-deficient for that, but a colleague's a colleague. If nothing else, it could have been one of us. Selfish, but that's how the mind works.

We've put an alert out for Healy. Picture in every paper, on every noticeboard. The first part of any murder inquiry is out of the way. We know who did it. Now we just have to catch him. Bloody frustrating that we had him here; locked in a cell too. And Jonah Bloonsbury decided to let him go. Don't know who to blame. Bloonsbury himself; Miller for putting him in charge in the first place; or me and Taylor for leaving him to it.

Taylor starts up.

'Right, people, here it is. I know this is hard, but we've

got to think straight, be professional. There's a dangerous man out there and we have to get him off the streets. We can be mad, we can be outraged, we can be depressed, we can feel guilty, whatever. But it can all wait. First off we have to be clear headed and we have to get our man.' He hesitates. 'And on that point – we all know we had him here and it was decided to let him go. If the press get hold of that... well, we're going to look bad, to put it mildly. So we keep our mouths shut. Tell no one. No wives, husbands, mothers, or whatever. Mouths shut.'

A few nods, most of us stare blankly at him or at the floor. No one's going to tell anyone anything.

'So, what have we got? Herrod took a call from Josephine Johnson yesterday morning, putting him on to Ian Healy. The sergeant went round there on his own. Put simply, he was an idiot.' Pauses, takes a deep breath. No friends of Herrod here to offend. 'Whatever the exact turn of events, it ended with the sergeant dead. Healy, realising we're onto him, disappears. From hair samples in the flat, forensics have confirmed that it was Healy who killed Ann Keller and Police Constable Bathurst. Some of us may wonder why Evelyn was killed, but it looks as if she was just in the wrong place at the wrong time.'

Looks around the room. Was that last comment directed solely at me?

Yes.

He's right, anyway. Forget about Crow and some great conspiracy. Bathurst goes to see Miller to give her confession; for whatever reason they end up in bed, as you do; on her way home in the middle of the night, Bathurst is stumbled upon by Healy, and that seals her fate. Shouldn't have been walking alone through the streets in the middle of the night when there was a killer loose. No conspiracy.

'Now Herrod. Three murders and our killer has gone to ground. We know he's our man, we need to know where he is. We need to speak to everybody that's ever met the guy. Family, friends, clients, whoever. Tom, you've just been down to his office?'

'Yep. Brought back everything we could find. Just about to go and look through it all, see what we can get. The PA's downstairs, trying to be stoic.'

'I'll speak to her when we're done.'

He stops, looks around the room again. Not one for speeches our Dan. My mind strays again to Miller, as he starts dividing up the areas of responsibility. Who's to look where, talk to whom. I know what I've got for the next few hours. Looking through file after file of Ian Healy's confidential papers. Landed with Morrow to help. It'll still be a long job. Look at the watch – almost seven o'clock already. Think of Peggy for the first time since this morning. Have to cancel again. She should understand. If she doesn't, then there just isn't any point, is there?

Too much is happening. Two women; a murder inquiry, which has now taken two colleagues; an old police conspiracy involving who knows how many clowns at the station. Too much at once. I just need a few hours to step back from it, assess the whole lot. Make some decisions, discard some of the garbage. But I'm not getting the chance. Every ten minutes there's something new. A revelation, a demand, whatever. At least today has simplified it a little. We're looking for Ian Healy, period. What I also need is for one of the women to tell me to take a hike – or both of them for that matter – and then things would be even simpler.

Switch back on for the wrap up.

'Right, people. You all know what you're doing. We need this sorted out quickly, so get out there and get on with it. '

Taylor walks from the room and the meeting breaks up. Trail out near the back, no one talking. There's a job to be done. Get back to my desk, Morrow comes trotting up.

'Right, Rob. Might as well sit at Herrod's desk. Seat should be cold by now.'

He raises his eyebrows, doesn't look too impressed. A dead man's seat. I push a box of papers over to him.

'What are we looking for?' he asks.

'No idea,' I say. 'Let me know when you find it.'

Lift the phone. Get the call to Peggy out of the way before I start. One ring and she lifts straight away.

'Hello?'

'Hey…'

'Oh, God, Thomas,' she says. 'Are you all right? I heard about Herrod.'

'I'm fine. He's not doing so well though.'

'What's going on there, for God's sake?'

'It's cool. Herrod was just stupid.' I'm all sympathy. Peggy didn't like him any more than I did.

'Well, just be careful.'

'I will. Look, I'm not going to be able to make it over tonight. This just keeps getting worse and worse.'

'I'm worried. I want to see you.' Start to object, she doesn't give me the chance. 'I'm not going anywhere. It doesn't matter when you come, I'll be in bed whatever time it is. Just come over and join me.'

What the Hell, it doesn't make any difference. Might as well sleep at their place as my own. Although, what happens if I've somewhere else to go tomorrow night?

'Sure. But really, don't wait up.'

'I won't.'

'OK. And as long as you're not going to be annoyed if I crawl in at half-five.'

'It won't matter.'

'OK. I'll be there.'

'Thanks, Thomas. The children'll be delighted to see you in the morning.'

All part of the plan.

'Aye, it'll be good.'

Say our goodbyes, hang up. Morrow's got his head buried in his pile of paper, good lad. If Herrod had still been there he would have been listening avidly to every word and not attempting to hide the fact.

Phone goes again as soon as I hang up. Internal.

'Hutton.'

'Thomas.'

Charlotte. Crap. Look up. Her office door is closed. She must have come back while we were in the meeting. I was wanting things simplified.

'Hi.'

I bet Morrow would want to listen to this if he knew who was on the phone.

'You'll be working late?' she says.

'No question.'

'I understand. Of course. But I was wondering if you could come over later?'

Come on... I don't need this. I'm supposed to go down to Helensburgh at three o'clock in the morning? I can't. Not tonight. Can't stand up Peggy again.

She's aware of my hesitation. Sounds anxious.

'Not Helensburgh. I've got a flat. Kelvinside. You could come over when you've finished.'

She sounds like a normal human being. Alone. Vulnerable.

Take a moment. You promised your ex-wife. Your possibly soon to be next wife.

'Things are just getting a little out of hand,' she says. 'I need to talk, that's all.'

Why now? Why tonight? Why can't she want to talk tomorrow night? Where's Frank when you need him?

'All right,' I say. Close my eyes, rub my forehead. Really, Hutton? Really?

'Thanks,' she says. 'I'll be here late as well. I'll speak to you before I go.'

She hangs up. Put the phone down. Stare at it. Wait for it to ring again with some other demand on my time for the middle of the coming night. When it doesn't, I lift the top paper off the pile and start to adjust myself to searching through the life and work of Ian Healy.

Haven't got two lines into it when the door to Bloonsbury's office opens and the broken man walks out. There are six or seven people in the room as he passes through and every one of us stops what we're doing to stare at the guy. Bloody eyes, face streaked and ugly. A mess. Appears to be walking in a bit more of a straight line than usual but his shoulders are hunched, shuffling gait. He stops halfway across the room. Has become aware that everyone's looking at him. Knows what we're all thinking. He catches a few eyes, but no one looks away. There's no one left in this station who couldn't look him straight in the eye now and tell him what they think.

Finally he looks at me and those eyes are bloody death; then he straightens up and walks from the room.

And if the man has any sense whatsoever, he won't return.

*

'I've been thinking about Crow,' says Taylor.

He looks tired. I'm not surprised. His wife has just left; he's been put in charge of a huge murder inquiry; instant results expected; under pressure. And besides, it's one thirty in the morning. And here's me, joined CID 'cause I thought it'd be nine to five.

'What about him?'

End of the day. Looked through all of the papers that I'm going to. Morrow and I found a few things we'll have to check up on, but that'll be for the morning. Taylor spent a good three hours with the PA, then sent her packing. She'd had the holidays off, then turned up for work as usual this morning. Healy was nowhere to be seen, no idea where he might have gone. And that was about it.

So. End of the day, last cigarette, last cup of coffee.

Then? Take your pick. Charlotte left just after midnight, slipping me the address as she went. So I've got a choice. Charlotte or Peggy, and I've promised them both.

Mind on the job. Crow.

'Why did he just vanish like that?' says Taylor. 'We'd started to think about him. Possible suspect, possible link between the two. We shouldn't lose sight of things. Saturday night we charged down there, kicking the door in. The fact that he'd run seemed to implicate him. Now, we've got Healy stamped over everything. So, do we just forget about Crow? Mark his disappearance down as coincidence?'

'There's no such thing as coincidence.'

'Exactamundo,' he says.

'So we need a connection between Crow and Healy.'

'Yep. You didn't see anything when you looked through Healy's files? A mention of Crow having dealt with any of his clients?'

'Nothing. But then, Morrow checked half of them, and he wouldn't have been looking.'

He holds my gaze for a moment, while the next part of the conversation – the part where he tells me I have to now go through all the paperwork Morrow looked at – then says, 'Not tonight.' Gee, thanks. 'Tomorrow morning. Have Morrow follow up whatever you dug up this evening. Don't need to tell anyone else what we're thinking.'

Taylor rubs his eyes. Half one in the morning isn't the best time for clear and logical insight.

'I don't know, Sergeant. We're missing something here. Something obvious.'

'Come on,' I say, 'we all say that. All the time. You can't know it until you know it.'

Rests his elbows on the desk and yawns.

'Sure. You get that from a Chinese fortune cookie?'

'I did. And there's more. Always take your clothes off before you get in the shower.'

'Very funny. Piss off and we'll talk in the morning.'

He stands up. Lucky sod is going home to an empty bed. Haven't decided where I'm going yet. Although, of course, I know exactly where I'm going.

'Any chance you spoke to Eileen Harrison today?'

I give him a quizzical look in reply.

'Don't look at me like that,' he says. 'You're always talking to women, or they're talking to you, or whatever the Hell you have going on. Don't look so *whatever could you mean, Chief Inspector*?'

I shake my head and start to head out.

'No,' I say over my shoulder, 'I didn't speak to Eileen Harrison.'

'Perhaps if she calls in sick again tomorrow, or we don't hear from her, you could go round and see if she's all right.'

'What? Seriously?'

'Yes. Look at my face. It's a serious face. There's enough weird shit going on around here for us not to at least make sure she's OK. Pretty weird her not coming at all, particularly at a time like this.'

Now there he has a point.

I don't reply and turn and walk back out into the main office. The quiet of the middle of the night; CID at rest. Look at the watch. A little over five hours and the shit'll be flying once more.

Pick up the car keys and start tossing the mental coin; knowing that if it comes down on the side of Peggy, I'll keep doing best of three 'til I get the right result.

33

Post-sex cigarette: the best there is. It might be a cliché, but it's right up there with sex itself and watching old film of Thistle beating Celtic 4-1. Cool, bitter, biting at the inside of your throat. Like a smoky single malt by a warm fire on a cold day. Lie back, breathe it in, stare at the ceiling. Forget everything. Savour the smoke and savour the remains of the delicious sensations still lingering in your loins and stomach. You feel the tiredness, begin to give in to it, let it sweep over you. Like waves crashing on the ocean.

'What are you thinking?'

You swallow a gallon of seawater. Just as well. I was about to nod off and drop the smoking butt end onto my chest.

'Just enjoying the moment.'

She places her hand on my chest, starts drawing circles. God, she's not about to get romantic on me? She kisses my shoulder, snuggles her head next to my arm. What the fuck?

'I'm glad you've been around the past few days, Tom. I've needed you.'

For all the bitterness and tough guy act, it still sounds good to hear it. Charlotte Miller needs Sergeant Hutton. Sort of thing you'd scrawl on your desk at school. If you were pathetic.

Quarter past four. Just had ball-breaking sex and feel relaxed for the first time in a couple of days. Had intended going round to see Peggy when I was finished, but now that I'm here, and absolutely exhausted, I've got a feeling I won't be going anywhere until it's time for work. Big Guilt means Big Denial. Try not to think about Peggy.

I keep waiting for Charlotte's guillotine to fall. Each time is more intimate than the last, however. Deeper into the mire. Falling in love. Me with her. Wrong person, wrong time, wrong planet.

I roll over on my side, away from her, and she curls her arms around me and presses against my skin, her breasts beautiful and soft against my back.

She says something else, her voice dreamy, but the tiredness has swept back in as I move onto my side, and I don't catch it. I try to pluck the words out of the air, but they're gone.

*

Fuck! Tuesday morning wake up call. Don't know what drags me from sleep, but I sit straight up in bed. Light outside, know I'm late without looking at the clock. Empty bed, damned woman already up and gone to work, leaving me lying here. Fuck. Dare to look at the clock. Aw, fuck. Fuck. Half past eight.

Look at my phone. Three missed calls, four texts, but the phone is on silent. I never did that. Must have been Miller. Miller put my phone on silent...

The station; Taylor; Peggy. They were all calling. Jesus. Where were Craig Levein and the First Minister, didn't they need me as well?

Fly into a frantic rush of cold water, toothpaste and last night's clothes. Out onto the street. Snowed in the night – a light covering. Nearly slip on the stairs. Have trouble starting the car, lurch out onto the road and within five minutes I'm stuck in traffic.

Keep looking at the clock as it gets ever later. Switch the radio on and off. Bad news, boring news, weather – I know it snowed! The phone rings again and I ignore it. And again.

Finally arrive well after nine-thirty. Run into the station – raised eyebrow from Ramsey – up the stairs and into the office. The usual hum of activity. In the centre of the room Taylor stands talking to Miller. They stop, look at me as I approach. Taylor looks as if he wants to thump me, Miller plays the part. The disapproving superior. I shrug my shoulders. No idea what to say.

'I'll leave you to it,' says the woman who five hours previously had screamed with lust.

Yes, screamed.

Taylor indicates his office and I follow him in. He sits behind his desk. Gestures for me to close the door. Starts up. Low voice. Mad.

'What the fuck are you doing?'

I can't explain.

'We've got a monumental case on here and you're lying in bed? And by the look of you, someone else's bed. Can you not leave it be for two *fucking* days while we get some work done?'

Wish I had some defence, but I've got nothing.

'Jesus, Sergeant, would you at least say something for yourself?'

I can't. He doesn't need to know about Charlotte.

He leans forward, elbows on the desk.

'Detective Constable Morrow's been in for the past two hours. Got some good ideas, doing good work. He's gone back out, on the job. Doing his damned job. Any more of this and it'll be your job he's doing. Get out there, and get on with it.'

Stupid, humiliated, feel like saluting. Think much the better of it.

'We're done, Sergeant.'

Right. Turn to go. Wait for the quieter words that a manager will often say to show they're not really mad at you. They don't come. Out the door, leave it open, and then back to my desk.

The papers that Morrow checked through yesterday are all still there, a pile on Herrod's desk. I lift them over, place them in front of me. There's a message beside the phone. *Can you call Peggy?*

Push it to one side, decide to think on it. What can I possibly say?

Lift the first paper and begin the trawl through for any

---

mention of Detective Chief Inspector Gerry Crow.

34

Spend three hours on all those papers that Morrow wasted his time on yesterday. Looking for the name of Crow, thinking about two women. It would be nice to be able to divorce your thoughts from that kind of thing, but I suppose we're all the same.

Peggy or Charlotte. Safe option, against the bomb waiting to go off. Keep making mental lists with the name Crow on them both, so I don't miss him if he crops up.

Points in favour:

Peggy. History; great sex; mother of my children; get my family back; I'm forty-four and it's about time I acted it; a warm, loving relationship, especially when the relationship with Charlotte is going nowhere – it'd be foolish to lose Peggy for something that might not last until teatime; Peggy makes good Jamaica ginger cake.

Charlotte. Great sex.

Try to tell myself that sex with Peggy is as good, but there's something extra with Charlotte. It could just be novelty, though. Maybe after twelve years it wouldn't have the same bite. Nothing dulls the appetite like familiarity.

I don't know. Head says Peggy, heart's divided, penis says Charlotte. That's about it.

I pick up the phone to Peggy eventually.

'Hello?' she says. Voice wary. Knows it's me.

'Don't hang up,' I say. Immediately onto the defensive before she can speak. Good move, Hutton, you moron.

She doesn't speak. Doesn't hang up either.

'I'm sorry. I just couldn't come over.'

'Where were you?'

Never was much of a liar, but I might as well give it a go. Easier over the phone.

'It was late. Middle of the night. And I know what you said, but there was no point. I needed the sleep, babe.' The old familiarity. I bet Brian called her *darling*. 'I'm sorry. It was half-four, I just went home, unplugged the phone, forgot to set the alarm and went out like a light. I know, I should at least have texted or something.'

No immediate reply. Not necessarily a bad thing. Don't say anything else. Wait and see.

'I just wish...' she starts off, stops herself. 'I don't know Thomas. Just be honest, for God's sake.'

'I'm being honest.' Missing the point as usual. 'Look, I'll come over tonight, I promise.' Close my eyes as I say it.

'Don't, Thomas. Don't...I don't know... I still want you to come. But come when you want. When you mean it.'

'I'll try and come tonight. Promise.' There I go again.

'Don't promise, Thomas.' Click.

Phone call over, just like that. No opportunity for more lies. Gun at my head right now, and I'd choose Peggy over Charlotte. But it won't last.

Back to work, try to think about Crow and neither of the women. Crow is just not as attractive a thought, however.

*

An hour later, and I've got it. Already early afternoon. Dying for some lunch. Morrow's been in and out, buzzing around like the good little detective. Good thing I like him.

Walk into the boss's office.

'Bingo.'

Taylor looks up. The man's actually going over some papers – not staring at the ceiling like he usually does. Must be taking his duties seriously. He's been out most of the morning, got in about twenty minutes ago.

'Close the door,' he says.

Do it, stand over his desk. Still feel that tension in the air.

'Hope you've got something, 'cause Morrow came up empty.'

I try not to be pleased. Start thinking like that, and I'll

be turning into Herrod.

'Crow and Healy. Beginning of last year. A rape charge. Crow was the arresting officer, Healy defended the accused. Somewhere along the line Crow messed up and the guy walked on a technicality. Of course, it doesn't say it, but it reeks of pay off. The accused was some big shot banker. What's a guy like that doing going to a no-hoper like Healy? Put on to him because he knows Healy's a man to do business with, presumably. Payment to Crow, he does the necessary damage, the guy's out of jail.'

Taylor stares at his desk. Rubs his chin with one hand, indicates the chair with the other. I sit down. He's sorting it out. I've already been doing that, and although it's what we were looking for, does it actually get us anywhere?

'So what?' he says eventually. 'What do we have? Healy and Crow know each other. Know the other's bent. How does it apply here? We've got the first half of the connection, now we need the second.'

Think straight, Hutton.

'Right. Crow and Healy worked together on at least one case. There might have been more, we don't know. The murder case last year we know was Crow. But there's no noticeable involvement from Healy.'

'Couldn't find anything on that?'

Shake my head.

'And now, we know Healy murdered Ann Keller and Evelyn,' I continue. 'We don't know if Crow has any involvement. And both men have disappeared. I talked to Crow, didn't suggest there was anything there. He did mention that he'd spoken to Herrod and Bloonsbury earlier this month, however. Now Herrod's dead too. And Bloonsbury's a mess. Might as well be dead.'

'Yes, but that's self-inflicted. I don't think we can go blaming Crow for Bloonsbury's condition.'

Sit up. A cohesive thought. First for three days.

'Maybe Crow's blackmailing him. Maybe that's why Bloonsbury and Herrod went to see Crow, 'cause Crow was threatening to reveal their part in the murder case.'

'How could he do that? He was guiltier than the rest of them put together. He was the murderer for God's sake.'

'Yeah, but look at the guy. He's wasted, down there in his dingy little cottage. You think he's going to think straight? Maybe he threatens Jonah with it. Jonah can't pay up, he knows he's about to be found out, and he does what any self-respecting drunk does. Hits the sauce. Meanwhile, Crow clears out so that when the shit hits the fan, he isn't around to catch any of it.'

'So, why hasn't the shit hit the fan yet? He's been gone three days.'

'He stopped somewhere to have a pint and is still stuck to the barstool? Who knows?'

'And where does Healy killing Herrod fit in?'

'I don't know. But if we can sort out the police end, we might find out. Where is Jonah?' I ask. 'If we just come straight out and ask if Crow's blackmailing him, d'you think we'll get a straight answer?'

Taylor rubs his forehead. 'I doubt it. Haven't seen the guy today.'

'She hasn't suspended him, has she?'

He shrugs.

'Maybe he's just taken a day off to try and sober up. Who knows? Maybe he'll come in tomorrow wearing a blue and red, skintight jump suit, with big yellow pants pulled over the top.'

'So, how about we just go round there and ask him if Crow's blackmailing him over the Addison case?'

'But what if he is? Where does Healy killing Ann Keller fit into it? If there's something going on between Crow and Bloonsbury, it doesn't have to involve Healy. A connection between Healy and Crow on a rape charge over a year ago doesn't mean anything, Sergeant.'

Deep breath. He's right.

'Anyway,' he says, 'the fact is that Healy killed those two women and now he's disappeared. He's the guy we've got to find.'

'So where do we start looking?'

———

192

'No idea.'

'So, how about we go and speak to Bloonsbury about Crow anyway. It might get us somewhere. If it doesn't, we're no worse off.'

Looks at his watch. Hope he's going to mention lunch. He doesn't.

'All right, we'll go with it. I'll go and see Bloonsbury. There's no point in us both turning up there like a delegation from Messed Up Coppers Anonymous, and if you go on your own, he'll tell you where to go.'

Nod. Fair enough. I'll get some lunch.

'You go and talk to your big shot accused rapist,' he says. 'See what he knows about Crow and Healy.'

'He's not going to tell me anything, is he?'

Stabs his finger at the side of his forehead.

'Use your napper. Be subtle.'

Subtle? I'm Scottish.

Stand up, ready to go.

'And you should call Peggy. She was looking for you last night after you left.'

Crap. 'What time?'

'I don't know. 'Bout two, maybe.'

Ah. Caught with my pants down. Every time. I'm such a useless liar. Walk out. Humble pie for lunch.

35

Be subtle.

Sitting in the waiting room outside the bank manager's office. Feels like a dentist's waiting area, except the magazines are more business orientated and the goldfish in the goldfish tank aren't goldfish – being of an altogether more exotic nature. Thick carpet – maroon, no pattern – cream walls. Wonder how I'm going to play this if I'm to get anything out of him.

As detectives go, I've always been reasonably good at sorting things out in my head, seeing possibilities, that kind of thing. However, when it comes to making witnesses give up that little extra, I'm useless.

The PA appears. Late forties, hair in a bun, blue suit. Leads me through the door into the banker's office, announces me as if I was attending royal court, then closes the door behind. Doesn't offer coffee.

The banker stands up from behind his desk.

'How do you do, officer? Please come in. Sit down.'

Check out the office as I walk to the chair. Expensive paintings, big plants, massive fish tank, the same rich carpet as the waiting room. Money. This is no banker dealing with the guy on the street and his deposit account of a hundred and thirty-five quid.

'How can I help you, Sergeant Hutton?'

'Won't take much of your time, Mr. Montague.' Had a geography teacher in first year called Montague. Hated him. Used to skelp you over the backside with the blackboard eraser. I could probably sue him now, if it wasn't for the fact he was murdered by one of the sixth years. Maybe I could sue the school. 'Just like to ask you a couple of questions about Ian Healy.'

He looks vaguely curious, like he doesn't recognise the name.

'Your lawyer,' I add.

'I think there must be some mistake, Sergeant. All my affairs are handled by Harper, McCalliog and Brown of Ingram Street.'

Affairs? Harper, McCalliog and Brown? Feel like arresting him for being an annoying twat with a posh accent.

Subtlety edged to one side.

'Rape case, last year. Janie Northolt, one of your employees. Harper, McCalliog and Brown didn't handle that affair.'

Patronising smile disappears off face.

'Oh, him,' he says. 'What about him?' Looks at his watch. 'I really am rather busy.'

'Perhaps then you could come down to the station later to answer some questions?'

He gives me the look. That one always shuts them up. Trying to throw his weight around, but he ought to know better. No one gets away with that for long in Glasgow.

'Very well, Sergeant. But I really don't see how I can be of any help.'

'You know Ian Healy is wanted in connection with the murder of a woman and two police officers?'

He nods. Of course he knows.

'We're just following up on all of his clients from the past couple of years. See what we can find.'

'Very thorough,' he says. His voice drips disdain.

What would I have to lose by punching this man in the face? Apart from, obviously, my job, and possibly my freedom for a few months?

'If all your affairs are handled by Harper, McCalliog and Brown, why did you go to a small-time lawyer like Healy to deal with the rape charge?'

Stares down his nose.

'It was a delicate matter,' he says, voice thinner than cat gut. Looks at his watch.

'It was also a pretty big matter. A rape charge from one of your employees. Aren't Harper, McCalliog and Brown competent to deal with big matters?'

His teeth clench behind pursed lips. Jaw pulses.

'The law may be black and white to you Sergeant, but there are some matters which you clearly don't understand.'

Right, that's it. Fuck you, you Lehman Brothers-worshiping fucktrumpet.

'Listen.' Lean forward. His head moves an inch or two back. 'I don't give a fuck about your sordid little rape. We know you raped her, we know you were arrested by Chief Inspector Crow, and we know you went to Healy because you found out he was a man who could deal with Crow. Money exchanged hands, Crow screwed up intentionally, and you walked.'

He starts to object, but I'm rolling.

'Shut it. I don't care about your rape. I don't care about the pay off, about any of it. All I'm interested in is Healy. The guy's a murderer, we need to catch him. I just need everything you can tell me about him. That's it. Where you got his name, if you know why there's a connection between him and DCI Crow. You can tell me now, or else there are plenty of people who'd be interested in your dodgy dealing with serial killers.'

Say it all in about five seconds. He fidgets. He fingers some papers on his desk. Toying with the idea, I suspect, of calling up some big cheese on the force with whom he plays bridge on a Tuesday, and telling him to get the low-life moron of a sergeant off his hands.

Fixes me with the look.

'I took it to Harper. He deals with my business.' That'll be Harper of Harper, McCalliog and Brown, presumably. Not Joe Harper, once of Aberdeen and Hibs. 'When he heard the name of the policeman involved, he said he had a reputation. That we might be able to deal with him. However, he didn't think it would be appropriate for Harper, McCalliog and Brown to get involved.' I bet he didn't. 'They mentioned the name of Ian Healy.'

'And you know why Healy and Crow were able to do

business together? Was there history?'

Now he looks smug. I've strayed into territory with which he is genuinely unable to help.

'Businesses trust me to take care of their money, Sergeant. They don't need to know how I do it, or my relationship with others in the banking world. I don't see that lawyers and policemen are any different, do you?' Point taken, but he continues to spell it out because he likes the sound of his own voice. 'I know nothing of the way these men work. I paid the money, I was released from that ridiculous and wholly unfounded charge.'

Class dismissed. The look says it all.

'Did you deal with Ian Healy on any other matters?'

'No, Sergeant, I did not, and I must say I'm finding all of this rather tiring. I am a busy man, so if you wouldn't mind taking your leave.'

Don't know how she knows, but the PA appears at the door and stands waiting for the uninvited guest to get the fuck out of Dodge.

I have to accept defeat. I can't possibly arrest them both, no matter how much I'd like to. Stand up.

'Just don't think of going anywhere in case we need to speak to you again.'

His face starts to go red. With anger. Hit the mark.

'As it happens,' he says, and you can hear him struggling to control his voice, 'I'm taking my wife to Austria tomorrow night to spend New Year in Vienna.'

We stare each other down. Like in a movie. Decide against annoying him further and retreat slowly from the office.

Out into the freshness of afternoon. The snow in the centre of town has turned to slush, but it still lies on the roofs. Low cloud and cold. Looks like it might snow again.

Grab a burger, having had a totally unsatisfactory sandwich on the way in, then head back to the office. Some time after three when I walk in. Taylor's in his office, feet on the desk, staring at the ceiling. Wonder if he's found our man. Should know better.

'Hard at work?' I say as I walk in.

Takes his feet down, straightens up.

'You're a fucking idiot, aren't you, Sergeant?'

'What'd I do now?'

Realisation kicks in. Didn't take the banker long to get on the phone.

'Be subtle...'

'The guy was an asshole. He was lucky I didn't–'

'Asshole he may have been, but I had Miller in here like a tornado. She seemed to think it was my fault.'

'Well, if you can't control your staff,' I say, with that cheeky grin I nicked from Ally McCoist.

I get the look in reply, then he puts his feet back on the desk.

'Well, before you offended the delicate rich person, did he tell you anything?'

'Nothing much. He was put onto Healy by his solicitors, Harper, McCalliog and Brown.' Taylor raises his eyebrows at the name. 'Said that Healy was known as someone who would do business with the police. But that's it. Or at least, that was all he was saying. Waste of time, I suppose. Still, I enjoyed annoying him.'

'Great, Sergeant. Well, you can go and annoy Miller now, 'cause she wanted to see you when you got in.' Looks across the desk at me. 'You've been in there a few times in the last week. You're not sleeping with her, are you?'

'I am as a matter of fact.'

He snorts. 'Aye, you wish.' Stares at the floor, runs a tired hand through his hair. 'Might have a go at it myself, now I've no reason not to.'

Quick change of subject.

'What about Bloonsbury,' I ask. 'You see him?'

'I did.'

'And?'

'He was drunk.'

'You ask him about Crow?'

'Got nowhere. He just started muttering about him being a useless bastard. The usual drunken ravings.'

'And the Addison case. You mentioned we knew about that?'

'Told me to fuck off and mind my own business,' he says, shaking his head. 'Don't know what the Hell we can do. Maybe bring him in, lock him up and deprive him of drink for a couple of days. But it's Jonah Bloonsbury, for goodness sake. Don't think Miller would go for it.'

'You're in charge of the investigation.'

'I'm sure there's a line in the sand, Sergeant, and arresting Jonah Bloonsbury'll be some way on the other side. We're just going to have to get our information from other sources.' He rubs his hand across his forehead. Looks tired. 'Right, away and take Charlotte across her desk, or whatever it is the two of you do in there.'

'See what I can do.'

He smiles as I walk out the room. Across the office, nod at Morrow, knee deep in documents. Wonder what Taylor's got him looking at now. Knock on Miller's door, walk in. She looks up, doesn't offer me a seat.

'Just had Jonathan Montague on the phone,' she says. Tongue coiled. About to unleash. Make a snap decision.

'Why didn't you wake me up today?'

'What?' she says, surprised. Annoyed at me for talking back. Like I'm in primary school.

'You left me sleeping and came into work. Knew I'd be late. What d'you do that for? And putting my phone on silent? Really?'

She doesn't answer. Stares back across the office. See her look behind me to make sure the door's properly closed.

'You do not go into the offices of people like Jonathan Montague and start mouthing off,' she says eventually. Ignoring me. Daring me. 'Especially not on ridiculous charges like the one you took to him.'

Feel stupid, but have to fight anger at the same time.

'And what was all that about DCI Crow?'

'It's still not right,' I say, choosing to employ her tactic of ignoring an awkward question. 'You may have put

Taylor in charge, but you're not volunteering the information on you and Evelyn…'

'You're not volunteering why you think Evelyn and I slept together,' she fires back.

What can I say to that? That I drove down to her house on Friday night like a lovesick little puppy. It's bad enough feeling pathetic, never mind everyone else knowing about it.

'I thought so,' she says to my next bout of silence. 'Don't think you're getting any special favours, Sergeant,' she adds with bite, 'there's plenty more where you came from.'

Won't have to open the door when I leave. Just crawl under it.

Stare each other down for a few seconds more but there's nothing else to be said. Turn to go. Wonder if she'll say something to my back, but she doesn't. Open the door and out into the freedom of the main office. Breathe the fresh air. Like stepping from a lift you've been trapped in for ten hours. Escaping a straitjacket.

Walk back to my desk wondering what other no-hope lead I can follow up, and why it is that Charlotte Miller has so quickly turned against me? Look at the time. Less than twelve hours since she was glad I'd been around the past few days.

Part of the game. And if she called up tonight and ordered my attendance at her bedside, would I have the guts to refuse?

36

Tuesday evening, on my way out the office. Contemplate leaving without checking in with Taylor, but decide I'd better. Find him in the ops room, leaning back against a desk, staring at the photographs on the wall of Herrod, Ann Keller and Evelyn Bathurst.

There's nothing to say. I stand beside him for a while, looking at the pictures in companionable and grotesque silence. The door is closed, we can't hear anything of what is going on outside. Absurdly, it feels peaceful.

'I need to get some sleep,' I say eventually.

He nods. Still nothing to say. Engrossed, but acknowledging that it's all right for me to leave.

'You should too,' I say, and he doesn't reply.

I almost pat him on the shoulder, remember it's not my place, then head to the door.

'On your way home can you call in and see Sergeant Harrison?'

He turns to look at me as I'm at the door. He reads the look on my face.

'She phoned in this morning,' he says. 'It was definitely her, so I don't think there's anything happened to her.'

I give him the *really?* look.

'It's just a bit weird,' he says, 'and I don't like it. So, go round there, knock on her door, make sure there's nothing I should know about. Then you can go home and get some sleep.'

Deep sigh – he's right, of course, and I need to stop being a dick about it – then I turn and head out into the night.

*

I stand at her door for more than five minutes. That's quite a long time to be standing at someone's door. Five minutes. Just do nothing for five minutes, then imagine you're standing at someone's door. Almost give up, but then she finally answers. Not sure how long I'd have given it. All the time I'm wondering how annoyed she'll be at me for dragging her out of her sick bed.

We stand in the cold of night, me illuminated by a streetlight, and her backlit by a small lamp in her hallway.

'Tom,' she says. 'Come in.'

She doesn't look ill, as such, but she does look fucking terrible.

I hadn't really envisioned going in. I hadn't envisioned anything beyond standing on her doorstep, making sure she wasn't dead, checking that she definitely had the plague or something, and then leaving.

On balance, *come in* isn't exactly a shock invitation though.

I follow her in, close the door behind me. We go into her front room, she sits down in a single armchair, I sit on the sofa opposite. The room is warm, there's a single lamp on in the corner. Quick check on the walls. Paintings. Good taste. Or, you know, so it seems to me. Like I know. There's a TV in the corner, but it's turned off at the wall. Looks unused.

'You all right?' I ask eventually.

'Feel like shit,' she says.

I nod.

'Flu or something? You want me to go to Boots for you? Call a doctor?'

'I've been sleeping with Evelyn.'

I look across the room. That's too far out in left field for me to be able to compute, so I don't even try.

'What?'

'We were.... You know, she was young, we just had this thing... It started at a station night a few months ago. It was just sex, you know. She called me her fuck buddy.' She lets out a sad, hollow laugh. I start to see Evelyn Bathurst and Eileen Harrison as fuck buddies. That's something I wish I could imagine in other circumstances. 'We barely even talked. Just saw each other every now and again for sex. You know what that place is like. Any place... You can't just go having sex with anyone, never mind a twenty-one-year-old constable. So, we never said anything to anyone, we slept together once in a while, and... that was it.'

Women talk to me. I said that, didn't I? I wish they wouldn't. But this is different.

'When was the last time?' I ask, and even under these circumstances I still feel like I'm asking that question with *And is there video?* appended.

'Friday night,' she says. 'She came to see me at... I don't know... just turned up in the middle of the night. We didn't usually do that. She came here at two in the morning, or something. She was upset but... we didn't talk... She didn't tell me what was going on, what it was about... she just wanted to take her mind off it. And I...'

She starts crying.

I'm not doing it, I'm not going over there.

'When did she leave?' I ask.

She wipes her hand across her face, tries to pull herself together.

'I just fucked her. I knew I should have given her the chance to talk, but I just fucked her. This vulnerable young woman... What does that make me?'

'It's not about you,' I say harshly. Jesus, Hutton. 'When did she leave?'

'Not long before she died,' she says. Barely keeping it together. 'She must have gone straight to the station, dropped off Forsyth's car, and then walked home...'

She loses it on the final phrase. Which is understandable, given that Bathurst never got home.

'I can't... I can't....'

And what she can't do is get the sentence out.

I stand up. What I can't do is... this. This thing. Sit here, talking to a colleague who's in tears. I should. I should be there for her, but I've seen enough upset people in my life, enough people weeping for the dead or the missing or the raped, or weeping for what they've done or what they haven't done.

She sits in the tearful depths of guilty despair, and I will join her in guilt and self-hatred by walking out on her. I can't help her. That's my excuse. What can a fucked up, melancholic arsehole like me do for anyone?

She didn't kill Evelyn. She hasn't done anything wrong, other than have a lot of people wondering who it was who slept with the constable, and one person – me – accusing the Superintendent of being the one to fuck the victim shortly before she met her fate.

I look down on Eileen Harrison for a minute or so. Not as long as I stood at the door, but still a long time, standing over a woman, watching her cry. Is she expecting me to say something? Sit beside her, put my arm around her, tell her that it's not her fault?

She's not expecting anything. She doesn't want anything.

I don't know why I stand so long. I'm never going to give her the slightest comfort. She's a big girl, in a big world.

Finally, I turn and walk quickly from the room, back into the hall, back out the front door. Once I'm outside I can no longer hear the sound of her sobbing.

I'll tell Taylor she needs the rest of the month off.

Of course, there's only one day of it to go.

*

Go home, destined to spend the rest of a lousy night at home in front of the TV. Decide to do the honourable thing and call Peggy, pleased that at last I can do something right by her. She tells me she's tired and she'll see me another night. I've asked for that. She'd caught me lying on the phone earlier on and had the decency not to tell me at the time. I deserve no less than to be turned away.

So that's me, a little before nine-thirty. A packet of smokes, fridge full of v&t, and a couple of pieces of toast for company. Dying to call Charlotte. Not sure why, other than the obvious. Do I want to apologise for accusing her of sleeping with Bathurst? Really? She seemed happy to let me think she had, although looking back, that seemed to be more my assumption.

Of course, I really just want to call her because I'm lovesick, which is pathetic, and induces even more self-loathing than walking out on Eileen Harrison did.

Finally, after an hour of crappy television and wandering thoughts, I lift the phone. No answer at the flat in Kelvinside, so I try Helensburgh. Phone lifts and before my beating heart wanders casually up into my mouth, Frank says hello. I hang up without speaking. Feel cheap, and wish I hadn't called.

So I sit for another two hours watching general mince and slowly getting drunk. I wonder about Crow and Healy and Miller and Bloonsbury and Bathurst and Harrison and every other bastard on the force. Are they all joined up in some great secret society, dedicated to murdering their own? Finally fall asleep and drift into dreams, where I'm back in the forest, and they're all there, in Serbian uniforms, chasing me, dogs unleashed. And Taylor's in amongst it all, one of them, with Morrow at his side.

Wake up to a discussion of pre-war Spanish sculpture at a little before three in the morning. Holds my interest for a while, then I crawl off to bed. Fall asleep before I can clean my teeth. Wake up to the alarm at seven o'clock, mouth like the inside of a golf ball, face you could fry bacon on.

Miserable as all fuck with it.

37

Wednesday morning. Last day of the year, and good riddance to it. Into the station at just after eight. Expect wild cheering from the studio audience that I made it in time, but silence all round. Hard little workers beavering away. Still feel as if I'm about an hour and a half late. I'm stopped by Ramsey as I'm about to head for the first floor. This is a man who never leaves his post.

'Aggravated assault, Sergeant. Domestic,' he says.

'No way, mate. Morrow's got to be around.'

'Already handed him a burglary on Main Street. No sign of Sergeant Harrison again, so...' he adds, looking down his list. 'Pretty much everyone's taken. You want to speak to Taylor.'

'Yeah. I'll give you a call.'

Up the stairs. I hate domestic assaults. Am still pondering what kind of cases I actually like investigating when I walk into Taylor's office.

'Ramsey wants me to do some domestic assault thing.'

He looks hellish. I mean, really... but then, why bother even mentioning it? Take everyone here and stick them out on parade and it would look like a zombie movie. We are all so completely knackered.

'Yes,' says Taylor, 'he does.'

'Do I have time to deal with a domestic assault?'

'Got to be done,' he says. 'Until Healy shows his hand, there isn't much for any of us to do. You got any brilliant ideas I'll go with them, but otherwise you might as well make yourself useful.'

I've thought of going on holiday. That was brilliant.

'Nope.'

'Right then,' he says, 'the domestic is all yours. You know it anyway, so you're the best person.'

'What d'you mean?'

He smiles. Don't like the look of this.

'Mr. and Mrs. Jenkins,' he says.

'You're fucking kidding me...'

He smiles. The pen in the eye brigade that I spent a day on last week. The couple where one was as bad as the other.

'What is it this time?'

'To put none too fine a point on it – he kicked the fuck out her. She's in the Victoria. He's got a bruise or two himself, so they say, but we don't know whether he did it to himself to make it look like she started it.'

'Jesus.'

'Exactly. The quicker you see to it, the quicker you can get back to our user-friendly serial killer case. If you need to bring the guy in, just do it.'

'Right.' Start to head out the door.

'You go to see Eileen?'

I stop. Deep breath. Turn round. I hadn't been sure what I was going to say at this moment, so I intentionally didn't give it a second's thought. I have nothing.

'Yes.'

I don't add to that, as if by presenting him with silence he'll decide to let me walk out without asking any further questions.

'You seem reticent,' he says, dryly addressing my silence. 'I presume you slept with her.'

Funny. I wish I had. The other reason I hadn't been thinking about her, of course, was because I was a complete and utter bastard and walked out on her without giving her the merest quantum of solace. Of all the times I've been a complete bastard with women... well, that's probably in the top ten. Although some of the others might dispute that.

'I didn't sleep with her.'

He makes a face like he's impressed. I keep the colourful retort to myself.

'And?'

'She's not well.'

'Jesus, it's like drawing teeth. Did you speak to the Sergeant and establish what's wrong with her, and when she's likely to be back at the station?'

Mind's gone blank. I'm just standing there thinking that I should probably tell him the truth, because it's pertinent to the investigation, but of course, I don't want to tell him because it's not my place to, it's Sergeant Harrison's place. Except she's not here.

'I can hear your brain working, Tom, I just can't hear what you're thinking, so perhaps you could verbalise?'

I feel empty. Brain shutting down, which is what it usually does when faced with a difficult verbal interaction. Has happened to me in court a couple of times, which is pretty fucking awkward, by the way.

'Sergeant!' he barks, and I do believe I'm just about to come out with some nonsense about her coming down with some virulent flu strain that must have traveled from Asia, when I notice his eyes divert and the look on his face relax. I slowly turn, expecting to see Miller striding across the office. Instead, we are greeted by the blessed sight of Eileen Harrison, fit and healthy and ready to go.

She stands in the doorway.

'I'm sorry about the last two days, Chief Inspector,' she says. 'I was pretty sick... both ends, if you know what I mean. Tried to come in the first day, and barely got out the front door. Thought I'd be better to sleep it off.'

He nods, looks appreciative at receiving a coherent answer.

'Thanks, Eileen, glad you're feeling better. Speak to Rob, and there'll be a briefing in about twenty minutes. You can catch up.'

'Thank you, Sir.'

She leaves, doesn't even look at me. I might not have been there. Well deserved.

'Notice how we spoke to each other,' he says to me, once she's gone. 'That was what we call a conversation. Whatever you say, I still presume you slept with her, particularly the way she blanked you there. That showed all the hallmarks.'

I open my mouth to protest, but really, what difference does it make? Turn to go.

'Take someone with you in case Jenkins is still feisty,' he shouts after me. 'Edwards or someone.'

Bloody marvellous. Got a feeling the guy's only got hammer blows for his missus and confident I could take him if I had to. Can't find Edwards anyway, so I head off on my own.

Beginning to think that it might be a good idea to get another job.

*

Back up to the office some hours later. Everyone looking fed up. End of term blues, I presume. The domestic was one of those things I wanted to wrap up as quickly as possible, but it wouldn't allow. Had to drag the guy in, spend a couple of hours on it. Booked him. Left him choking quietly with rage in a cell. Now we need to find out what his wife wants to do about it. She'll probably want him released so she can kill him.

Morrow is still at Herrod's desk, doing that detective constable thing. Checking through masses of paperwork with more enthusiasm than is warranted.

Slump down behind my desk, we acknowledge each other. I'm confronted with an accumulation of paperwork that needs sorting out. Mounting ever further as the week goes on – none of it being of any concern to the primary investigation. Stare at it for a few seconds. Decide that's all the time I've got to give to it today.

'What have you got?' I ask.

He answers without looking up.

'Looking through all Healy's crap for cases Justin Edwards worked on. Getting nowhere,' he adds.

'Why Justin?'

'Haven't you heard?' he says, raising his head.

'I've been in with the domestic for the last two hours.'

Hairs rise on the back of neck.

'Killed in a hit and run this morning on the way in. Died on his way to hospital.'

I stare blankly ahead, don't know what to think. Edwards. Doesn't immediately hit me. Confused. Need more information. Gesture with my hands for him to keep talking. Where's the voice gone?

'Blue, 07 reg Astra. Stolen from outside a shop in Rutherglen late last night. Found abandoned on the Blantyre Farm Road. Don't know what the car was used for, if it was anything other than to kill Edwards. Might have been a hit, might have been an accident. I'm checking through this stuff, see if I can find anything, anyone that wanted him dead.'

His fiancée after she found out about him getting his kit off at the Christmas night out.

Stupid thought. Then, of course, I think about Crow.

Could it have been Crow? Killed Edwards for the same reason he killed Evelyn. But then, we know Healy killed Evelyn.

'Where's the boss?' I ask.

'He and Bloonsbury have been in with Miller for about half an hour.'

'Jonah? When did he appear?'

'About an hour ago. Clean shaven, walking in a straight line, change of clothes.'

'The fuck did that come from?' I ask and he shrugs. We stare at each other for another few seconds, then he goes back to his paperwork.

Need to think, and to have something sensible to say to Taylor when he emerges from the war council.

Three officers dead and an obvious connection leaps out. The Addison case. Only Bloonsbury and Crow are left. One of them could be the killer – Crow the big favourite; Bloonsbury has had trouble taking a piss the last week – or is there someone else who knows about the five of them and is taking them out one by one?

But it doesn't make sense. We know Healy killed

Evelyn and Herrod. So where does he come into it all?

The door to Miller's office opens and out come Taylor and Bloonsbury. And Morrow was right. The guy looks human. Still got the indentations on his lips where the bottle has been attached for the past week, but at least he's not staggering. He veers off to his office, Taylor heads for me. Looks extremely pissed off.

'Lunch, Sergeant?' he barks.

'Only half eleven.'

Stops and looks down at me.

'I'm going for some lunch. Are you coming?'

Not one to refuse a warm invitation. Drop what I'm doing – which is nothing – and walk after him as he marches out the door.

38

Sitting in a strange little café in the middle of Hamilton. Food ordered, cups of tea in front of us. Taylor didn't open his mouth on the way over here; just drove too fast. Listened to Bob the whole way. When we started, *Sad Eyed Lady* was playing, and it hadn't finished by the time we got here.

We both ordered chicken pie and chips; presume he's as pessimistic as I am about the possibilities of getting a good result on the food front.

'So how come Bloonsbury showed up?' I say eventually. Can't sit here all day holding each other's dicks, not talking about anything.

Taylor drinks his tea, staring at the floor. Thinking.

'Maybe he is Jesus after all,' he says.

Gets a disapproving glance from the waitress who places our pie and chips in front of us.

'Risen from the grave,' he adds. 'That's what Jesus does after all. It's his thing.'

Dig into the pie, delighted to find it's not too offensive. Chips are soggy though, and not hot enough. Pieces of limp tomato hog the side of the plate.

'So, what's with the anger then?'

He grimaces as he tastes the chips.

'You hear about Edwards?' he says.

'Yep.'

'Think the same thing I did?'

'Crow.'

'Exactly,' he says. 'Crow.'

He crams his mouth full of chicken pie and sits chewing morosely. Washes it down eventually with some tea.

Waits until he's got more pie in his mouth before he starts up again.

'I decided I might as well raise the thing with Miller. So I said, 'Heard a rumour about the Addison case.' She looks at me funny. 'I heard that rumour too,' she says. 'Don't believe everything you hear.' So I says, 'Well how do you explain the murder of three of the officers involved inside five days?' 'Coincidence,' she says, 'it does happen.' You know the tone. I mention that Crow has vanished, and that we'd found a connection between him and Healy. She says she knows, which of course she does because you blundered into Montague's office like some sort of fucking cowboy.'

Thanks.

'And she doesn't care,' he continues. 'Meanwhile, Jonah just sat there like... fuck, I don't know. A sack of shit, that's what. I told her I thought we should be checking it out, she says there are better things for us to spend our time on. 'Jesus has some better ideas,' she says.'

'Jesus?'

'Yes, Jesus! Keep up! I'm going with a resurrection metaphor here, it's not hard... Jonah apparently used his day off to sober up and think brilliantly.'

'Ah. And what exactly might those ideas be?'

'Aw, God, you know. The usual crap. Doppelgangers and photographs and disinformation. But you know, and they used to know 'n all, that's not what cracks it. It's gut instinct. Jonah used to have it and so did she. Even if it was just the instinct for the best person to sleep with.'

She's certainly lost that.

'So why won't she let you get into the Crow thing?'

He continues to wolf down his chicken pie, leaving the chips where they belong. Points an angry fork.

'Why d'you think? Doesn't want to open up old wounds. If it gets out, she's going to look bad, and we can't have that.'

Stab at the food. Chips are chips, and I'm not about to leave them, no matter how awful.

'She knows the score then?' I ask. 'The whole thing? Crow the murderer, Bloonsbury the conspirator.'

He shakes his head.

'Don't know. It would be unbelievable if she did. Even she couldn't take protecting the force's image to those lengths, could she? Fuck.' Shakes his head again; finishes off the chicken pie. 'No, I don't think so. Wanting to make her station look good, fine. But the Addison thing was about Bloonsbury and Crow getting a pension.'

'What if she'd only found out in the last few days?' I say. 'She might not want to bring it all out into the open. Not at a time like this.'

'How's she going to have found out in the last few days?' he asks.

'Evelyn.'

He finishes off his tea and starts looking around for something else to eat.

'You going to eat the rest of that pie?' he says.

'Yes.'

'So we're back to Miller having been Bathurst's lover the night she died,' he says. 'I'm just not sure about that.'

It's time. I've been putting it off long enough, although I'll still have to skirt around the stuff about Eileen. It's up to her to bring that particular nugget to the table.

'Well, I don't think they... they didn't sleep together or anything, but she went to see her. Evelyn went to see Miller.'

'How d'you know that?'

He looks annoyed already. Course, he's been annoyed since we left the station.

'I went down to see Charlotte on Friday night. Forsyth's car was parked outside.'

'In the name of... What...? What...? Why the fuck were you going to see Charlotte?'

I sort of shrug. Don't know how I'm going to say this without it sounding utterly ridiculous.

'You're not sleeping with her, are you, Hutton? Don't tell me you are actually sleeping with her?'

I just nod. He looks at me with slightly gaping mouth. Still got a bit of chicken pie on his tongue, a couple of bits in his teeth.

'I do not believe it,' he says, and there's no doubt that's the truth. 'Am I the only bloke in that entire station who hasn't slept with that fucking woman?' The man looks incredulous. I've managed to impress him. 'How long's this been going on?'

'About a week.'

'Every night? Just the once? What?'

'Christmas Eve, Saturday, Monday.'

'Fuck.' He lets the word drift off into nothing. He lifts my cup of tea and drains it. When his mouth drops open again, the pieces of chicken have gone. 'That's where you've been all these mornings. Jesus. What's she want with someone like you?'

'There's just been something between us since I accidentally saw her breasts a few months ago. It's been an elephant in the room kind of thing. An itch needing to be scratched.'

He's peering at me, as if I'm some kind of weird exhibit in the zoo.

'How, in the name of fuck, did you *accidentally* see the superintendent's breasts?'

'It just sort of... happened... But, I'm telling you, they were great breasts, and I've been thinking about them ever since then, and every time I looked at her, she knew I was thinking about her breasts, and weird though it sounds, obviously she was thinking, *the sergeant's thinking about my breasts*, and it was getting her excited – or at least curious – and she just had to give it a try.'

'Or three.'

He lets out a long sigh. I hide behind my mug, with raised eyebrows, even though it's empty. Even now, as we're having this conversation, I'm thinking about her breasts.

'All right,' he says. 'You've been banging the superintendent. Wonderful. Not actually relevant to the investigation, of course. So, Evelyn went to see her on Friday night, she also had lesbian sex on Friday night, but

215

not with the superintendent…?'

'Yes.'

'So, she spoke to Miller, presumably about the Addison case, although we don't know, and then she went off somewhere else to some lover.'

'Yes.'

'And do you know who this lover was?'

I stare across the table, lowering the mug. I'm really not going to answer that, but then I don't have to.

Eileen Harrison: the only known lesbian at the station, the two days off work, coming back after the visit from the other sergeant… it all plays out in his eyes as he looks at me, and then he nods. His face goes blank, he leans on his hands, then rubs his face.

'So we've had officers running about for the past five days trying to find out who Evelyn slept with just before she died…'

'It's just the way it's worked out,' I say.

He looks unimpressed with that. Unimpressed with me, and Eileen Harrison.

'You could've told me, at least, that you knew Bathurst had been to see Miller. Why didn't you say?'

I really don't have an answer for that.

'You wanted it to be your own little secret? Was that it? Is it more than sex, Sergeant? What are you saying?' I'm not saying anything, you're saying it all for me. 'You think you've got some sort of chance with her? You want to be Mr. Miller? Fuck, Tom, what are you thinking?'

He's hit the nail on the head. He is a detective after all. I just sit there looking like a lump of lard.

'When are you seeing her again?'

'Don't know. She was pissed off about the Montague business. Think she might have dumped me.'

Don't know how pathetic my voice sounded just then. He shakes his head, the anger leaves his face to be replaced by a smile. Starts to laugh. Wonder what he's doing, but it becomes infectious and I join him. He's right to laugh at me, after all, I deserve it.

'She just used me for sex,' I say, and we both end up wetting ourselves laughing for a couple of minutes over the absurdity of me and Charlotte Miller.

If you can't laugh, what can you do? Bastard.

When we get ourselves back together, he asks the obvious question.

'What was it like then?'

I would've asked him the same thing if the situation had been reversed.

'Awesome,' mundanely, is as good as I can do.

He looks appreciative. 'I expect it probably would be.'

The waitress hovers nearby, Taylor orders another piece of pie, no chips. She disappears again. He smiles, shakes his head, rolls his eyes, says, 'God, I should have ordered more tea.' Calls over to her, raises his cup. She nods.

Glad I've told him at last. And it takes some more of the edge off this pointless infatuation. I needed a good kick in the arse to start getting over it, and her reaction to the Montague business was a reasonable start. Taylor pishing himself laughing at me is also what I needed.

'So, you think she's dumped you because of Jonathan Montague?'

'She hasn't said as much, but I reckon that's about it.'

'She's probably sleeping with him 'n all.' He smiles. 'Three times in six days, you lucky sod...'

We sit in silence for a moment. The second piece of chicken pie arrives, suspiciously quickly. Really, did they even have time to heat that up in the microwave?

Taylor doesn't seem bothered by the indecent haste, and tucks straight in.

'So, Charlotte's mad about you going to Montague. She knows it's because we're checking out Crow. Evelyn has told her the whole story...'

'We assume, we don't know.'

'Whatever. She doesn't think the Addison case has anything to do with this, despite the three deaths, and so she doesn't want us digging away at old wounds. Leave

---

217

them be and concentrate on finding Ian Healy.'

'Or,' I say, 'she knows they're connected because she's part of it. Wants to ensure we don't discover the truth.'

'Too scary, Hutton. Crow, fine, 'cause the guy's sick. But Miller. If that's the case, why not just put herself in charge of the case when she removed Bloonsbury?'

'She tried that.'

'What do you mean?'

'She said she was doing it. I threatened to reveal the fact that Evelyn went to see her on Friday night; told her to put you in charge instead.'

He looks at me, forkful of chicken pie in hand.

'You're fucking kidding me?'

'Nope.'

'Jesus, Hutton, you're full of little secrets. Anything else you'd like to tell me?'

'Well, it was odd, because at the time that I was ordering her about – and let's be clear, I was a lot less forceful than that sounds – I assumed she'd slept with her. So, even though she hadn't, she still thought the fact that they'd seen each other the night Evelyn was murdered was enough of a reason to withdraw from leading the investigation.'

Taylor nods away as he continues to wolf down the pie.

'Yep, that might be significant. Anything else?'

'Don't think so.'

'Good. I think I've heard enough secrets.'

I gesture to the waitress that I'd like some more tea.

'So what are we going to do?' I ask.

He spears another piece of pie.

'We're going to ignore her and go after Crow. Go back down to Arrochar later this afternoon. Speak to a few people, do a more thorough search of that horrible little house of his, and we're going to work out where he went.'

The tea arrives.

'Magic,' I say.

39

Some time after four o'clock. The evening has already arrived, but still the country is bright with the low cloud and the snow lying on the ground. Hogmanay, the usual busy night ahead. Nevertheless, it isn't like it used to be around here, that's for sure. Anyone's granny will tell you that. All that running around and first footing; turning up at the house of total strangers with a bottle of White & McKay in your hand; singing strange songs without words which could be Cole Porter as much as Harry Lauder; all that has gone. We've become a nation of people who sit and watch rotten TV, and complain endlessly about how awful it all is and how New Year just isn't what it used to be. As if it's everybody else's fault but our own.

No lousy TV for us tonight, though. We're on the hunt for Crow, and after a few hours wasting time chasing reported sightings of Ian Healy, we're back on track. Might be the wrong track, but I have a feeling.

In the last two days nearly ninety people have reported seeing Ian Healy. Sounds good? It's a gigantic waste of time. If they'd all come from the same place, we'd be fine. But, as is always the case, we've had calls from everywhere. Down south as well, as his picture went out on the national news.

So Ian Healy is this week's Elvis. Working a petrol pump in Wolverhampton; sitting on a bench in Hyde Park; throwing up over the side of the Mull ferry in choppy seas; playing golf in Nairn.

That's the trouble with putting out photographs – you get all sorts of clowns calling in. Same last week with the photofit, which turned out to be a pretty poor resemblance of our man. Every poor sod with no one to talk to wants to phone the police.

Problem is that it only takes one of those calls to be

right; you can't ignore any of them. So I had four hours checking up on spurious calls from around Glasgow.

Bloonsbury charged around for a few hours until he hit the wall about three o'clock. Didn't see him do it, but you could smell the whisky on his breath, see it in his eyes. Can't keep a fool away from his drink for long.

Just before I left, I got another call on the Batphone from Charlotte. What are you doing tonight, Thomas? Frank's in Poland. Why don't you come down?

Seriously...

Not sure what she's playing at. Fortunately, however, I'm not going to fall for it as badly as before. I'm not completely over the hump, so it doesn't mean I won't go down there, but at least I'm starting to become sceptical. Recovery in small stages.

Anyway, the waste of an afternoon is behind us and we head on down to Crow's house. We can talk to a few of the people in the vicinity and not just the repugnant neighbour. Do a more thorough investigation of the house, look beyond the porn and empty beer cans, see if there's any note of where his ex might be.

We get to the house not long after five. Step out of the warmth of the car into the chill of night. Stop and look out over the loch. No cars on the road, low cloud and the snow muffling any sound. Silence. More snow in the air, but it hasn't started to fall with any force. The loch is still, hardly a wave washes upon the shore. The mountains covered in white. Beautiful. Scotland in all its silent, scenic grandeur. Clean and fresh.

Hear the faint murmur of the TV set from the house next door. Wild cheering from some awful quiz show. The moment is gone. We turn back to Crow's house. The snow-covered path virginal. He hasn't been about today, but then we hardly expected him to be.

'Right then,' says Taylor, 'let's get it over with.'

Up to the front door, push it open and into the house of fun. Lights on. Doesn't look as if anyone else has been in the place since we were here on Saturday night, which is good.

And so for another hour and a half we plunge back into the seedy, low-tech world of Detective Chief Inspector Gerry Crow. Go over everything, a much more thorough search than before. Look for scraps of paper, address books, telephone numbers, anything. Down the back of the sofa and armchairs, clearing out drawers, every filthy nook and every revolting cranny trying to find what we can. And at the end of it we've got an old book with old numbers of people he probably hasn't spoken to in years, plus a couple of addresses and numbers on bits of paper which long ago fell behind cushions and into holes. The sad state of Gerry Crow – no friends, and no life barring the putrid collection of illegal pornography.

Sitting in the lounge at the end of it. Lights on, watching the snow fall. Dying to step out into the cold.

'Almost feel sorry for the bastard,' says Taylor, and I know what he means. But, as I've said before, he's not a man to inspire sympathy.

'Still like to stick him in jail, mind.'

'Aye. Right, I'm going to make some of these calls,' he says, taking out his phone, looking over the meagre list of numbers. 'While I'm doing this, you can start the house to house. Begin with next door if you like.'

'Can I arrest him?'

'Feel free. Just remember you'll have to fill out a report.'

Good point.

Taylor starts to call the first number; I head out into the cold. Snowing quite hard. Feels clean. Almost seven o'clock; wonder what the clown with bad hair is going to be watching on the TV tonight.

I ring the bell and wait for the explosion. Should have brought my truncheon.

Ring the bell again. Can picture the old man inside, tutting and cursing, swearing at his wife. If he knew it was me, he probably wouldn't even answer; then I'd get the chance to break the door in, wave a piece of paper at him pretending it's a warrant, and ransack the place. Might do that anyway.

Door opens. Hold out the badge.

'Detective Sergeant Hutton. We spoke on Saturday.'

He looks at me with silent, rude curiosity.

'About your neighbour, Crow.'

He lets out a long breath. 'Right,' he says.

'You seen him recently?'

'I told you before, he fucked off. And I wish you'd do the same.'

He starts to close the door. Put my foot across the line, hand to the door.

'Listen, granddad,' I say sharply, 'you either answer the questions properly this time, or I'll get a warrant and a team from CTIS, and we'll come down here and rip your damned house to shreds.'

He hesitates. The cry comes from the living room – 'What are you doing, you stupid cunt? Close the fucking door!' – glances over his shoulder, then comes out onto the front step, closing the door behind him.

'What d'you need, 'cause I'm watching the telly?'

It worked. Not often these days that people so quickly crumble at the threat of a search warrant.

'I need to know the last time you saw Crow, exactly what he said when he called you, if he'd had any visitors, anything. Think about it, take your time.'

'What's that useless bastard been up to, then?'

'It doesn't matter. Just answer the questions.'

He lets out a long sigh. Wants to show what a huge favour he's doing me.

'Me and the missus don't sleep so good, you know? Me with the sciatica, and her with the arthritis. Right bastard that sciatica, son, and they doctors don't know shite.' Patience. 'So we're usually awake in the middle of the night. Saturday morning, I don't know what time it was, maybe one o'clock, something like that, I hears a noise, you know. Something going on next door.'

'What kind of noise?'

'I don't know, do I? Was I in there?'

'Fine. Go on.'

'I heard the door slam, and I looks out the window. Seen him drive off up the road.'

'Which way?'

'Up yon. Loch Fyne way, you know.'

Right. Getting somewhere. Didn't head back to Glasgow.

'So when did he call you?'

'In the morning sometime. Can't remember exactly when. Eight o'clock or something. Maybe earlier. Bastard got me out of my bed.'

'What'd he say?'

He shakes his head, sucks his teeth. I kind of hate this guy. But then, I hate most of the people I have to question.

'No' much. Says he was going away for a few weeks, could I look after the place. I mean, really?'

He laughs bitterly, and I don't blame him. Crow's place would be best looked after by an arsonist with ten gallons of fuel and a Zippo.

'How'd he sound?'

'How did he sound? The fuck?' He looks over his shoulder at the closed door, a wistful glance. '*Lethal Weapon 3*'s on.'

'Come on, Grandad, it's shit. You're involved in the real thing here. Much more interesting. So how did he sound?'

'Ach, I don't know. I didn't speak to him much, you know, but he sounded… different. Hard to describe. With a cold, or breathless or something. Look, I'm no' one of they psychiatrist bastards, one of they educated bastards. I'm a working man. Forty year in the postal trade.'

'That'll explain the sciatica.'

'Aye, it does, but d'you think the Post Office wants to know about it? Do they fuck.'

'Anything else you can tell me?'

'Aye, there is. My balls are getting frozen off. Can I go back inside now?'

And we've reached our limit.

223

'Sure, on you go.'

He grunts some sort of base insult or other and slams the door. I turn away, just as Taylor emerges from Crow's place.

'Get anywhere?' I ask.

He looks up at the snow, lets the flakes land on his face for a moment – a few seconds of cleansing – and then looks over.

'Spoke to three people. First, Julia, the ex. She hasn't heard a thing from him in five or six years. Says that if we find him, we've to remind him of his alimony responsibilities.'

'Some chance.'

'Yep. The other two, don't know who they were. Wouldn't say, but we can check them out. Just a couple of shady guys that Crow does his dirty work with, I suspect. They both sounded pissed off at the mention of his name. I'd guess he owes them money, and neither of them knows where he is. What about you?'

I point in the direction of the Rest and Be Thankful.

'Left at about one on Saturday morning and went that way.'

He looks into the snow, along the road which runs beside Loch Long, then rises up the hill away from the loch, giving way to turn-offs which offer at least three choices of what route to take. The snow is already thick on the road and hardly a car has passed along it since we arrived. Only a fool would head up into the hills on a night like this; particularly when the man we're following went five days ago, and his trail will be colder than the water in the loch we're standing at the head of.

Only a fool...

'You're going to follow him, aren't you?'

He laughs.

'Seriously, Sergeant, it was five days ago.'

'What then?'

'You're going to go and interview some more of the neighbours, while I go back inside and watch the tele.

224

Lethal Weapon 3's on.'

'That can't be what's happening.'

He smiles, makes a gesture for me to get on with it, and then turns away and walks back into the house, closing the door behind him.

40

Get back into the house half an hour later. Frozen to the bone, in need of a hot drink. Or alcohol. Find Taylor with his feet up watching one of those shows on BBC3 with a name like *Too Young To Kill Your Mum* or *Under 10 And Pregnant*.

'Anything?' he says.

'They all thought he was a creep. Some of them had stories to tell, but nothing relevant. What about you? You find out who the bad guys were in *Lethal Weapon 3*?'

'You might be surprised to hear I've been working.'

'Shocked.'

'Put a call through to all the stations in the surrounding area. Asked them to go out looking for Crow's car, call if they found anything.'

'I'll bet you were popular.'

'Just used my natural authority.'

Have a picture of fifteen desk cops trudging out into the snow, cursing him with extravagantly colourful words of dissent.

'So what if he drove outwith the surrounding area?'

'We'll do it tomorrow. But if it's nearby we can go looking for it tonight. So we sit and wait. Give them an hour or two. Told them to call in with nil returns. Fine, he could be anywhere, but if his car's in one of the smaller towns out west here, then we might get him.'

'Couldn't we go and sit in a bar somewhere?'

'We're going nowhere. Park your arse. There's some warm McEwan's beside the settee.'

Thanks.

And that's it for a long time. We sit and wait, enduring awful television as we go. The phone rings every now and again with the occasional station informing us they've checked the one carpark in their one carpark town; but the rest of the time we're quiet, as Taylor shows a peculiar liking for watching shows about teenagers who hate their parents and shows about teenagers who are parents. Says it helps him understand our clientele.

About an hour and a half into the ordeal, when we're on the point of giving up, we get the one we're waiting for. Dunoon. The local Feds have found Crow's car parked up a small street at the back of the town. Taylor gets the location, tells them to leave it as it is, and that we'll be along to check it out ourselves.

So, a few quick calls to warn off the rest of the search party, and then we're back out into the snow. Along Loch Long away from Arrochar, slither up the Rest and Be Thankful, down and along Loch Fyne, past Strachur.

The snow lessens as we go, but Taylor's concentrating on not driving off the road, while I let my mind wander through a variety of women. Peggy, Charlotte, the relatively forgotten Alison, even Eileen Harrison. Still feeling like a complete shit, and deserving of the opprobrium that will probably come my way at some point. Maybe just in Hell, when I get all that's coming to me.

We get to Dunoon, drive past a chippie on the way in, and the very idea of the smell proves too intoxicating. Fish suppers all round, and then we resort to the satnav to find the right street. Satnavs are another invention that make me wish I was living in the '50s.

What is wrong with those fucking people who drive into a lake, or into the middle of a wolf-infested forest, and say, *it's not my fault*? The satnav is just another way in which the human race can abdicate any sense of personal responsibility.

So we step out into the snow and the cold, still finishing off our dinner. Good fish supper too – crispy batter, tasty piece of fish, right amount of salt and vinegar, chips deep-fried to perfection.

We stand looking at the car. Kicking the tyres, various other forms of external examination, while we eat the last of the meal – Taylor a little behind 'cause he was driving.

'So, what?' I say to him. 'He got the ferry over to Gourock? Got the train up to Glasgow?'

'Fuckit,' mutters Taylor, as he drops a piece of fish into the snow. Bends down, scoops it up, pops it into his mouth before it gets too cold. 'No, doesn't sound right. What would be the point?'

'Trying to throw us off his trail.'

'Would he even think we were on his trail to that extent?' he says.

I finish off the fish supper, stuff the paper into my coat pocket and wash my hands in the snow. Light up a cigarette. That post-fish supper nicotine experience.

Taylor fishes around in his pocket and tosses me a small black book. Crow's life in sixty small pages.

'Check through that. Look for anything in this area.'

Get to it in the dim light of the streetlamps, while Taylor continues to circle the car kicking at various parts, nothing left of his dinner but chips. Finally says, 'You any good at breaking into these things?'

Look up from Crow's seedy list of acquaintances. Horrified to see that I'm down there.

'Herrod was your man for that.'

'Dead now.'

Good point. Lose interest in the book because I'm not getting anywhere; wander around the car. The lock on the boot looks pretty rusty, and since it's a hatchback that'll allow us access to the whole thing.

'Get a crowbar and jemmy the boot lock, or put in a window,' I say.

He finishes off his chips, looks around for a bin, then scrunches up the paper and tosses it to me.

'Find a bin, eh, Sergeant?' he says. I cram it into my other pocket. 'I've got something in the boot you can use for that. Break the lock, it'll make less noise. No point in arousing the suspicions of the local constabulary if we don't have to. I expect Charlotte's slept with most of them 'n' all.'

Hilarious.

I retrieve the small crowbar from the boot of Taylor's car.

'I could eat another one of those,' he says, as I return laden with crime committing goods.

'A second fish supper?'

'Yeah.'

He sounds remorseful as he says it, like it's a failing to admit to gluttony. Two fish suppers in quick succession. No matter the temptation, the second one is likely to be a disappointment.

Hold the cigarette between my lips, speak without managing to drop it into the snow.

'Well, I think we'll regret it, but why not? A second fish supper...' pause for that bit of extra effort, 'might just be called for,' I say as the lock springs open.

Take another long draw on the smoke, remove the cigarette from my mouth.

'Might have a haggis supper this time.'

Put the cigarette back in my mouth, lift the boot...need both hands, it's so rusted and stiff.

The boot opens, we stare at the contents, obvious despite the dim light. An unpleasant smell drifts out. The cigarette falls from my mouth into the snow.

'Fuck...'

Taylor reaches forward and pulls at the head of the corpse that lies bundled in the back of the car. It does not move to his touch, so we both pull at the body more vigorously. It is stiff and unyielding, but eventually we manage to yank it over, and the head comes round to meet us. Eyes and mouth open.

We stare at it for a while. Neither of us knows what to say. We've spent the last week and a half not having any idea what's going on. We pieced together what we could and came up with some sort of connection. And now everything that we thought made sense has been tossed out the window.

'Jesus,' says Taylor. 'I mean, seriously...?'

41

Still thinking of Jo. Always thinking of Jo. He doesn't realise that Christmas has passed, such labyrinthine paths has his mind wandered down. Still sees himself giving Jo a Christmas present, cuddling Jo under the duvet on a cold Christmas night, the lights of the tree twinkling in the corner. *All I want for Christmas is Jo.*

Head twitches. If only he can find her.

How long had she been missing before he realised? How many days had he stood outside her house waiting for her to come back before he discovered that she'd gone for good? How many days? How many wasted days? How far could she have gone in that time? Time to go anywhere in the world.

He didn't know why she'd left. Why had she left? Why would anyone in her position leave like that? She had someone who would do anything for her, who would love her and run after her and do everything for her, who would keep her warm and safe, who would protect her from the perils of modern city life, which are legion.

How could she walk out on him like that? What kind of thoughtless, selfish slut had she been? Maybe when he finds her, when he finally gets to give her a present, it won't be jewellery and it won't be clothes or chocolates or flowers or tickets to the Royal Concert Hall. Maybe it will be pain. Payback pain for the pain that she's inflicted on him, for reasons he cannot understand. Payback pain for Jo.

He is cold, cold to the bones. Hasn't had anything to eat for two days. He was fed at first, but now that's stopped. Forgotten what food tastes like, forgotten the warmth of it as it slides down his throat. Water and the occasional shot of J&B is not enough. The whisky burns and warms, but still he does not like the taste; nothing can change that.

His wrists were sore, but eventually the numbness came to take the pain away and now he feels nothing; except for the occasional trickle of blood down his arms after he tries to wrestle himself free. Knows the way to no pain is to stay still, but sometimes he is gripped with a desperation to get away. Jo is out there – sweet Jo – and she needs him. He knows she aches for him the way that he aches for her. Imagines all kinds of things happening to her, and the anger wells within him at the thought of it, at the thought of him not being there to protect her.

There are so many criminals and dangerous psychopaths out there. And here he is, imprisoned, and there's nothing he can do about it.

The anger passes. He thinks of a quiet Christmas afternoon. Lights sparkling on the tree, Bing Crosby singing. And Sinatra and Nat King Cole. Coal crackling in the fire. Holding hands, his ring around Jo's finger.

His hands around her throat.

42

There's never a ferry when you need one.

Heading back to Glasgow, the long way round from Dunoon; back the way we came. It's going to take at least a couple of hours in this weather, and we could call someone in Glasgow to do our work for us; but who's that going to be? Who do you call when you've just found your prime suspect dead in his own car, leaving you suspicious of the two most senior officers at the station?

Crow looked as ugly in death as in life. I can't think of anyone I'd feel less sorry for, having found them long dead. We alerted the locals, but asked them to keep it under their hats for a few hours. Do the necessary, but don't go phoning Glasgow with the news, 'cause Glasgow already knows.

Still plenty of snow on the ground, no talk in the car. Taylor concentrating on not driving too fast for the conditions, leaving me to concentrate on what the Hell is going on. Can think of only two options.

Out onto the dual carriageway past Balloch before the snow gives a temporary respite and driving becomes easier. About twenty minutes left of the year, and I can't wait to be done with it. As if tomorrow's going to be any better.

Taylor speeds through the night. Decides it's time we talked about it. Gerry Crow, dead in his own car.

'You worked any of it out?' he asks.

Gather the thoughts, try not to say them all at once.

'If Crow had anything to do with the other deaths, there must have been some accomplice who's now taken care of him. Alternatively, and more likely, he had nothing to do with it and has been dealt with the same as the others, as part of the same deal. Forgetting Ian Healy for a second, 'cause I've no idea where he fits in, of the original gang of five only Bloonsbury is left.'

'Yep.'

'So, is it that Jonah's been taking care of all his co-conspirators, or does it mean that someone else is going after them all and Jonah's next in line?'

'Miller for instance,' he says. 'Or, dammit, I don't know. Since she knows about the Addison case then maybe she's going to be the next victim.'

'So who do we warn? Bloonsbury or Miller?'

'Maybe they're in it together.'

Maybe they are. Nothing would surprise me now.

'And what about Healy?' I say.

'I can't work that out. We know he killed Ann Keller and Evelyn. Herrod was killed at his place. I don't know. Maybe he's working with Bloonsbury. Jonah did let him go after all. Could be they did a deal.'

Stare ahead into the thick mist of night. We need to be talking, but it's in the vague hope that we stumble across something relevant, rather than the actual possibility of working anything out.

'He realises Healy's the killer,' I say. 'At the same time, he's wanting to get rid of all his co-conspirators, so he enlists Healy's help. Threatens to arrest him if he doesn't do his dirty work for him, something like that.'

'Jonah Bloonsbury,' says Taylor, bitterly. 'Still don't believe it. That theory's still got to be on the sidelines. If he was going to shaft them, why get the help of a psycho? How are you going to control a guy like that? Why not just do it himself?'

We pass through Dumbarton, still not much traffic, a few flakes of snow in the air, three quarters of an hour short of our destination. We're heading for Bloonsbury's house, although what will we say if we find him sitting there, a dram in his hand and angrily proclaiming his innocence?

'No proof,' I say to him.

'What?'

'We've no proof. Of any of it. It's all speculation.'

233

He nods. 'I know.'

'We could be miles off the mark, pissing in the wind. Here's a scenario: Healy kills Keller, then Evelyn. Just in the natural course of his duties as, I don't know, the next Tobin. Josephine Johnson puts Herrod onto Healy, and he gets his comeuppance when he goes to see him. Healy, realising we're on to him, fucks off. The next day, Edwards is killed in a hit and run. It happens. Pretty big coincidence, but why not? Meanwhile, some ugly confederate of Crow with whom he does business, gets fed up with our horrible ex-colleague and does away with him. There are probably a thousand people out there who wanted to see Crow dead. So, five deaths and Jonah Bloonsbury has nothing to do with any of them.'

Taylor stares into the white gloom. He likes the sound of it, I can see that. And it doesn't sound too far-fetched either. A little, perhaps, but not as outlandish as Jonah Bloonsbury enlisting the help of a psychopath.

'Perhaps you're right. Hope you're right. Can you imagine the stench of this if Bloonsbury's our man?'

'Maybe we've been getting ahead of ourselves,' I say. 'So, there's been a coincidence or two. It happens. We'll charge in there to find Jonah sitting alone, getting quietly drunk along with Jools Holland.'

He drums his fingers on the steering wheel.

'I don't know, Sergeant...'

We've talked ourselves in a circle, as you do. He descends into silence. Time to mention the other thing that I ought to have mentioned a few hours earlier.

'So...' I say, 'I've also got Charlotte Miller to think about.'

'What d'you mean?'

We hit the Erskine Bridge; and somewhere bells are ringing to herald the arrival of the New Year. Party. The snow starts to thicken once more.

Here goes.

'She asked me down there tonight. Frank's in Poland, apparently. I mean, who goes to Poland?'

He looks at me. Fortunately not for too long, and turns back to the road.

'And were you going to tell me this sometime?'

'I'm telling you now.'

'Seriously, Sergeant.'

What with him being right to be annoyed, I naturally go on the defensive.

'What's the problem? You're jealous?'

'Fuck me. Where were we two minutes ago with this discussion? There are four officers dead. If it's not coincidence, if they're all dead for the same reason, and if it's not Bloonsbury who's done it and he's next on the list, it could be Miller. She knows you know. Why else would she ask you down there?'

He may be right, but I have my defensive annoyance to think about. 'If she was going to do it, then why not do it before now? She's had plenty of opportunity.'

'I don't fucking know, Sergeant. Just ask yourself why she's banging you in the first place.'

'I told you! Because of the incident with her breasts!'

I look at him. The very act of describing the incident with her breasts as *the incident with her breasts*, makes me smile, but Taylor ain't smiling.

Silence again. And he's right. The incident of the breasts doesn't really explain why a superintendent is going for the likes of me, yet it still doesn't make sense that it should be to keep me quiet. I didn't know a thing about any of this when I first went down there on Christmas Eve.

Nothing to say. The journey continues in silence; and the snow falls in ever more furious flurries, so that by the time we arrive in Hamilton we're driving through a white mass.

Haven't been at Bloonsbury's house since he had a bachelor poker party two weeks after Beattie moved out. Really it was a poker/porn movie/drugs/alcohol/prostitute party. Standard police fare. Filled the house up with a bunch of us, raided the warehouse and got what he could, dragged in a couple of tarts that they'd picked up specially the night before. You know the deal: 'come round and do the lot of us tomorrow night or you're nicked.' Happens all the time. Anyway, sad to say, Detective Sergeant Hutton was in the midst of it all. Hammered out of my face, losing a fuckload of cash at the cards, standing in the queue for the women. God knows what number I was in line. Not a proud moment in my career.

Some things are best forgotten.

Pull up outside the house, get out of the car into the cold. Up the path, the tangled mass of dead vegetation that is the garden still evident despite the snow. Wonder what state of decay the house is going to be in.

The place is quiet. No lights, no sound.

'He's either out, or he's collapsed on the floor,' says Taylor as he rings the bell.

'Probably out somewhere collapsed on the floor,' I say. Pull my coat closer around me. Makes no difference. It's freezing.

He rings the bell again and we stand and wait. In vain. Tries the door handle. Locked.

'You ready to put the door in again?' he says.

'You're kidding?'

'Come on, Sergeant, we're not standing out here all night waiting for the guy to wake up or come home.'

'But he could've nothing to do with it. He might just be drunk. How's it going to look if we go breaking into his house and nothing comes of it?'

He gives me the Chief Inspector look.

'Sergeant, break the fucking door down. I'll take the responsibility. Just do it. If someone's taking them all out, Bloonsbury could be lying in there dead, anyway.'

Let out a long breath. Here goes. Glad I've got my boots on.

Foot up, kick hard at the lock with the soul of my boot. The door gives slightly, while I lose my balance, slip and fall on my backside. Into a soft bed of snow. Taylor ignores me, puts his shoulder to the weakened door and pushes it open. Looks back.

'Come on, Sergeant, off your arse,' he says, and walks into the house. Puts on the hall light, looks up the stairs.

'Jonah!'

I dig myself out the snow, brush it off best I can, walk into the house.

'Jonah!' he shouts again.

Dead quiet.

'Right, up the stairs, Sergeant, I'll do down here.'

Taylor walks off into the sitting room – the scene of a vast majority of the poker party – while I head up to the bedrooms, scene for another part of the poker party. Three bedrooms, with a bathroom at the end, if I remember correctly.

Have a vaguely embarrassed feeling, walking into the house of someone who may well be perfectly innocent. Half expect to find him in bed with someone from the station, and I'm going to feel like an idiot.

To the top of the stairs, stop and listen. Nothing.

'Jonah, you there?'

No reply. Feels creepy now that I'm here, even with the lights on. Vaguely unpleasant smell in the air. Wonder if it's death. Don't think so. Assume that anywhere Bloonsbury lives is going to smell vaguely unpleasant.

Walk along the top landing, floorboards creak beneath my feet. Past the regulation police photo – the young Jonah with the Secretary of State for Scotland of the day. Ian Lang by the looks of things. His glory days were that long ago.

Push open the door to the front bedroom.

'Jonah?'

Turn on the light. The place is a shit tip. The sort of state your room is in when you're sixteen and your mother's forgotten to tell you to clean it up for the last year. The man lives like a pig. Hate to think what sort of lifeforms Taylor's going to come across in the kitchen.

Walk into the room, start poking around his things. Clothes everywhere, blankets tossed off the side of the bed. Sheets and pillows stained. Wonder if he's changed them since the whores were here along with all the guys from the station. By the looks of things, not.

Think I feel it first, rather than hear it. A noise; a whisper of sound. Niggling. Feel it in the shiver down my back. Drop the jacket, the pockets of which I've been looking through. Stand still. Silent. Taylor maybe.

It comes again. A murmur of noise. The next bedroom. A strange sound. Not like a man or woman's voice, but still human. A whimper.

Wish I had a gun again. Ought to start carrying these things around, but still the noise is not threatening. Out into the hall, and now I can hear it more clearly. Feel the pain of it. Hairs rise on the back of my neck.

A noise from downstairs. Taylor stumbling into something, a low curse; calls out for Bloonsbury again.

Stand outside the other bedroom. A second's hesitation. Push the door open, no idea what I'm going to find. Half expecting to see a dog whimpering in the corner.

Light on.

Jesus Christ. The smell hits me as much as the sight of what is in front of me; get that instant shock, like needles of water under a freezing shower.

Ian Healy, manacled to the wall. Unshaven, cheeks drawn, barely recognisable from the man I spoke to a week ago. He's naked, his arms attached to the wall above him, and from these he hangs limply. His feet can touch the floor, but they offer no support. And around his feet are several days worth of faeces, urine and vomit.

Take a step back, try to ignore the smell. He squints from the light, and then looks at me. Acknowledgement flickers across his face, a word tumbles silently from his lips.

'Boss!' I shout, 'think you'd better get up here.'

43

Can hear Taylor labouring up the stairs. I'm about to plough my way through the human detritus on the floor to let Healy down, when I decide to wait for the boss. Healy might look like a shitshow shambles of a human being, but he's still a killer. Ann Keller at least, although the truth of the second and third murders is beginning to kick in. Taylor arrives, stands at my shoulder.

'Jesus,' he says to my back.

Finally, after a week and a half of speculation and haphazard supposition, we have something concrete. A piece of living evidence up on the wall which is all the proof we need of Jonah Bloonsbury's involvement in the murders of three other officers. *Jesus* just about hits the nail on the head.

'This is medieval for fuck's sake,' says Taylor. 'You got your keys?'

'Remember what this guy did to Ann Keller.'

'We don't know he did anything to anyone.'

'Maybe the rest was a set up, but how did Bloonsbury get on to him in the first place? This guy killed Ann Keller. Think about what he did to her before you go letting him down.'

He looks at Healy. Healy stares blankly back. At a guess I'd say he has no idea what we've just been talking about. Dead eyes, mouth attempting to smile.

'How long have you been here?' asks Taylor.

Nothing.

'Healy, how long?'

A whispered word passes his lips, drops out into the room, unintelligible.

'What was that?' says Taylor. Voice still harsh. No time for naked psychopaths on walls.

Healy's lips move again, and this time we can hear it.

The chill of the croaking voice.

'Jo,' he says. 'Tell Jo.'

*

The threads of a story come from time to time together and make a picture in the web.

Another one of Charlotte's favourite quotes. Very appropriate.

Half an hour later and we're back on the road. Called Ramsey and told him to get a few of the lads round. Impressed the delicacy of it all upon him. No one's going to like the truth of this. Got him to start the search for Bloonsbury and to have the guy brought in. Who knows what gutter he'll be lying in at the moment? Also told him that we'd take care of telling Miller, which is where we're heading right now. Down to Helensburgh, back the way we just came. Stopped for petrol and provisions in case we get stuck in the snow, and on our way.

Eileen Harrison showed up at Bloonsbury's place before we left, still looking dazed. Not sure that her expression changed that much on seeing Healy, but she was looking so completely out of it that her expression didn't really have anywhere else to go. There were three constables with her to take care of Healy, just in case the guy decided, or was able, to get funny.

Brief discussion in the car before Taylor shut up to concentrate on driving through the blizzard. We'd asked a few questions of Healy, but he was in no fit state to answer anything.

The pieces fall together, scraps of rubbish into a bin. Maybe it all starts when Crow tries to bribe Bloonsbury. That's a guess, but we know they had dealings in the last month, and it's a reasonable stab. Bloonsbury begins to panic about the truth of the Addison case getting out. Great career finally flushed down the toilet, starts to wonder what to do about it.

Meanwhile, Healy murders Ann Keller. The same

night, Evelyn finds out the truth about Addison. Maybe Bloonsbury gets wind of that, maybe not. Maybe he knows she goes to see Miller. Anyway, I put him on to Healy, he talks to the guy, realises he's our killer. Hatches his plan. Decides he'll get rid of all his co-conspirators. Who knows how quickly he worked it all out? So he gets hold of Healy some time after he'd tried it on with that clown of a woman in Rutherglen.

Early hours of Saturday morning Bloonsbury goes down to Arrochar, takes care of Crow. Bundles him into the back of the car, drives to Dunoon. Gets back to Arrochar and his own car somehow. Stole another vehicle perhaps. Having dealt with Crow he then comes up to Glasgow and kills Evelyn. Not sure how he knows where to find her, but then she was between her home and the station, not that much of a stretch. Does to her what Healy did to Ann Keller, planting evidence to incriminate Healy.

Next up, he knows somehow that Herrod has been put onto Healy by Josephine Johnson. He waits for him, stabs him through the chest. Then the following day he does for Edwards in a drive-by murder.

The story so far. Don't have too much proof of it all, but it falls into place. Feels right, and there have been plenty of times when Bloonsbury's not been around the station.

So we have Jonah Bloonsbury, come to this; and the confirmation of that hanging on the wall in his spare bedroom. Healy had been there a few days, Jonah's been at his house in that time. No set up, no bullshit, Bloonsbury's our man.

Feel empty. Hollow. Don't want to be in the police tonight. Don't want to be here. If your life's going to be this shit, you might as well be living in one of those shit countries that don't even function, where despair is all-consuming, where despair isn't just defined by being unable to afford to renew your Sky subscription. Every one of us is going to look awful when this gets out, and there'll be no one on the force thanking Taylor and me for having discovered it.

Which brings us to the last big question. The involvement of Charlotte Miller. Which side of the tracks are we going to find her on? We could have phoned her, but this is the sort of thing you have to say to someone's face. Gauge the reaction.

Don't really start talking about it until we're over the Erskine Bridge, the snow has cleared and we're both chewing on nasty ham and cheese sandwiches we picked up at the petrol station. Nearly two o'clock.

'How we going to play this?' I say eventually.

He waves the sandwich at me.

'Why'd we even buy these, Sergeant? They're minging.'

'It was after midnight. What choice d'you think there was?'

He grumbles, continues to eat.

'Not sure, is the answer to your question,' he says. 'Been considering letting you go in yourself as planned.'

'To see if she kills me?'

'More or less.'

'Thanks.'

'Don't think it'll work,' he says. 'I mean, if she doesn't know anything about it, then she'll drag you into bed and I'll be left sitting in the car freezing my balls off. And we'll both look like idiots when we have to tell her the truth. So, we'll just go in there, tell her what we've found. We think Jonah's been killing off everyone who knows about the Addison business, which means that she might be next on the list.'

'And what if she's in on it and, I don't know, pulls a gun?'

'Don't see it. What's her motive? Sure, if the Addison stuff got out it'd look bad, set her back a year or two, but how is she supposed to know if some of her officers are murderers? And she's Charlotte Miller, for God's sake. She can fuck and connive her way out of anything. She doesn't need to conspire to murder her own officers.'

Takes the left fork at the lights, heads down towards

Helensburgh. I have to agree with him. The woman I've become close to in the last week isn't any confederate of Bloonsbury. What he's done is sickening, but he's such a mess of a man that however much your belief is stretched, there's still some credibility about it. But Charlotte Miller?

'And if she is in on it,' he continues, 'which I really doubt, what's she to gain from doing anything to us? It's already out about Bloonsbury, everyone knows. No, if she's implicated, she'll deny everything, get hold of Jonah and kill him so that he can't talk. That way, she suffers minimum damage.'

Sounds right, but this is such a mess you never know.

'So where's Jonah got to?'

He shrugs. 'God knows. Lying in a ditch. If he realised from what I said earlier today that we were on to Crow, maybe he's just done a runner. Off to London to sleep under a bag with the rest of his kind.'

'Or he could have come down to Helensburgh to kill Miller. The last of the people who know.'

'*We* know,' he says. 'He's still got us to take care of.'

Given the alacrity he's shown in polishing off the others, that's not the most comforting thought. Imagine my death at the hands of a crazed Jonah Bloonsbury. A drunk Jonah Bloonsbury. But the Hell with it, maybe death would be best at this point. The victim police officers will undoubtedly be hailed as brave heroes – like every other person who dies these days – while those officers not murdered during the course of this investigation will all be castigated for being a collection of criminally-inclined, incompetent losers.

Still pondering what it would be like to have a sword driven up through your insides, embedding you to a wall in the manner of the late and little-missed Herrod, when Taylor pulls up outside the mansion. Stops the car, switches off the engine. Looks at me.

'This is it, Sergeant. Now, I know you usually have sex when you come here, but on this...

'Hilarious, sir.'

He smiles and gets out of the car. I follow, stepping into deep snow, once again feeling the cold cut through the thin lining of the jacket. Look up the path to the house. A couple of lights on, but don't see her face pressed against a window watching out for me. If she was expecting me, I'm a good deal later than she'd have thought I'd be arriving.

Push open the gate at the bottom of the garden, start the long walk up the path.

'Hope she's in,' says Taylor.

'And alone,' I add. 'And unarmed.'

'Jessie,' he says.

44

Stand on the doorstep, where I've been twice in the last week. Different kind of nerves tonight. Had hoped by this age I'd stop feeling nerves, but that doesn't appear to happen, no matter the shit that's gone before.

About to ring the bell.

'Wait,' says Taylor.

'Second thoughts?'

'Got a feeling in your guts, Sergeant?'

He's right. Police instinct. There's something wrong. Don't know what, don't know how. Just a feeling, but there's so much work done on the back of feelings like this. Something in your stomach; the hairs on the back of your neck; that extra sense that stops you walking into the unexpected, stops you getting a knife in the belly.

'You want me to kick the door down again? That'll keep our arrival a secret.'

He gives me his Chief Inspector look, reaches out, tries the door handle. The door, in mockery of my dramatic suggestion, clicks open.

Give each other a *right, zip it* look, and walk into the house. Close the door silently behind and stop and listen.

Nothing.

Lights are on in the hall. Door to the lounge is open and we can see the faint red of the Christmas lights, although the tree is out of sight. He gestures to me to check out the rooms on the other side of the hall and I start tentatively looking in the first one, as he goes into the lounge.

A library, the sort of room that normal people just don't have in the house. Rows of books that will remain forever unread; a writing desk untouched by human hand; an old-fashioned globe from a time when the Far East was a vague mass, and Manhattan was a swamp; a small lamp burns in the corner, for whatever reason. To aid the investigating officer, perhaps.

Walk through the room to the door at the far end. Gently. Open it, into the next. In the dim light cast by the small lamp in the library I can see the outline of the billiards table. The overhanging light above the board dominates the room in its shady darkness. Nothing to see here. Through the room and into the one behind – the room at the back of the house.

It's dark in here, the dim light from the library not penetrating. Looks like a sitting room, the large TV in the corner. 46" screen. This will be where Frank comes to watch the Rangers on those rare occasions he can't make it to the game. Through the room to the door on the other side, after a cursory glance. We're looking for Charlotte, not carrying out a close scrutiny of the place.

Back out into the hall. Taylor already coming out of the kitchen. Shakes his head, indicates up the stairs with his thumb as he walks past.

It's a big hall, allowing a large sweeping staircase to run up the left-hand side; elaborate balustrade, which includes a figurehead at the top of the stairs. You'd think it might be a composer or something equally pretentious. But it's worse – it's some old Rangers player from the forties or fifties. George Young, someone like that. God, but Frank's a sad fucker. I nearly laughed the first time I saw it. Decided that he deserved to have had me sleep with his wife. Walk up behind Taylor – not a creaking floorboard to be heard – and he stops for a look at the small figure. Not a word, shakes his head, walks on.

He stops on the landing and we stand and listen. Nothing again, the house still silent. Don't know exactly what it is we're looking for. The sound of someone being murdered? The screaming sounds of sex? Can't be that – I was the one lined up for the job.

'Bedroom?' he asks quietly.

Point along the hall. Feel a tingle of excitement at the very mention of it. The thought that Charlotte will be lying in there waiting for me. Don't think she's going to be too impressed with me turning up with company. Can hear her saying, 'Think you couldn't cope, Sergeant?' Can also hear her losing her temper. Begin to have my doubts about just walking into the house unannounced. The gut feeling is still there, but Charlotte Miller is the boss after all, and she's about to have two clowns standing on the threshold of her bedroom. Uninvited.

'You sure about this?' I say to him, voice as low as I can get it. 'Maybe we should go back and ring the bell.'

'Man up, Sergeant,' he says.

Stand outside the door. Look at Taylor. For all his hard words, can see he's not quite as sure as he wants to be. Not a sound from within. What if we just barge in there and all she's doing is sleeping? We're going to look like idiots. And I'm definitely killing off any chance that I've got; although my brief infatuation has already burned at its brightest and is waning.

'What are you expecting to find?' I whisper.

I can see he's definitely not as sure as he wants to be. But still, the guy's wife has only recently left him, and we're all at our most reckless when that happens. Just looking for something else to go wrong.

He shrugs. This is it. He opens the door, hand to the light switch, steps into the room. I blunder in behind, and the two of us stand there like a couple of Action Men.

Except there is no Action Man outfit for making a complete dick of yourself.

Charlotte stirs, raises her head from the pillow. Her eyes blink the sleep away and she sits up. Looks at us like she can't quite comprehend what it is we represent. The sheets fall away from her and she's wearing the same top she wore the first night I came here. Can see the wonderful outline of her breasts.

Not the time, Hutton, not the fucking time!

We stand there like a couple of puddings waiting for her to say something, even though the onus really ought to be on us.

'Chief Inspector?' she says eventually. The look on her

face is moving slowly from surprise to lack of understanding, on its way to outrage. Taylor better make this good, 'cause I'm keeping my mouth shut.

He hesitates, but knows he has to say something.

'We've got to speak to you about DCI Bloonsbury,' he says.

Interesting.

She gives him the withering, reduces-constables-to-jelly stare. Taylor's got an in-built force field against it, and I'm just trying to hide behind him, like Ron and Hermione squeezing under Harry's invisibility cloak.

She pushes the sheets away and stands up out the bed. The top slithers down her thighs, but not before she's allowed us the briefest glimpse of pubic hair, smooth and sensual thigh. Get that weird feeling at the back of my throat. Right place, wrong time.

Shakes her head, eyes still squinting into the light.

'What the fuck are you doing, Dan? What time is it?'

'About two,' he says. Good command in the voice. The guy is not a bit intimidated. Balls of steel.

She gives me the same look – obviously unaware that I'm protected by Taylor's balls of steel force field – then turns back to him.

'And you couldn't phone?'

Doesn't bat an eyelid, Taylor. Very impressive.

'Thought we should see you in person.'

Another angry stare. Giving it her best, but she must know it doesn't work with him.

'The doorbell?'

He doesn't immediately answer. Come on, Dan, think of a good one. Have no idea what he's going to say, and then he does the obvious and completely ignores the question.

'We found Ian Healy,' he says.

The eyes light up, the face does a variety of different things. She takes a step forward.

'Where?' she says.

'The Chief Inspector's house.'

'What?'

'Bloonsbury had him prisoner in his house. Had had him there for a few days by the looks of things.'

She's giving him a different kind of stare now. Sits down on the bed, shaking her head. Then the hand goes to the forehead and she starts rubbing. Stress. The bane of our times. This is a reasonable time to be stressed, however. We can almost hear this piece of information, and what it entails, running through her head. Or maybe she's already thinking of her own position. How she's going to explain it to the media, to the Chief Constable; how much will she have to bear the burden of responsibility?

If she already knows that Healy's been imprisoned at Bloonsbury's house, as one of our theories went, this is a command performance.

Looks up after a while. Can see the lack of assuredness in her eyes.

'Go downstairs and wait in the lounge. I'll be down in a minute,' she says. 'Fix yourselves a drink,' comes as an afterthought. A good afterthought. I need it.

We stand there staring at her, but we're already dismissed. The allure of a woman in her pyjamas, or a reluctance to let her out of our sight. Don't know. Finally Taylor leads and we walk out. Miller and I exchange a glance, but I can't even begin to try to read it.

Surprised to find my legs are still fully functional. Along the hall and down the stairs, past the bust of Wullie Thornton or whoever it is.

'Don't know how you do it,' I say to him, when I presume we're well out of earshot. 'It's like you've got this superpower.'

'Piece of piss, Sergeant,' he says as we walk into the lounge. 'You've just got to remember which one of you has the balls.'

'I have my doubts about that.'

'Got to use your napper. If we'd discovered nothing amiss, the minute it got nasty I just needed to drop in the bit about Healy and Bloonsbury. The shock of that was always going to completely alter the situation.' He raises his eyebrows at me to get my approval. I stare at him. Good point, but it wouldn't have stopped my legs from being jelly even if I'd thought of it.

Head for the alcohol.

'I need a drink. Want a single malt? They've got some decent stuff.'

He stands in the middle of the room, staring at the remains of the fire – a single low flame still struggling to escape the ashes – illuminated by nothing but the red glow from the Christmas lights.

Check the ice bucket and find it fully equipped. Hmm... On the one hand, that seems a bit odd. On the other, ice!

Make myself a v&t, half and half. Take a long swallow. Cold and warm and smooth and sharp, the perfect drink.

'They've got some Lagavulin here,' I say. 'You like that shit.'

He's staring at me, forehead knotted, eyes squinting in the dim light.

'There's something not right,' he says.

'What d'you mean?'

He looks around the room, but mostly it is in warm darkness. Red glow, faint shadows. Still.

'Don't know. Just something...' Lets his voice trail off.

Looks away, into dark corners. I forget the drink for a second, follow his gaze. Have the first inclination of tension; a shiver down the spine. A suspicion of sound, of movement. Swallow. Muscles tense. Waiting.

'Get the light, Sergeant,' he says.

And then the movement from behind the seat by the tree. The words barely uttered, no time for me to get to the light switch. A brief agitation in the dark, the flurry of an arm, and something flies through the air and thuds into the side of Taylor's head before he can duck out of the way.

He falls back, crumples to the floor. The chair is pushed aside into the tree; the figure appears from behind.

Heading for Taylor, knife glinting red. The tree topples over, all tinkling balls and rustling tinsel; the shadows roll around the room with the falling light.

Can make out the ugly face of Jonah Bloonsbury, contorted in exertion; can smell the whisky as his breath is angrily exhaled. He is almost on top of Taylor, unmoving on the floor. Throw the drink at him. The weight of the liquid shifts the flight of the glass, but still it hits him on the side of the head. Makes him turn, stumble, and before he can attack Taylor, I'm on top of the guy, hand to his wrist, lifting it up, stopping the stab of the knife.

Fall back, wrestle each other onto the floor. Gritted teeth, can smell the man. Still not thinking straight, propelled unprepared into the middle of the fight. He starts to drag the knife down. Stronger than me, always knew that. Brings it closer, and now all my efforts and thoughts are at stopping it. Six inches from the top of my head, even closer to his. But he has control, I'm totally defensive. Defensive. Think of the best way to play football, the best way to do anything. Go on the attack. Risk it. For an instant. Switch energies, and with everything I've got I bring my head up into his face. Miss the knife by a fraction. His nose and teeth crunch under my forehead, and I feel it as much as he does. But I'm ready for the shock, he isn't. The briefest second, that's all I have. Control his wrists, bring the knife down sharply. Feel the warm embrace of his neck around the blade as it plunges into him just beneath the chin. Instantly the fight goes from him, the body rests heavily on top of me. The chest still heaves, can feel the blood begin to pulse from his neck. Sickening, dark, warm. Push him off me, and struggle to my feet. Can hear his gasping on the floor, the deep breaths, accompanying low moans from Taylor lying next to him.

Light.

The room is full of it and Miller is standing in the doorway looking at the scene in the wasted middle of her sitting room. Taylor struggling to sit up, red running down his face from a bloody wound; Bloonsbury lying on the floor, hand over the wound in his neck, the knife still cradled in the hand which stabbed him – I should take it off him, not thinking straight, don't do it; and me standing over them, blood across my face and the top of my coat.

Her mouth is open, but there's nothing coming out. Nothing to say. A well-placed profanity might be in order. She looks scared, I'll give her that. Taylor starts to struggle to his feet, and I step over Bloonsbury towards him.

'I'm all right,' he says, holding his hand up. 'You'd better call an ambulance for him.'

'What happened?' says Miller eventually. Voice shattered. Bloonsbury continues to moan on the floor. Should be more wary of him, but he's been knifed in the neck. Still not thinking.

'He was waiting,' I say. 'It's him who's been killing off the others. Evelyn, Edwards, Herrod. Even that bastard Crow.'

'Crow?' she says. Completely lost.

'Everyone that knew about the Addison case. Presumably you were next.'

She stares down at him, open mouthed.

'Jonah?' she says. Thinks he's dying.

His head lifts for the first time. Ignores me and Taylor, looks straight at her. The movement of his neck restarts the blood flow. Steady pulse. His voice, when it comes, is hoarse, choking with blood. Hate-filled.

'Fucking bitch,' he says. 'Bitch.' Blood spits from his mouth.

The look on her face changes. Shock to anger. Eyes burn. Seen the look before.

'Christ,' she says. 'I knew I should have done something about him ages ago. Look at the state of this. I'll get an ambulance.'

Look at the state of *this*? What? The carpet?

She begins to walk from the room.

'Don't you turn your back on me, you bitch. Don't you run my life… then turn your fucking back…'

———

Did he say run? Or ruin?

She hesitates, turns. Bloonsbury has hauled himself onto his elbows, breaths coming from him in great gasps; panting; gurgling. Taylor and I watch it, uninvited guests.

'Get back here you fucker,' he wheezes at her, voice seemingly on the point of giving up. She stares down at him, all the contempt that anyone could muster in those eyes.

'Fuck off, Jonah,' she says. Words spat out, and she starts to turn away.

I look at him, not really sure what's going on. He's still got the knife in his hands. Have a brief moment, see what's going to happen. Strange vision. And it paralyses me for a hundredth of a second.

From nowhere Bloonsbury finds the strength. Picks himself up, knife clutched firmly in his hands. Almost slow motion. Blood spills from the wound in his throat; he is covered in it. Leaps towards Charlotte, knife back, every last effort into taking his revenge. She senses the rush of movement behind her, turns her head. Time for the briefest flash of panic across her face.

But he's a dying man. As the knife is on its downward sweep towards the middle of Charlotte's back, I'm on top of him, wrestling him to the floor, and he collapses beneath my weight. The knife falls from his hands, lies useless and blunted on the carpet.

I look up at her, at that impassive face. Panic gone, no trace of fear. Can't read a thing into it. Push myself off Bloonsbury, and the blood gurgles in his throat from some desperate dying breath. Pick up the knife; Taylor and I stand and stare at Charlotte.

She gives all she gets. Bloonsbury might just have implicated her in all of his crimes, but she'll know whether there's any proof out there. The actions of a drunk psychotic aren't going to see anyone incriminated.

'Thank you,' she says. Small voice, but steady.

I nod. Don't say anything. Taylor and I just stare at her in the brightly lit silence. He fingers the wound on his head.

A bauble topples from the Christmas tree with a tinselly shiver, settling on the carpet. Bloonsbury suddenly coughs a bloody cough, a strangulated breath wheezes from his body. Silence broken, the spell dispersed.

'I'll call an ambulance,' she says, because she has to. Although might not she want Bloonsbury to die where he lies?

There's something in her eyes, then she turns and is gone from the room.

Look down at Bloonsbury. Too late for an ambulance anyway, the man is dying. From the hands of Detective Sergeant Hutton. I'd like to be able to say that he's the first man I've killed, but I can't. On good days, on days when I can block out the past, when I can turn the past into another lifetime, those are the days when I could say he's the first man I've killed. There aren't many of those days.

I look at Taylor. We are uninvited guests. Silence over the house. A clock ticking somewhere. For some reason I start wondering what Frank is doing, and will he care?

'Go and listen, Sergeant. Make sure she calls an ambulance. And the local station,' says Taylor.

'Yep.'

45

Three o'clock, New Year's Day. Watery sun low in the sky; bright afternoon with the snow still thick on the ground, frost already in the air for the night ahead. Clear, chill, fresh, a beautiful day.

Sitting in the car across the road from the old family home. Have been sitting here for over twenty minutes. Can't decide whether or not to take the giant step across the road. I don't deserve for Peggy – or for any of them – to take me back, but if I go over there, clutching the small bunch of flowers that currently lies on the passenger seat, then take me back is what they'll do. Despite being a total car crash the past few days, my future is there if I want it.

Caught a couple of hours sleep, some time between five and eight. Woke up feeling as completely shit as I have for the previous few days. Looks like the case is largely closed, but it'll be months, or years, before the stench of this vanishes; and I can still feel the warmth of Bloonsbury's blood pulsing over my hand.

The Great Detective, Glasgow's one-time police hero, lies in the morgue at the Victoria. Died on his way to hospital, and they brought his body up this morning. Died at the hands of Detective Sergeant Hutton. I said to someone that he was the first man I'd ever killed, but not with any conviction.

Checked out some things this morning. Our suspicions were pretty close to the mark, and anything new we've discovered has confirmed our theory.

Learned from Josephine Johnson that she spoke to Bloonsbury first on Saturday. He told her to call Herrod the following day. Set him up right from the off. Poor girl unknowingly played her part, Herrod walked straight into it. Bloonsbury knew his man, knew he would charge round there on his own. White knight. Waited for him, then butchered him. Butchered his own man.

I can't understand it, because I would've thought Herrod would've been all right to keep his mouth shut. But who knows what was going through Bloonsbury's mind the last few weeks?

Found details of a car stolen from Dunoon late Friday night or early Saturday morning. Turned up in Arrochar. Fits the bill for Bloonsbury having dealt with Crow.

What else do we have? They're going back over Evelyn's body, see if they can find any trace of Bloonsbury on there; now that they know what they're looking for.

Taylor interviewed Healy for a couple of hours. I didn't sit in on it. He wavered all over the place; psychotic to reasonable to switched-on lawyer to deranged killer. And through it all, an obsession with Josephine Johnson. To hear him speak, their relationship bordered on Romeo and Juliet for tragedy, and to Paul Newman and Joanne Woodward for longevity. An obsessive personality that had needed an outlet, and had found it in a woman who had run away from him. He didn't seem to think she'd run away for good, and that at any moment she might return. He thought there were a variety of reasons she'd left, but had admitted there was a possibility she'd done so because she was a 'bitch-slut intent on fucking as many other men as possible', which was why he'd had to punish her.

Can you believe anything such a man tells you? He said he was taken by Bloonsbury after he blundered into the woman's flat in Rutherglen. Thought he must have been followed. Pretty messed up in those manacles, so he lost track of night and day, but we know how long he was there.

Ian Healy should be locked up for the rest of his life, but who knows these days? Gets a decent lawyer and he'll probably have the jury feeling sorry for him because he was kidnapped by the police; and they'll let him off. We'll get enough evidence on the guy to convict a multitude of murderers, but you never can tell. Lawyers, lawyers, everywhere, with names to make, CVs to enhance.

We found Bloonsbury's prints in Crow's house and on the car that was used in the Edwards hit and run. Drunk Jonah; didn't even think to wear gloves. You just don't think to do it as an officer, do you? When you get prints, you check them against those of known criminals – not against your own men.

So Bloonsbury is guilty as charged on all counts. And dead with it, which is good. All the best villains get it at the end. Saves on the trial costs, and means there isn't going to be any screw-up in the courtroom with some fucking jury.

And now that Bloonsbury's gone to Hell and taken his secret with him, where does that leave Charlotte Miller?

She sat watching it all in the middle of the night, as the ambulance arrived and whisked away the dying man. Guzzled expensive brandy; bottled in Roman times. Hid behind her masque of wealth and shock, all carefully constructed. Safe in what knowledge? That there was no connection between her and Bloonsbury, or this: every step of the way, after every action she has taken, she has wiped the board. There will be nothing out there to point the finger in her direction.

Can you convict anyone on the actions of someone like Jonah Bloonsbury? Maybe it was the final act of petty revenge from a dying man. To make it look as if she'd colluded with him all along. That she'd let him into her house at the end, rather than him letting himself in or breaking in. The front door was left open, remember, but that could point either way.

Yet what other proof do we have? We had our suspicions before we went down there, and the way Bloonsbury acted suggested she was part of it. But that was it. It could be that our continuing investigations will unearth something, but we both know she'll have been more thorough than that.

And so, today, she left us to it. No attempt at interference. Appeared at the station for twenty minutes.

The Chief Constable turned up – all shiny buttons and stinking of drink – then left with a smile far from his face, ten minutes later.

She called me into her office just before she went. I stood in front of her in that office for the fifth time in a week. Wary rather than nervous. Wondered if I was going to hear a confession.

Not a chance.

'I'm going away for a few days,' she said.

Just a few days? I thought. Those days will likely stretch to weeks, the weeks will stretch to forever.

'Need time to think. Get my head together. Chief Constable thinks it would be a good idea. Let things settle. The last few days have been rather hard on the station,' she said. Rather hard? Go on, Charlotte, tell it how it is. 'It all seems like some great conspiracy.'

That's exactly what it is, darlin', I thought. And there's a good chance you're at the centre of it all.

She looked at me for a few seconds. Don't know what she was expecting me to say. Was she looking for sympathy? But I didn't give her anything. There was nothing to say. Taylor and I both suspect her of involvement, and we'll do everything to get evidence of it.

My bet, however, is that there'll be nothing to find.

We're left to wonder what went on between her and Jonah Bloonsbury. Maybe it goes back all the way. Sixteen years ago, to his first moment of glory and a chase across open moorland. Must have started sometime. Maybe the two of them have been in it together all along, riding the back of the other. And while Bloonsbury couldn't cope and floundered in an ocean of whisky, Charlotte Miller rode the high seas. Was going to go all the way.

'Would you come with me?' she said. A quiet, nervous voice, but I wouldn't believe that voice now no matter what the tone. Still, that request was out the blue. An electric shock. But whereas before it would have been a shock from an entire power grid, now it was like static off a jumper. 'Now that it's over, you should be able to get some time off. I'm sure Dan wouldn't mind.'

Dan would go mental, love, I thought. But there was nothing to worry about. There was no way I was going anywhere else with Charlotte Miller. Standing in front of her desk was as far as she was ever going to take me.

'I don't think so,' I said. Still too many things to sort out. And even if there weren't...

She swallowed. Took it well. Knew what I was thinking, I'm sure.

And that was that. She didn't say anything else; I turned my back on my infatuation of the past week and walked from her office. Closed the door behind me. That's a tried and trusted metaphor right there.

A couple of minutes later she swept out of the station. No goodbyes. We couldn't exactly lock her up just because Bloonsbury tried to kill her, but I would bet now if we find something and want to bring her in, she'll be very difficult to get hold of.

And that's just about it. Some questions answered, some not. A few leftovers, such as the man who currently rots in prison on the Addison murder charges from last year. The crimes of Gerry Crow – although that's all hearsay. Maybe it was Bloonsbury all along. Who knows? It'll be for someone else to work out what to do with that guy.

We're done, and I'm left sitting across the road from my ex-wife, waiting for something. Maybe it's for one of them to take the decision out of my hands. For one of them to look out of the window and notice the car parked across the road. For one of them to decide whether to draw the curtains or come over and invite me in.

At the back of my mind – despite all the stupidity of being infatuated with Charlotte Miller – I was presuming that I'd end up back here, that I'd be walking in through that door. But last night I killed a man, and it wasn't the first time. It was the first time in seventeen years. And while seventeen years is a long time, it's not nearly long enough.

I always thought that when I met the right woman, I'd talk to her. My part in the Balkan war. I'd let it all out, a great tumble of awful reminiscence, spewing forth, unstoppable, ending with me in tears and a wreck on the floor. And for years I thought it would be Peggy. For years. And maybe even this past week I thought it would be Peggy.

But sitting here, across the road from her house, I know. I don't think I was lying to myself when I first thought she'd be the one. I genuinely believed it. Now, however, I know for sure. Not today, not tomorrow, not next week. And some time soon, after I move back in, I'll wake up jabbering and sweating and panicking in the middle of the night and she'll look at me and be afraid, and she'll hope that I'll talk to her, and I'll see it in her eyes. The sure and certain knowledge that I won't. The sure and certain knowledge that there probably is someone out there in whom I'd confide, but that it's not her.

I see a movement in the front room, and suddenly I know that I can't be sitting here waiting for them to make the decision for me. I have to leave.

Engine on, into first, and smoothly away from the side of the road. Grasp the steering wheel firmly, because my hands are shaking. Look at the clock. Must have been an hour that I sat there. Late afternoon, New Years day.

Automatically flick the music on. Bob. *Idiot Wind.*

Jeez, that line about not knowing peace and quiet in so long. There we go.

Time for me and Bob to hit the nearest pub.

By Douglas Lindsay

The Barber, Barney Thomson

The Long Midnight of Barney Thomson
The Cutting Edge of Barney Thomson
A Prayer for Barney Thomson
The King Was in His Counting House
The Last Fish Supper
The Haunting of Barney Thomson
The Final Cut
Aye, Barney
Curse of The Clown

The Barbershop 7 (Novels 1-7)

Other Barney Thomson

The Face of Death
The End of Days
Barney Thomson: Zombie Slayer
The Curse of Barney Thomson & Other Stories
Scenes from The Barbershop Floor

DS Hutton

The Unburied Dead
A Plague of Crows
The Blood That Stains Your Hands
See That My Grave Is Kept Clean
In My Time of Dying
Implements of the Model Maker (2021)

DCI Jericho

We Are the Hanged Man
We Are Death

DI Westphall

Song of the Dead
Boy in the Well
The Art of Dying

Pereira & Bain

Cold Cuts
The Judas Flower

Stand Alone Novels

Lost in Juarez
Being For The Benefit Of Mr Kite!
A Room with No Natural Light
Ballad in Blue
These Are The Stories We Tell

Other

For The Most Part Uncontaminated
There Are Always Side Effects
Kids, And Why You Shouldn't Eat More Than One For
Breakfast
Santa's Christmas Eve Blues
Cold September